ULTIMATUM

Antony Trew

CHIVERS
THORNDIKE

This large print book is published by BBC Audiobooks Ltd, Bath, England and by Thorndike Press, Waterville, Maine, USA.

Published in 2003 in the U.K. by arrangement with Robert Hale Limited.

Published in 2003 in the U.S. by arrangement with Robert Hale Limited.

U.K. Hardcover   ISBN 0–7540–7306–8   (Chivers Large Print)
U.K. Softcover   ISBN 0–7540–7307–6   (Camden Large Print)
U.S. Softcover   ISBN 0–7862–5669–9   (General Series)

The text of this Large Print edition is unabridged.
Other aspects of the book may vary from the original edition.

Set in 16 pt. New Times Roman.

Printed in Great Britain on acid-free paper.

British Library Cataloguing in Publication Data available

Library of Congress Cataloging-in-Publication Data

Trew, Antony, 1906–
    Ultimatum / Antony Trew.
        p.   cm.
    ISBN 0–7862–5669–9 (lg. print : sc : alk. paper)
    1. Palestinian Arabs—England—Fiction. 2. Terrorism—
Prevention—Fiction. 3. Nuclear terrorism—Fiction.
    4. London (England) Fiction. 5. Large type books. I. Title.
    PR9369.3.T7U47 2003
    823'.914—dc21   2003053305

'It is important to recognize that organized terrorism is a form of war—indeed it is rapidly becoming the most persistent and effective form of war.'

'There is nothing more dangerously naïve than the belief that "it can't happen here".'

'. . . advocates of the "soft" line argue that almost any concession within reach should be made if it saves one innocent life. Yet if terrorists' blackmail succeeds once, it will certainly be tried again—with more dreadful threats and more extreme demands.'

LORD CHALFONT
in *The Times*, 10th April, 1975

CHAPTER ONE

It was cold and dark and the rain came in swathes, carried by the wind. In the glare of the headlights it seemed to the driver in the transporter's cab like the folds of a muslin curtain, opaque here, transparent there.

A loom of light showed over the hill and he saw the motorcycle escorts swerve in behind the leading Panhard AML scout car. The loom resolved itself into twin lights which came swiftly towards the convoy.

'Bastard,' growled the transporter's driver. 'Expect he's drunk.' The oncoming lights were dimmed and he said, 'That's better.'

'He's scared,' said the lieutenant. 'Seen the escorts?'

The car passed, going slowly now. A silver Mercedes with West German number plates.

'Boche,' said the transporter's driver. 'No wonder. They're all pigs.'

The third man in the cab said, 'That's an old-fashioned view, Durand.' His forced laugh didn't hide the note of censure. Durand was silent. It was better not to cross swords with people like the superintendent. He concentrated on the road, glancing for a moment at the driving mirror where the rear escorts showed up wet and glistening in the Mercedes' headlights, jets of spray leaping from their tyres, the

1

motorcyclists weaving in behind the tailing Panhard, its armour bright with reflected light.

Above the noise of the transporter's engine and the whine of wet tyres, Durand heard the voices of the armed guards in the bunker-space behind him. Two there, four more in the transporter itself. Except for the lieutenant all, like himself, men of the CRS—Corps Républicain de Sécurité; all, like himself, in civilian clothes.

It was a formidable escort for the grey packing cases in the big transporter, numerous as they were. It had been like that all the way from Carcassonne where the convoy had halted for the guards and escorts to change. That was where he'd taken over.

At the briefing they'd been told the operation had a high security classification. They'd not been told what was in the packing cases, nor where they'd come from. Presumably the men relieved outside Carcassonne knew that, but they wouldn't have known where the convoy was going.

Clever, thought Durand. Well organized. But not his business. They'd been warned at the briefing not to talk. For him that had been unnecessary. He always kept his mouth shut. It had taken time to get to where he was. He wasn't going to hazard that. He pulled at the harness of the shoulder-holster, easing the pressure under his arm. The superintendent lit a cigarette. Damn him, thought Durand. It's a dirty habit. Stinking the cab out like that.

The rain fell more heavily, hissing down, crackling against the windscreen with a sound like breaking tinder. He switched the wipers to FAST, concentrating on the road, watching the tail-lights ahead looming and receding. A signpost showed up through the rain: N568: ARLES 43 KM—MARSEILLE 41 KM.

'Forty-one kilometres to go,' said the lieutenant. 'Not long now.'

'Slow part's still to come,' said Durand.

The superintendent switched on the map-light, held his wrist under it. 'Ten to three,' he said. 'We'll be there within the hour. Won't be much traffic in the early morning.'

'Hope you're right.'

Discreet white lettering on the doors of the driving-cab indicated that the transporter was the property of François Berthon et Cie, Chatillon-sous-Bagneux.

*   *   *

At Martiniques the convoy left the Route Nationale and followed the loop road to the coast. It was one which carried little traffic in the early hours of morning. After Carry-le-Rouet they began to shed the escorts. First to leave were the Panhard scout cars. There were no farewells, no exchanges of signals as the armoured cars reduced speed and disappeared into the darkness. When they'd gone the transporter turned north-east and made for the Route Nationale. Once on it the four outriders dropped away and the transporter swung east, heading for Marseille. The rain had stopped but not the wind.

Not long afterwards a civilian motorcyclist with leather jacket and red helmet overtook at moderate speed. Once ahead he throttled back remaining a hundred metres or so in front. Before long he was joined by another. This time the helmet was yellow.

In the cab's mirror Durand saw the lights of two motor cyclists following behind. The four leather jacketed riders with their bright helmets, each of a different colour, kept no particular station, accelerating and breaking from time to time, their relative positions constantly changing. It could not have been apparent to passing traffic that these men were an armed escort of the CRS.

*   *   *

They were well into the built-up area on the western side of Marseille where rows of sodium street lamps shed orange light over wet streets and anonymous façades. The air was heavy with the fumes of traffic and industry and the pungent smell of city streets after rain.

The superintendent held the plan under the map-light, a fingernail marking the transporter's position. 'We're coming up to Rue d'Anthoine,' he said. The traffic lights turned red, the transporter's hydraulic brakes hissed and it came to a halt. Beyond its bonnet the leading motorcyclists sat on their machines, stolid and motionless, the lights of the transporter exaggerating the bright colours of their helmets. Above the dull rumble of the Berliet's diesel could be heard the throb and roar of motorcycle engines. Their riders, impatient to go, were revving the powerful engines in staccato bursts.

'It's green,' said the superintendent.

Durand nodded but said nothing. Why should he? He, too, could see. He engaged gear, released the handbrake and clutch and depressed the accelerator. The engine note rose and the Berliet moved forward.

'Turn right into the Rue d'Anthoine,' said the superintendent.

The hauling unit turned in a wide circle, the towed body of the articulated vehicle tracking round behind it. It was seven minutes past four and Marseille was still asleep. There was little traffic, mostly farm trucks bringing in produce, and cars carrying night-shift workers home. Here and there an occasional cyclist struggled against the wind, or if it was behind him sat bolt upright making the most of it.

Towards the bottom of the Rue d'Anthoine they turned left into the Boulevard de Paris, soon afterwards right into the Boulevard Dunkerque to make towards the Gare

5

Maritime.

'Right at the next traffic light,' said the superintendent. 'That'll take us down to the gates on the Quai Lazaret.' They passed a stationary patrol car of the Gendarmes Mobiles, but its occupants appeared not to notice them.

The lieutenant opened a briefcase and with the aid of a torch took out some papers. 'The shipping documents,' he said, 'and my identity permit.'

'Got yours ready, Durand?' asked the superintendent.

'Yes. Below the instrument panel.'

'Right,' said the superintendent. 'I'll do the explaining. Leave it to me.' He didn't add that none would be necessary. The CRS had briefed senior port officials. The transporter would be passed through the dock gates without examination or delay subject to production of the shipping documents and port identity permits for its crew. The permits identified the three men as employees of François Berthon et Cie, haulage contractors of Chatillon-sous-Bagneux in the Department of the Seine. The faked permits had been prepared by the CRS for the men in the driving-cab. The six armed guards did not need them for they could not be seen. Officially they were not there.

*   *   *

The dock gates on the Quai Lazaret showed up in the distance.

'Flash your lights,' said the superintendent. 'Slow down.'

Durand did so. The four motorcyclists accelerated quickly away, leaving the transporter behind.

Durand turned the Berliet sharp left and a gendarme waved them to stop under the arc-lights at the gate-house. A port official came from it and beckoned. The superintendent climbed down from the cab, shipping documents in hand. He greeted the man and together they went into the gatehouse. Two more officials sat at desks.

'The papers,' said the superintendent, holding them forward. 'And my permit.'

The port official shifted a Gauloise from one side of his mouth to the other, examined the permit, shot a quick glance of enquiry at the superintendent and passed it back. 'Good,' he said. 'Now the consignment notes and the export authority.'

The superintendent handed over the shipping documents. The port official stopped, holding them under the desk lamp, turning the pages with bureaucratic deliberation. 'Agricultural machinery,' he said, sucking at the Gaullois. 'To be shipped in the *Byblos*.' He consulted a berthing chart. 'She's lying in the Joliette Basin. Wharf Seven, Berth D. Here,

7

see?'

The superintendent moved across to the berthing chart. 'Yes,' he said. 'I see.'

The official rubber-stamped and initialled the documents. 'Right,' he nodded. 'She sails at daylight.'

The superintendent took the documents, went back to the transporter, climbed into the cab. 'We can go,' he said. 'She's in the Joliette Basin, Wharf Seven, Berth D. I'll direct you.'

Durand grunted and the Berliet rolled forward. The superintendent lit a cigarette, sighing as he exuded clouds of blue smoke. 'Did the gendarme check your permits?'

The lieutenant said, 'Yes. There was no trouble.'

'Good,' said the superintendent. 'I didn't think there would be.'

*   *   *

The Berliet nosed down the roadway between the warehouses, past A Berth then on past B and C. In a hundred metres or so it swung left.

'That's her,' said the superintendent. 'Pull up alongside. Ahead of the crane.'

'Small, isn't she?' said the lieutenant. An undistinguished coaster lay in D Berth, puffs of diesel exhaust coming from the grubby white, red-banded funnel. The name *Byblos* and the port of registration BEIRUT showed up on her stern. The scene was brightly lit by

8

cargo clusters in the ship and arc-lights on the warehouse. There was no sign of life but for two men at the inboard end of the gangway.

Durand parked the Berliet ahead of the crane. A man in a peaked cap appeared on the deck of the coaster. 'Move her back, opposite number two hold.' He pointed to the hold immediately forward of the bridge superstructure. The crane came to life, its motor humming as it back-tracked along the rails, the jib turning in the direction of the coaster.

Durand backed the Berliet towards the crane, stopping when the man in the peaked cap shouted, 'That'll do.'

The superintendent and the lieutenant got out. Durand pulled a lever under the dashboard and the roof of the transporter rose slowly on side-hinges until it was fully opened. A motor in the crane whirred and the jib swung back until the cable and lifting hook plumbed the open transporter. The hook descended and the men in the transporter hitched it to the wire sling on the packing case. The crane driver pulled the lifting lever and the case came clear. The jib swung outwards towards the coaster and hovered over number two hold, the crane driver obeying the signals of the man in the peaked cap.

The men in the hold who received and stowed the grey packing case saw that it came from Duquesne Frères et Cie, manufacturers

9

of agricultural machinery at Ouvry-sur-Maine, in the Department of the Seine. It was consigned to a well-known firm of distributors in Beirut, D. B. Mahroutti Bros, and it was the first of sixteen of various shapes and sizes to be transferred from the transporter to the ship.

*   *   *

While the off-loading was taking place the superintendent and the lieutenant went on board the *Byblos*. In the captain's cabin they conferred earnestly with the men who'd been on the gangway when the transporter arrived. They were Syrians and both spoke excellent French. Much of the discussion was of a technical nature and in this the lieutenant took a prominent part. Documents signed, felicitations exchanged, the superintendent and lieutenant returned to the transporter where off-loading had now been completed.

The entire operation had taken less than an hour. It had been watched from beginning to end by a bearded young man concealed behind a lifeboat on the boatdeck of the *Byblos*. A livid scar ran from the base of his right ear down the neck into his collar. Much of the scar was concealed by the beard and long black hair. He was a member of the coaster's crew. A new one, he'd signed on as galley-hand only two weeks before. That was the day the coaster had left Beirut for Marseille.

CHAPTER TWO

'She sailed this morning at daybreak. Nayef's message came at five o'clock. That is why I sent for you.' Mahmoud el Ka'ed's intense eyes searched the faces of the eleven men and a girl gathered round him in the cellar. They were sitting on wooden benches at a table which did service of sorts as a workman's bench. The cellar, low-ceilinged and poorly lit, smelt of old drains and decay. From somewhere came the tic-tac of dripping water. In the corners there were broken chairs, an old chest, a pile of threadbare carpets, a stack of cartons and a heap of rubbish.

Unpromising though the place was it had the advantage of being a 'safe house'. An anonymous building between the Boulevard Saeb Salaam and the Rue Bechara el Koury in the area of the Safa Mosque, it was far enough from the sprawling refugee camp to the south of Beirut to avoid sporadic air strikes by the Israelis and the close attention of their agents. It was one of several 'safe houses' they used for their meetings.

The voice which had spoken was low pitched, almost gentle—and misleading because it was not at all in keeping with the character of its owner. Tall, slim, hollow-cheeked with flowing moustache, it was his eyes, concealed now behind dark glasses, which revealed the man they called El Ka'ed— the leader. They were eyes which glittered with fierce energy.

'Nayef's message gave the dimensions. I have already passed them to Youssef. Zeid will let us have details of the markings as soon as he arrives.'

After his listeners' predictable murmur of excitement, Ka'ed said, 'The ship is coming direct. The agents say she will arrive in five days. That is on Friday morning.'

A pale, cadaverous man wearing horn-rimmed glasses said, 'When is zero hour?'

'Between two and four in the morning. The nearer to two the better. The moon will have set. The operation must be completed before daylight.' He looked towards the end of the table. 'What news have you, Assaf?'

Assaf Kamel had long hair, tired eyes. 'Colonel Rashid Dahan will arrive on Friday morning with four Syrian officers,' he said. 'They are coming from Damascus by car, travelling in civilian clothes. On arrival they'll disperse before going to the Syrian Embassy. Each will make his way independently. By order of the Ministry of Defence the port authority has given them the use of a transit shed near the Port Captain's office, Shed 27. They will drive two of Mahroutti's trucks down to the ship to pick up the load. The trucks will be kept in the shed overnight, guarded by the

Colonel and his officers. The next morning—
that's Saturday—they'll go to Damascus. They
are not prepared to leave the consignment on
board the *Byblos* overnight, and they are
unwilling to make the journey back in
darkness.'

'Good,' said Ka'ed. 'That is very good.' He
looked at Kamel with approval. This was a
man for whom he had both admiration and
affection. Kamel's sleepy looks belied his
character. He had served in the Syrian army
for several years as an arms expert and had
long experience of bomb-disposal work. Apart
from these qualifications, invaluable to the
Soukour-al-Sahra', he had shown himself to be
brave and steadfast.

There was a long silence, Ka'ed
contemplating the serious intent faces. What
were they thinking? What did they feel? They
didn't look alarmed or afraid. Least of all
Jasmine, the girl. She had an immensely
calm face but he knew she was hard,
notwithstanding her good looks.

He spoke to Kamel again. 'Let me see the
photos, Assaf.'

Kamel handed them over. Ka'ed went
through them slowly. He selected one,
compared it carefully with the face of a young
man on the far side of the table. 'Ammar Tarik
certainly has the Colonel's features,' he said.

The girl looked doubtful. 'Ammar is
younger and less handsome.'

13

The men laughed. Tarik shrugged his shoulders. 'Ask Assaf. He has seen us both.'

Ka'ed leant forward, looking down the table. 'So, Assaf. What do you say?'

'Yes. Ammar *is* much younger, but the resemblance is strong. They are of the same build, though the Colonel is heavier. He has a big stomach.'

Ka'ed looked at the girl. 'Make-up is your job, Jasmine. What do you think?'

'He'll look like the Colonel when I've finished with him. Don't worry.' She examined the photograph of the Colonel. 'I see what Assaf means about the stomach. But we can fix that. It's no problem.'

'Good.' Ka'ed rubbed the underside of his moustache with a knuckle. 'Assaf, tell us what you know of the Colonel. His house in Damascus. Where it is. What it looks like. His wife and children and other relatives. Tell us about the servants, too.'

In a deep throaty voice Kamel told them what he knew and it was a good deal for he'd spent a week in Damascus learning what he could about the Dahan family, photographing them with his Minolta spy camera, listening to their conversation at night through an Epines 258 XVe directional mike and amplifier while he sat in a car close to the open windows of the house.

When he'd finished Ka'ed said, 'You've done well, Kamel. You always do.'

There was some discussion then about the movements of a ship called *Leros*, after which Ka'ed gave them a thorough briefing. At the end of it each knew exactly what had to be done and when. Timing was an important part of the operation.

It was after midnight when they broke up and left in twos and threes to go their separate ways. When all had gone but Ka'ed's bodyguard, Abdu Hussein, he turned off the lights and they climbed the stairs to the street. It was warm, the sky bright with moon and stars, and there was little traffic. They walked towards Rue Shahla, keeping a careful lookout, conscious of the Walther 7.65 mm automatics in their shoulder-holsters, the combat knives in their belts. There were many who would have liked Ka'ed dead—and they were not only the Falangists and the Israeli secret agents who abounded in Beirut. In earlier days his face had been heavily bearded. Now, clean shaven, with moustache and dark glasses, few would have recognized him as Marwan Haddad, the name by which he had been known in the PLO. It was, as it happened, his real name.

At the University College of Beirut he had read philosophy and political science and there made the contacts and friendships which led him into the ranks of the Palestine Liberation Organization. At first a devoted disciple of Yasir Arafat, he'd later become disillusioned

15

with the leader's diplomatic strategy, his caution and what Ka'ed regarded as fatal lack of militancy. After quarrelling with Arafat, Ka'ed drifted from the centre to the extremist flank. There he became an embarrassment to the PLO leadership and attempts were made to discipline him.

Predictably, he broke away with a handful of followers and established a splinter group, Soukour-al-Sahra'—the Desert Hawks. The choice of name was not without significance. He made no secret of his policy: intransigent militance, unremitting violence, escalating terrorism. He believed implicitly in Mao's philosophy: 'Power comes from the barrel of a gun'. Step-by-step diplomacy, the Geneva Conference, Kissinger's attempts at an Arab-Israeli détente were, he was convinced, a waste of time.

Under Ka'ed's leadership Soukour-al-Sahra'—the SAS—had embarked on a widespread campaign of bombings, hi-jacks, kidnappings, bank hold-ups and assassinations. What funds they needed came from these operations, the ingenuity and success of which caught the imagination of many young Palestinians who, like Ka'ed, were impatient and believed that militant action was the only way to secure an independent Palestine. Like him they were ready to die for their cause; indeed they did, for the SAS suffered casualties, though nothing like as many as they

16

inflicted.

By late 1975 they had grown into a well-organized highly effective extremist group working outside the umbrella of the PLO. And they were beginning to make themselves felt, not only in the Middle East but in the chancelleries of the Western World.

Mahmoud el Ka'ed knew he was responsible for this. Not that he thought overmuch of his successes. The political objective was still too far from attainment, the real achievement yet to come. It was upon this that all his energies—what his enemies called his fanaticism—were now bent as he prepared what he liked to think of as The Final Solution.

CHAPTER THREE

The undistinguished-looking coaster with the red-banded white funnel entered Beirut Port in the late evening and berthed at the eastern end of the new basin in St Georges Bay.

There she lay, small and inconspicuous, dwarfed by the ships of the Messagerie Maritime, the American Export Lines, the Hellenic Mediterranean and the Khedive Mail Lines, and other vessels larger and more important than she was. But at least this was her home port and most of her crew lost no

17

time in getting ashore that night to be with families and friends. Among those who remained on board were the two Syrians who'd signed for the grey packing cases in Marseille at the time of loading.

The bearded young galley-hand with the scarred neck was one who did go ashore. Outside the port gates he took a taxi to the Safa Mosque. He paid it off and walked, following a circuitous route, bound for the rendezvous where he was to meet Ka'ed. Often he looked back to see if he was being followed.

*   *   *

At eight o'clock on the night the *Byblos* arrived in Beirut Port the hatches on number two hold were lifted, a crane manoeuvred into position, two Benz six-wheeler trucks came alongside and the sixteen grey packing cases were transferred to them. On either side of their driving cabs the trucks were lettered 'D. B. MAHROUTTI BROS'—and below that 'Agricultural Machinery'. No other cargo was off-loaded that night. Soon after the six-wheelers left the quay the two Syrian passengers came ashore.

In a dark shadowed alleyway between transit sheds a man had been watching the off-loading. Shortly before it finished he went to the back of the shed and picked up a motorcycle. He wheeled it down the length of the sheds to a point where he could watch the roadway along which the trucks would travel.

Before long he heard the sound of their engines. Soon afterwards they passed. He started the motorcycle and followed at a safe distance. The trucks travelled down towards the western side of the harbour, crossed the road which led to the main gates, turned right, then left, and stopped outside a large shed near the Rue de Trieste. It was not far from the Port Captain's office. The area was poorly lit but the man astride the motorcycle, motionless in the shadows, saw dark shapes climb from the trucks and slide open the doors of the shed. The six-wheelers were driven in, the doors shut behind them and he heard the slamming of bolts. Later two men arrived on foot. They knocked at the small door beside the main doors and were admitted.

The man wheeled his motorcycle back towards the railway lines, pushed it across and started the engine. He followed the route he'd come by until he reached the road to the main gates. He turned into it, passed through the gates and made off into the city.

*   *   *

There were stacks of cargo of various sorts in No. 27—the dimly-lit shed where Colonel Rashid Dahan and his officers were talking to the two late arrivals. All wore civilian clothes. The Colonel and those who'd come in the trucks with him were dressed as workmen.

'Was the journey all right, Roumi?' he enquired.

'Successful but not very comfortable. We had bad weather in the Gulf of Lyons. It made us sea-sick.'

The Colonel smiled, showing fine white teeth. 'All part of the day's work for soldiers.'

'We gave thanks to Allah that we were not sailors,' said the younger of the two.

'Any questions asked in the ship?'

'No. The captain had been told we were Mahroutti's representatives. That this was an important and valuable consignment. Irrigation equipment of a new type for the agricultural settlement at Bekàa. That we had been sent to supervise its handling and stowage. The rest of the crew were not interested.'

The discussion with the late arrivals continued for some time. Eventually, having agreed with the Colonel that they would proceed independently to Damascus on the following day, they left the shed and disappeared into the darkness.

*   *   *

The Syrian officers sat on packing cases, talking in low voices, some smoking. It was still

20

only ten-thirty. Too early for sleep. They knew an uncomfortable night lay ahead. It was warm and the air in the transit shed was stuffy, pungent with the smell of copra, bags of which were stacked in a far corner. The only places to rest were the driving cabs of the Benz six-wheelers.

'It will be a long night,' said the Colonel, reading their thoughts. 'We shall take it in turns to rest. I don't think sleep will be possible.'

'Except for Azhari,' said a young officer. 'He passes out like a light. And snores.'

Azhari protested and there was a ripple of laughter.

Beneath their clothes, Colonel Rashid Dahan and his men were armed with Stetchkin 9mm automatic pistols. They had been supplied to the Syrian Army by the Soviet Union.

*　　　*　　　*

In the early hours of morning there was knocking on the doors of the transit shed. Dahan alerted his men and went to the door accompanied by Azhari. He saw by his wristwatch that the time was seventeen minutes past one.

'Who is there?' he demanded.

'Abdul Hassami, Assistant Port Captain,' came the reply. 'I have an urgent message for

21

Colonel Rashid Dahan.'

The Colonel nodded to Azhari and took up a position beside the door. The hand he thrust into his jacket clasped the butt of the 9mm Stetchkin. In one quick motion he opened the door and shone a torch in the face of the man standing there. He was wearing the uniform of a senior port official.

'I am Colonel Rashid Dahan,' said the Colonel. 'What is the message?'

'You are wanted on the telephone, sir. Your wife is calling from Damascus.' The port official hesitated. 'I am sorry, Colonel, but there has been an accident. It is your son, Omar. Your wife has just returned from the hospital.'

'In the name of Allah!' The Colonel stiffened, the colour draining from his cheeks. 'He's . . .?' he gulped. 'He's not dead?'

'No, sir. But she says it is serious. His bicycle collided with a car.' Hassami paused, looking sorrowfully at the Syrian. 'Please follow me to the port office, sir.'

The Colonel's energy seemed to drain away, his knees felt weak and his head spun. Omar was his eldest and favourite son. Only a few weeks back the boy had celebrated his twelfth birthday. It was then the Colonel had given him the new bicycle. With an effort of will he cleared his mind. 'Yes,' he said. 'I'll come. One moment, please.'

He hurried over to the trucks. 'Take charge,

Aramoun,' he said. 'There is an urgent telephone call for me from Damascus. From my wife. Omar has had an accident.' His voice trembled with emotion. 'I must go to the port office. I won't be long.'

'Of course, Rashid.' The man who spoke was a major, the Colonel's second-in-command and close friend. 'I am sorry. May Allah be merciful.'

Dahan stared at him helplessly, turned on his heel and went back to the door. He stepped outside and joined the port official. Together they set off down the roadway between the sheds.

'It is not far,' said Hassami. 'A few minutes only.'

The Colonel was too shattered to say anything.

At the end of the shed the roadway turned towards the harbour. They followed it until Hassami said, 'Down here, sir. It's a short cut.'

They left the road and walked down a darkened alley between sheds, the port official leading. Over his shoulder he said, 'Your wife mentioned that it was a new bicycle. A birthday present.'

'I know,' said the Colonel heavily. 'I wish I had never given him the accursed thing.'

'You cannot blame yourself.' Hassami added, 'It is the will of Allah. We are almost there.'

'Good,' said the Colonel. It was the last

word he was to utter for at that moment he was struck over the head from behind and slumped to the ground. Two men loomed out of the darkness as the Assistant Port Captain leant over the recumbant figure. 'Well done, Ammar,' he said to one of them. 'Move fast now.'

Ammar Tarik handed the cosh he was holding to Hassami who took up a position at the top of the alleyway, while the new arrivals stripped the unconscious Dahan of all he was wearing save his underpants. Tarik took off his own slacks and shirt and changed into the Colonel's clothes. 'I don't mind the make-up,' he whispered, 'but this padding is awkward.' He passed his own slacks and shirt to the other man. 'Look after these.'

'It's not for long,' said his companion, making the clothes into a bundle. 'Pity there's no light. I'd like to compare you with him.' He looked at the almost-naked body on the ground.

'Right,' said Tarik a few minutes later. 'I'm ready.' He let out a low whistle. They heard the scrape and shuffle of feet at the top of the alleyway.

'They're coming,' said the other man. The unconscious Syrian began to moan. Tarik dropped down beside him, clamped a hand over his mouth to muffle the sound. The men in the alleyway arrived, led by the Assistant Port Captain. 'Ready?' His whisper was urgent.

Tarik said, 'Yes, Mahmoud. But he's groaning. My hand's over his mouth.' Hassami knelt and in the darkness it seemed to Tarik that he was striking Dahan in the chest. The thumps were followed by coughing and a gurgling sound. The Colonel's body twitched spasmodically then lay still. Hassami stood up. 'I had to,' he said, putting the Colonel's 9mm Stetchkin into a pocket of his uniform jacket. 'He might have identified me.'

'You had no choice.'

There was hurried consultation, the assistant port captain issued instructions and the men disappeared into the night. When they'd gone he wiped the blade of his knife on the Colonel's underpants, replacing it in the sheath on his belt. The knife had been a problem for Mahmoud el Ka'ed. It did not fit easily under the tight jacket of the uniform he was wearing—the uniform of an assistant port captain.

CHAPTER FOUR

In the Israeli Embassy, not far from Kensington Palace Barracks, the Ambassador was talking to Ezra Barlov, head of the intelligence section. 'So Kahn believes it is imminent. On what authority?'

'On information gathered by Tel Aviv.'

'Who are these people?'

'Difficult to say. It hasn't yet been possible to establish their affiliations. We didn't know about Spender Street until comparatively recently.'

'How did Kahn get on to them originally?'

Barlov dropped his spectacles, made much of bending down to search for them—how could he tell the Ambassador that Samia Khayat, the Palestinian girl working in the London office of an insurance company with extensive Middle East interests, had in recent months become a close friend of Sandra Hamadeh, a girl working in the same typing pool, who shared an apartment off the Bayswater Road with her brother?—how could he explain that Samia Khayat was Rachel Margolis, an Israeli agent 'planted' in London five years ago? Deep cover was sacrosanct.

Barlov retrieved the fallen spectacles and returned to his chair. 'I'm afraid that's something Tel Aviv hasn't told me, Ambassador.'

The older man looked mildly embarrassed. 'I'm sorry. I shouldn't have asked. Now—you say Kahn thinks this is the target?'

'He rates it as probable.'

The Ambassador threw his hands up in a token of despair. 'Jakob Kahn's probables and possibles.'

26

Barlov's thin face broke into a smile. 'It's not a bad way of assessing the risks. Courses of action open to the enemy.'

'And he believes the people at Mocal are involved?'

'He thinks it's possible. That's why they're under surveillance.'

The Ambassador, a plump, fatherly figure, folded his arms, leant back in his chair. 'Tell me about Mocal.'

'The business is called Middle Orient Consolidated Agencies Limited. Import, export agents. For the last three months they've occupied premises at 39 Spender Street. Two offices on the ground floor. Before that it was a shell company bought for next to nothing by the three Palestinians who run it.'

'What is known about them?'

'Very little really. We know what each of them looks like, the names they use. All new to us. We've no previous history of any of them. They've been in London for some time, at least six months—that's Hanna Nasour—and one of the men, Najib Hamadeh, as long as two years. We're satisfied the business is a phoney.'

'But, good cover.'

'That's the idea.'

'On what evidence, Barlov?'

'They don't seem to do any business.'

'And this operation? What does Kahn think. Bomb attack?'

27

'Probably. At least an attack with explosives. Possibly bomb or bazooka.'

The Ambassador got up from his desk, took off his glasses and cleaned them with slow deliberation. 'What do you propose to do?'

'Kahn wants the premises bugged.'

'Is that possible?'

'It is.'

'When?'

'In the next twenty-four hours.'

'I hope nothing goes wrong, Barlov. We can't afford a Watergate.'

'There is no prospect of the Embassy being involved, Ambassador. Ascher and his people have excellent cover and they are highly professional.'

*   *   *

From the bay window of the small apartment near Vauxhall Bridge he could see over Lambeth Bridge to the Houses of Parliament and Westminster Bridge. Beyond that the Thames faded into the mists of an autumn evening. He was enjoying its tranquillity when he heard the sound of a key turning in the lock. He took the Mauser automatic from his shoulder-holster and stood against the wall. The door opened and a young woman came in.

'Hi,' he said. 'You're late.'

'It was Johnnie Peters. He wouldn't let me go.'

'Your scene?' He put the revolver back into the shoulder-holster.

'Not really. He's all right. Very jealous and inquisitive. Wants to know what I do, where I work.'

'Have you told him anything?'

'Nothing, Shalom. He thinks I'm a freelance journalist. That I work at home and dart about looking for stories. I help him to believe that.' She sat on the studio couch. 'He thinks there's another man.'

'How d'you get him off that?'

'By telling him there isn't.' She looked at him in a curious, puzzled way. 'That's true, isn't it?'

Shalom Ascher shrugged his shoulders. He was a burly, bearded, stooping man in his early thirties. 'Don't ask me. How should I know?'

'Actually, the best way of stopping his questions is to let him talk about himself. Like most men. Their favourite subject. They talk, you listen. As long as you've got a pair of ears, a reasonably passable face and body, they're happy.'

'You're a cynic, Ruth. Anyway, watch it. He may not be as stupid as you think. Works in an advertising office, doesn't he?'

'Yes. On the creative side, he says. Not a very important number, I guess. Don't know why I bother really.' She poured herself a coke. 'Like one?'

'No thanks. Why *do* you bother?'

29

'Biological fact. Woman needs man. I've been in London for six months. Not allowed to mix with our own people. He's available. Life has to go on.'

'Don't get emotionally involved. You can't afford that.'

'I don't have to. I'm tough. You know that.'

'Do I? I wonder.'

She stood up, picked up her bag and coat. 'See you.' She went through the door into her room.

He sighed. Ruth Meyer was an attractive woman. Too attractive really. Ascher liked her a lot, but feared involvement. It didn't go along with the work they were doing, so he did nothing about it. But he didn't care much for the idea of Johnnie Peters. Shaking off what he suspected was jealousy he went back to the window, leant on the sill and looked down the Thames once again. He decided it was useful therapy for a man with a lot on his mind. Daylight had almost gone. With narrowed eyes he focused on the stream of traffic silhouetted against the lights on the bridge beyond the Houses of Parliament. It looked like a glowing caterpillar moving along a luminous branch, the buses the moving arches of its back.

He heard her come back into the room. 'They're fortunate,' he said, keeping his eye on the river.

'Who?' The studio couch squeaked as she sat down.

'The British. To have London, Westminster, the Thames, the bridges. This view. It always reassures me. Like their institutions. The Commons, the Lords. Reflects the character of the people. Solid, unchanging.'

'Nothing's immutable.' She put down the paper she'd picked up. 'Least of all Britain.'

He moved away from the window and sat at a small table. 'Right, let's get on with our own problems.' He yawned, stretched his arms in one big gesture.

She slid on to the floor, sat with her back against the couch. 'Let's have it,' she said. 'What happened from twelve to four?'

'Nothing much. Normal routine. They went out just before one. For lunch, shopping, whatever. Hamadeh and Souref got back at fifteen minutes past two. Hanna Nasour came along soon afterwards.'

'Were they carrying anything?'

'Hamadeh and Souref had newspapers and a plastic carrybag from Music-Box in the Strand. An LP I expect. Hanna came back with a Marks & Spencer shopping bag. Couldn't have been much in it, the way she carried it. She also had a newspaper and what looked like a bag of fruit.'

'Any deliveries?'

'No parcels or packages. Zol joined me at four. We sat and chatted. At four-ten a postal messenger delivered a telegram to Mocal. I handed over to Zol a few minutes later and

31

left.'

'Wonder what was in the telegram?'

'Haven't a clue.'

'What a business that must be,' she said. 'Limited all right. No customers. No deliveries. No dispatches. No bank account. No telephone. Practically no mail. A staff of three sitting on their backsides doing nothing. It doesn't add up.'

Ascher shrugged his shoulders. 'How do you know nothing? Maybe they play backgammon, make love, drink coffee, whatever. That can be a tough routine. And because it doesn't add up—well, that's why we're here.'

'Lucky them.' She laughed dryly. 'No. They're Arabs. It will be very serious. Endless discussion of the project. How they are to do it? On what day and at what time? And who with. You know.'

'Don't underrate them, Ruth. They've a cause and they're ready to die for it. Makes them a tough proposition.'

'Well, what are they waiting for? I know Jakob says there's something brewing. Believes they may be involved. But it doesn't look like it from here.'

'That's why we've got to get a bug in there. They're not going to have parcels coming into the place with "Explosives" written on them. The postman's not going to drop letters on the pavement with coded messages for us to pick up.'

She stood up, pulled her hair forward over her shoulders and went to the window. 'What happens tonight?'

'I relieve Zol at eight o'clock. He has something to eat, then comes here. At eleven he goes back to Spender Street. You get there at midnight. I take the tools in. He brings the bugs and a tape recorder. You bring another recorder and the spare tapes. Okay?'

'Yes. Mind if I go to the pictures first?'

'Johnnie Peters?'

She smiled. 'Yes. He wants me to see *Emmanuelle*. Says it's erotic but beautiful. Thinks it would be good for me.'

'Considerate of him. What time does it finish?'

'About ten-thirty.'

'Be sure to lose him soon after that. We don't want him tailing you down Spender Street.'

'Don't worry. I know how to get rid of him.'

'How?'

'A woman's secret, Shalom.'

'Okay. But we've got some too. Don't take chances.'

He lit a cigarette, his eyes following the smoke as it drifted to the ceiling in whispy spirals. 'Now, where was I? Sure. We move into Mocal around three in the morning. Soon as we've checked all's clear. You stay in Fifty-Six keeping a lookout. Anybody, anything, odd turns up you alert us. Use the radio-cab code.'

'Radio-*taxi* code,' she corrected. Ascher's last assignment had been in the United States.

'Same thing.' He shook his shaggy head. 'We've already cased the place. The door has a mortice lock with Yale backup. No trouble.'

'Bolts?' she suggested.

'There aren't any.'

'Did Ezra have that checked?'

'Yes. Sent in one of his lot, meter reading, ten days ago.'

She came back from the window, sat on the floor again.

'Tell me more.'

'We'll allow fifteen minutes to look round the place. Another ten to fix the bugs. Ten to test. We talk, you check the tape. That's thirty-five minutes. Soon as you give us the okay we come back to Fifty-Six. Any problems?'

'Not yet. After midnight'll be Tuesday. Should be quiet around three.'

He nodded, looked at her absentmindedly as if he were thinking of something else. 'We'll have to watch it. Leaving the office and coming into Spender Street when it's all over. Best come out separately. Could be the odd fuzz about.'

'There's no law against working overtime in your own business,' she said. 'Even in Britain.'

'We'll be careful all the same.'

Narrow, winding, little-used, Spender Street was one of those quaint old London thoroughfares which seemed no longer to

34

serve any useful purpose. Situated in the triangle formed by Leicester Square, Covent Garden and the Savoy, and more or less equidistant from them, it snaked a brief course between small, smoke-grimed buildings, most of them struggling for tenants since London's great fruit and vegetable market had moved from Covent Garden to Nine Elms.

Number 56, an old decaying structure of two storeys and basement, was as small and unimportant as the street on to which it faced, but for the Israelis the two offices they rented there were vital. One of these was a general office, the other a stockroom. The sign on the passage door read *Ascher & Levi, Music Agents*. Once through it, callers were confronted with stacks of LPs and singles in colourful sleeves, hundreds of cassettes, a library of catalogues, two tape-recorders, a hi-fi, desks, chairs, a typewriter, filing cabinets and a telephone.

The windows were fitted with venetian blinds, and from them the Israelis could watch unseen the ground floor premises across the street. Their particular interest was number 39, a dark, dingy, brick-fronted place, coated with years of London grime. On its windows, opaqued in dark green enamel, the name MIDDLE ORIENT CONSOLIDATED AGENCIES LTD was lettered in gold.

CHAPTER FIVE

Mahmoud el Ka'ed and his men separated on emerging from the alleyway where they'd left the body of Colonel Rashid Dahan. Though they were all bound for the rendezvous behind Shed 27 they went by different routes, swiftly and silently, the sound of their footsteps muffled by rubber-soled shoes. The chosen place was a recess between two stacks of timber, well shielded from passers-by. As each man arrived, no more than a dissembled shape in the night, he answered Ammar Tarik's whispered, 'eight-two-one', with, 'five-three-nine', the challenge and reply for the night. Ka'ed and his bodyguard, Abdu Hussein, were the last to reach the rendezvous. Ka'ed saw that the time was 1.48 am.

'Issam and Abu Ali,' he called in a low voice. The men's answering 'Here' was barely audible in the darkness.

'Go now,' he said. 'One to each end of the shed. If you are not back by two o'clock I will assume it is all clear. Then we move in. When you see us come on to the loading platform, you join us.'

'Yes, Mahmoud.'

'In the name of Allah be silent. Your lives will depend upon it.'

They moved past him and out into the

night, and Ka'ed touched their shoulders in a gesture of affection. Like the rest of the party each had in their overalls a Walther automatic with silencer, a cosh in one hand, a combat knife in the other. They were dressed as dock labourers, but for Ka'ed who still wore the uniform of an assistant port captain.

* * *

It was 2 am. Issam and Abu Ali had not returned.

In the recess Ka'ed whispered, 'Ready, Ammar?'

'Yes. We are ready.'

'Move now. We shall follow.'

Ammar Tarik with two men slipped out and made for Shed 27. Soon afterwards, on hearing Ka'ed's muted 'Come', the other men followed him into the darkness.

The moon had set but the sky was bright with stars, the night air warm. From distant quays came the hum of machinery and the noise of cargo working by the night shift. Occasionally the far-off shrill of stevedores' whistles pierced the thin curtain of sound.

* * *

Movement could be discerned on the loading ramp along the front of the shed. Dark shapes, hidden in the shadows, pressed against the

37

walls near the main entrance. Others moved along the ramp to join them until there were eight in all.

When the last man was in position, Tarik knocked on the door. He heard voices in the shed, then footsteps making for the door.

A man called out, 'Is that you, Colonel?'

Tarik replied, 'Yes,' and moved to the edge of the loading ramp, five or six metres from the door. He leant over the side, looking down into an empty railway truck on the spur-line feeding the ramp. Behind him he heard bolts being drawn, the sound of a door opening, a voice calling, 'Colonel?'

Without turning, Tarik—dressed in the Colonel's clothing and looking very much like him—hissed, 'Sheesh!' and beckoned to the man at the door to join him.

The Syrian officer came towards him, automatic in hand. He had gone only a few paces when he was struck down by two men who came from the shadows. Within seconds they had stabbed him in the heart and pushed his body into the empty truck. Tarik turned, went back to the half-closed doors.

*   *   *

The Syrian officer who had answered the knocking was Major Aramoun, the second-in-command. Captain Azhari and the other officers had taken cover behind the trucks in

38

accordance with Aramoun's orders. They saw him go to the door and call out, 'Is that you, Colonel?' They heard the answering, 'Yes,' saw him unbolt the door, hesitate and step out, his Stetchkin automatic at the ready. As the door swung back on its hinges he was lost to sight. There were sounds of movement outside. Soon afterwards the door opened again and they saw the Colonel standing in the entrance. With fingers to his lips he signalled silence, while the hand holding the 9mm Stetchkin beckoned them. Worried and mystified, Captain Azhari ordered the lieutenants to go to the Colonel at once. Azhari then took cover behind a truck, some fifty metres from the door. Pistol in hand, he kept a sharp lookout.

The Colonel was still visible, standing outside the door with his back to the shed. He was stooping as if to be less conspicuous, apparently watching something to his right. Major Aramoun was out of sight.

While Azhari watched, the two lieutenants reached the door. The Colonel moved to the right, the lieutenants followed, and all three passed out of the captain's field of vision.

Puzzled and tense, Azhari waited. Suddenly, and with disturbing clarity, he heard the sounds of a struggle, thumps and a sharp cry, quickly muffled. Moments later men came pouring through the door into the warehouse. Azhari fired three shots and saw a man fall. The Syrian ran round to the front of the truck and jumped into the driving cab. He made frantic efforts to start the engine, hoping in his moment of terror to get the engine going and crash the truck through the closed doors of the shed. But it was a forlorn hope. The intruders were already banging at the doors of the Benz cab. In desperation he put his hand on the horn button but nothing happened, and he realized he'd not switched on. He turned the key as a man smashed the window next to him. Azhari saw the menacing barrel of an automatic pistol, shrank away, lifting his weapon in a futile gesture of defence. As he did so, he was acutely aware of two things: the automatic pointing at him was fitted with a silencer, and a spurt of flame was coming from its barrel.

*   *   *

Not long after Ka'ed and his men had killed Azhari, a black Benz six-wheeler was driven up the ramp into the shed through the now open doors. On either side of the cab it was lettered in white D. B. MAHROUTTI BROS, beneath that in smaller letters, 'Agricultural Machinery'. With the aid of a fork-lift truck, two grey packing cases were taken from the new arrival and substituted for two in the trucks already there: one from each of them. These were among the smaller packing cases which had been transported by the *Byblos* from Marseille to Beirut, but they were identical in size, colour and markings to those just brought into the shed.

The substitution complete, the bearded man with the scarred neck—lately galley-hand in the *Byblos*—climbed back into the driving seat of the Benz. One of Ka'ed's men joined him. The Benz moved ponderously out of the shed and down the ramp. The bearded man steered it across the railway lines and along the service road to the junction with the main road. There it turned right and rumbled down towards the dock gates.

Ka'ed and his men dragged the dead bodies of Major Aramoun and the lieutenants back into the shed, took the Walther automatic with spare magazines from the body of Abu Ali, placed papers in his jacket and hung an identity disc about his neck. With his combat knife Ka'ed slashed the dead man's face beyond recognition. He wept as he did so for they were old friends and Abu Ali had been one of his first recruits. When he'd finished, his men shut and locked the doors and with them he disappeared into the night.

*　　　*　　　*

Colonel Rashid Dahan's body was discovered by a dock labourer soon after eight o'clock in the morning. The police were at once called. There was no ready means of identifying the

41

body which had been stripped of clothing but for its underpants. It was taken to the mortuary and examined by a forensic surgeon who pronounced death to be due to multiple stab wounds. The police assumed the motive for the murder to have been robbery.

At that stage, owing to the secrecy which had surrounded the movements of the Syrian officers and the Benz trucks, no thought was given to any connection between the dead man and the Syrians in Shed 27. Indeed their presence there was known only to the Port Captain and his immediate assistants. It was a good deal later, when he learnt that one of the Mahroutti trucks had left the docks with a consignment of agricultural machinery in the early hours of morning, that his suspicions were first aroused. With the police he went to Shed 27. The doors were locked and there was no response to knocking, so they broke in and found the bodies of Major Aramoun, Captain Azhari and the two lieutenants. In addition, that of a man whose face had been mutilated beyond recognition. The documents in his pockets and his identity disc showed that he was an Israeli soldier. It was at this stage they realized that the almost naked body found that morning near the Port Captain's office was Colonel Rashid Dahan's.

The police counted sixteen grey packing cases in the Benz six-wheelers. A quick check with the *Byblos*'s chief officer confirmed that

42

this was the number which had been off-loaded. Exterior examination of the packing cases indicated that none had been opened or in any way tampered with. A check with the police at the Port Gates revealed that the Mahroutti Bros truck which had passed through in the early morning had the same registration letters as one of the two trucks still in Shed 27. The Chief of Police and the Port Captain lost no time in reporting what they'd found and the conclusions they'd drawn to their respective Ministers—Defence and Transport.

That night the Lebanese Minister of Defence telephoned his opposite number in Damascus on a scrambler line. The Syrian Minister having expressed shock and indignation, they were soon in agreement that Shed 27 had been the target of a particularly brutal Israeli commando raid. The Syrian Minister suggested that since the packing cases had not been removed or tampered with, the raiders must have been disturbed and obliged to call off their operation.

The Lebanese Minister pointed out that whoever might have disturbed them must have done so unwittingly, for no report of any sort had reached the port authorities or police.

The Syrian Minister agreed that this was difficult to explain. He undertook to fly down a party of officers on the following day to take over the consignment and move it to

Damascus by road.

The Lebanese Minister told him that Shed 27 was now being guarded by police, reinforced by an army unit. Everything possible was being done to prevent a repetition of the events of earlier in the day.

The two ministers agreed it was imperative to keep the news of the attack from the media for as long as possible, and to ensure that the contents of the packing cases should remain a closely-guarded secret. In the meantime, said the Syrian Minister, an urgent meeting of his cabinet would be called to consider the diplomatic action to be taken vis-à-vis the Israeli Government.

CHAPTER SIX

In an old junk yard in Sinn-el-Fil, a poorer quarter of Beirut, two men worked on the engine of a vintage Renault. But for occasional rubbish scavengers and children looking for a place to hide, few people came that way. No weapons could be seen but the men were armed.

Inside the shed a single bulb on a worn flex hung from a roof-beam. In its uncertain light could be seen a big Leyland pantechnicon which took up one side of the shed. BADAGUI CO. SAL was lettered in black on its yellow sides. In the warm air of afternoon the atmosphere in the shed was pungent with the smell of diesel oil and tyres.

Two grey packing cases stood on the dirt floor near the far end where a man was busy at a bench. He was working by the light of a camping torch. Not far from him three men and a girl were examining a large steel cone with the aid of an inspection lamp. It lay on a wooden trestle, near it a fork-lift truck. Beyond the yellow Leyland an armed man stood on guard.

'One point seven-five metres,' said the bearded man with the neck scar. 'Heavier than it looks. Screening accounts for most of the weight.'

'I thought it would be much bigger,' said the girl, Jasmine Fawaz. 'They *are* in pictures.'

'The pictures show you the whole thing. This is the warhead—just one section. Each Pluton has four units. The warhead, the guidance package, fuel tank and rocket engine. I used to work on the final assembly. Putting the lot together.'

'Did you enjoy it, Zeid?' She looked at him with curious eyes.

'It was very interesting. I suppose that's always enjoyable. But I was going to say—about size—when four sections are put together Pluton is seven-and-a-half metres long. All up weight 2350 kilograms. A lot of that is fuel. There were four Plutons in the

45

Byblos consignment. More are coming in other ships.'

'Fortunate we only needed a warhead,' she said.

Adel Khoury, a gloomy round-shouldered man, pointed to the grooved locking device in the base of the cone. 'This is where the detonator is attached. When Kamel is ready we'll fix it.' Khoury had taken a degree in physics at the American University in Beirut. Later he'd gone to the Massachusetts Institute of Technology, and during vacations worked on nuclear reactors with General Electric.

Ka'ed yawned. He'd had virtually no sleep for twenty-four hours. 'Let's have a look in the van.'

They followed him over to the Leyland. He opened the loading doors and got in, trailing the lead of an inspection lamp. The others followed, ranging themselves round the stack of Bokharas and Kashans. The carpets were 2.75 x 1.85 m making a solid stack 1.5 m high.

The men rolled back the upper layers to reveal a rectangular cavity in the centre of the stack. Its area was somewhat larger than the area of carpet remaining.

Jasmine Fawaz shivered. To her it looked like a mass grave awaiting coffins. A latticed aluminium frame supported its four walls. In the centre, between the cross bracing, there was another aluminium frame. Ka'ed lifted the top half. 'It's shaped to hold the warhead

46

firmly in position once it's locked down,' he said.

The girl looked doubtful. 'Is the bale strong enough with so much of the centre cut out?'

'Yes.' He took off his dark glasses, cleaned them with a tissue. 'The whole bale's reinforced laterally and transversally with aluminium rods. You can't see them but they're there. It's a very strong structure.'

'What about weight?' said Abdu Hussein, thinking what wild eyes Ka'ed had.

'Much the same as a standard bale of carpets of this size. The volume of material cut out is several times greater than the volume of the warhead. The weight of the warhead plus the aluminium reinforcing is only fifteen per cent more than the weight of the material cut out.' He replaced the top half of the frame. 'A tightly-compressed bale of carpets is a heavy item.'

Jasmine said, 'How many carpets are there?'

'Eighty-five.'

She shook her head. 'And we mutilate most of them. How sad.'

'They cost us nothing.' Ka'ed shrugged his shoulders. 'We took them.'

'Like we take everything.'

He went to the open doors of the pantechnicon. 'Hey, Zeid,' he called.

The man at the bench answered, 'What is it, Mahmoud?'

'As soon as you and Kamel have finished,

bring it across with the fork-lift.' He turned to Tarik. 'Got all the baling gear ready?'

'Yes. Hessian, hooping bands, mechanical bander, marking materials, stencils. All okay.'

'Good.' Ka'ed climbed down from the Leyland and joined the man at the work-bench. For some time he watched in silence. At last he said, 'Nearly finished, Assaf?'

Assaf Kamel did not look up from what he was doing. His eyes were fixed on the tip of the soldering iron from which a whisp of vapour issued. 'Not long now,' he said. 'I'm annealing the leads for the timing gear and emergency detonator.'

Ka'ed saw from his watch that it was close to six. The Leyland would take the bale out that night under cover of darkness. The sooner it was away from there the better.

Zeid Barakat came to him. 'Mahmoud,' he said. 'I'm still not happy about the morality of this.'

Behind the dark glasses Ka'ed's eyes narrowed, his voice hardened. 'If you want to worry about morality, Zeid, worry about the morality of those who took our country from us.' He put his hand on the bearded man's shoulder. 'I know how you feel, but you must get your priorities right. We are at war. We have to do things we don't like doing. This morning we killed five Syrian officers. There are no greater supporters of an independent Palestine than the Syrians. War makes for

48

terrible decisions.'

Barakat smiled in a restrained, humourless way. 'You are right, Mahmoud.' He drew a hand across his eyes. 'It's a mood. It will pass.'

'You are not alone with your conscience, Zeid. There is always a struggle in our minds. We mustn't lose our resolve in weakness and sentiment.'

*　　　*　　　*

The attacks on Shed 27 had taken place in the early hours of Wednesday, 6th October. Notwithstanding the efforts of the Lebanese authorities to keep the news from the media, the following morning's edition of Beirut's *Al Hayat* ran a headline: ISRAELI COMMANDO UNIT ATTACKS BEIRUT PORT? Beneath the double column headline with its mark of interrogation appeared the report of a clash between Lebanese units and an Israeli commando force—presumably seaborne—believed to have penetrated Beirut Port during the hours of darkness on October 5th/6th. It was rumoured said the paper guardedly, that the raiders had been driven off after a number of men had been killed.

This sketchy, somewhat inaccurate account was enough to indicate that someone had talked. The Ministers of Defence and Transport were furious but the secret was out and during that day, smelling a sensational

49

story, the media men began casting for a scent. One of them, Pierre Gamin, accredited to Le *Monde*, found it and went racing down the trail.

* * *

It was after ten on the morning of Thursday, October 7th, when the yellow Leyland entered Beirut Port and proceeded to the berth where the Hellenic Mediterranean Lines' ship *Leros* was lying. A vessel of medium size, she carried both passengers and cargo. The Blue Peter fluttering at her yardarm indicated that she was to sail that day. The journey would take her home to the Piraeus via Latakia, Famagusta and Iraklion.

The driver of the Leyland backed it up against the loading platform behind the transit shed. The man accompanying him went into the office with the shipping documents. When he came back the doors of the Leyland were opened and dock labourers manhandled the big hessian-wrapped bale on to the platform where it was picked up by a fork-lift truck. The vehicle turned and purred its way back into the shed, looking like some primeval monster carrying its kill.

The man with the shipping documents climbed in next to the driver. 'Right,' he said. 'Let's go.' The Leyland travelled slowly down the service road between the sheds before turning left and disappearing from sight.

The fork-lift truck carried the bale through the shed to the platform on the far side where stevedores were busy with cargo slings and nets feeding the cranes. The driver put his load down, turned the fork-lift and steered it back through the shed.

The canvas labels sewn on to the bale showed that it was consigned to Dimitri Ionides & Co., 181 Pastropoulos Street, Athens, and included an injunction to 'Stow in a Dry Place'. In due course, stevedores put slings round the bale and a crane transferred it to number 3 hold where it ended up in the *Leros*'s 'tween decks.

*   *   *

One of the passengers who boarded the ship shortly before sailing that afternoon was the bearded, scarred man.

*   *   *

About the time the Leyland was delivering its load in Beirut Port, a party of Syrian officers accompanied by paratroopers drove the Mahroutti Bros trucks out of Shed 27 and began their journey to Damascus, some 110 kilometres to the north. None of the Syrians was in uniform. They had left behind in the shed the formidable but discreetly hidden overnight guard supplied by the Lebanese Army.

The trucks were preceded and followed by two black Citroëns. The civilians in these cars, which passers-by would not have associated with the trucks they were escorting, were security police. The Minister of Defence was not taking any more chances while the consignment was on Lebanese territory. The Citroëns would keep within reasonable distance of the trucks until the Syrian border was reached, and there would be discreet surveillance by the Syrian Air Force, overflying the Lebanon with the knowledge and consent of the government in Beirut.

*   *   *

'Pernod. No water, much ice.' The Frenchman slid his empty glass across the counter of the bar in the Hotel St George. Through the windows he could see over a wide arc of the Mediterranean. Ruffled by the wind, its cliché blue showed frills of old lace where incoming seas spilled against the shore. To the east lay the port with its array of masts and funnels. A skimmer buzzed across the harbour, leaping and bumping, its wake describing a foaming white line which faded slowly into the sea from which it had come.

The barman poured the Pernod on to a mound of crushed ice, added a slice of lemon and pushed the glass back to the Frenchman. 'Three twenty, m'sieu,' he said impersonally, his eyes elsewhere in the manner of his kind. The Frenchman took a wad of Lebanese notes from his pocket, peeled off four and handed them across. Without waiting for the change he took the Pernod and walked through to the foyer. There he went to a phone booth. He lifted the instrument and the girl on the hotel switchboard answered.

'Paris, France,' he said. 'Seven-five-zero-four-double-four.'

'One moment, m'sieu.'

He waited, arranging mentally the order of what he had to say. His thoughts were interrupted by the girl. 'There is a delay, m'sieu. The lines are busy.'

'How long?'

'Thirty, perhaps forty, minutes.'

'*Tiens*,' he said. 'I'll wait in the bar. Call me there through the barman. Please don't page me.'

'Your name and room number, m'sieu.'

'Pierre Gamin,' he said. 'Room two-three-nine.'

*   *   *

The delay on the Paris call was longer than expected. An hour and twenty-seven minutes elapsed before the barman put down his phone, looked across to where Pierre Gamin

53

was sitting and nodded. 'Your call, m'sieu. Booth seven.'

The Frenchman went through the foyer to the booth and lifted the phone. 'Hullo,' he said.

'Hullo, Pierre. How are you?'

He recognized the voice of Jules Boyer, doyen of the Middle East desk in the Paris office. 'Fine, Jules. Listen. This is urgent. Duquesne Freres et Cie, Ouvry-sur-Maine, Department of the Seine. Got it?'

'Yes. We're taping it anyway. Carry on.'

'Good, Jules. They make agricultural machinery?'

'Yes. Big people.'

'A consignment from them for D. B. Mahroutti Bros of Beirut arrived from Marseille in the *Byblos* two days ago. It was off-loaded at once and taken in two of Mahroutti's trucks to Shed 27 of this port. Mahrouttis are important distributors of agricultural machinery in the Lebanon. Head office, Beirut.'

'So where's the story?'

'Listen, Jules. For God's sake don't interrupt.'

'Mahroutti's trucks were locked in Shed 27 for the night with their load.'

'So?'

'This morning's *Al Hayat* has a banner headline over two columns: quote, Israeli Commando Unit attacks Beirut Port interrogation mark, unquote. Below the headline they report rumours of a seaborne raid by an Israeli commando unit on the night of fifth/sixth October. Israelis believed to have penetrated the dock area but to have been repulsed after several had been killed.'

'Have you checked the story?'

'Yes. There seem to have been no witnesses of any fighting. But something did happen in Shed 27 that night.'

'How do you know?'

'There were armed guards in the shed with these trucks. They were found the next day. All were . . .'

At that stage the call was cut off and the voice of the girl on the switchboard came through. 'I am sorry, m'sieu. There is a fault on the line.'

'*Merde!*' said Gamin. 'It should be now. Listen. Please get me that number again. As soon as you can. It is urgent. Please.'

'I will try, m'sieu. But it will take time. The lines to Paris are very busy. Where shall I call you?'

'As before. In the bar.' He put down the phone and stepped out of the booth.

Two men came up to him. One tall and thin with dark glasses, the other short and stocky with shadowed jowls.

The thin man said, 'Monsieur Pierre Gamin?'

'Yes,' said the Frenchman.

From an inside pocket the man produced a plastic-covered identity card. 'Deuxième Bureau,' he said. 'Please come with us, m'sieu. They wish to talk to you at headquarters.'

'Talk? About what?'

The thin man shrugged his shoulders. 'I have no idea, m'sieu.'

Pierre Gamin was not as astonished as he tried to appear. He'd foreseen the possibility. That was why he'd given Réné St Clair of *Paris Match* a letter to Virginie, Gamin's wife, for delivery that night in Paris. Inside the letter was a sealed envelope addressed to Jules Boyer.

Réné St Clair had left Beirut on an Air France flight about the time Gamin's first telephone call to Paris came through. The letter to Jules Boyer contained all that Pierre Gamin had intended to say in that call . . . and rather more.

CHAPTER SEVEN

At noon the two Benz trucks belonging to D. B. Mahroutti Bros shed the escorting Citroëns. Shortly afterwards they reached the border posts at Masnaa. There, having completed the necessary formalities, they were passed through. A few kilometres on they were joined by an escort of Syrian armoured cars.

These kept sufficiently far from the trucks, two ahead and two following, to allay curiosity. It was, in any event, a road on which military activity was commonplace.

Little more than an hour after leaving the border the motorcade arrived safely in Damascus.

*   *   *

At eight o'clock that night the Lebanese Minister of Defence, at home changing for an official dinner, received an urgent call from Damascus on a scrambler line. It was an awkward time for the Minister who was in his bath and already somewhat late, but since the caller was the Syrian Minister of Defence he at once went to the phone. In a somewhat agitated voice his caller informed him that the Mahroutti Bros' trucks had arrived at the Military Ordinance Depot between one and two that afternoon. Later, when the packing cases were opened, it had been found that two of them contained scrap metal of the same weight as the equipment missing from them.

The Lebanese Minister, having expressed astonishment and dismay, was quick to grasp the point. 'So there has been substitution,' he said.

'Yes. It was evidently the purpose of the Israeli attack. Of the two packing cases that are missing one contained a warhead, the other the detonating component. I understand they are always kept apart until the weapon is assembled for operational purposes '

'So they've got a warhead but no delivery vehicle.' The Lebanese Minister paused. 'I wonder if that's what they wanted. After all, they have the Lance missiles.'

'Yes. There's no way of knowing. It may be they were interrupted, or they took the smaller packing cases because they were more easily transported.'

The Lebanese Minister said, 'How would the Israelis have known which contained the warheads and detonators?'

'In the same way they learnt about the consignment,' said the Syrian Minister. 'Their intelligence service is highly efficient. Somehow, somewhere, there has been a leakage.'

'Not at this end, I assure you,' said the Lebanese Minister. 'The nature of that consignment was known only to the Prime Minister, the Minister of Transport and myself.'

'Of course, my dear Bakkal. We accept your assurances without question. The leakage could well have taken place at the French end. However, it is most unfortunate that the Israelis were able to reach Shed 27, kill all our people there and remove the packing cases without detection.'

Conscious of the implied criticism, the

Lebanese Minister said, 'It was indeed unfortunate. It is to be the subject of a full enquiry. But you will recall that when I offered to provide a Lebanese military guard you assured me your Syrian officers would not require assistance.'

'Quite so. We were anxious not to draw attention to the consignment. This dictated our policy. And still does.' He paused. 'I am sure you will agree, my dear Bakkal, that there is nothing to be gained by recrimination. The situation is too serious for that. Particularly in view of the report published by *Al Hayat* this morning. That really has complicated matters.'

'I agree. We are taking strong action. But newspapers are newspapers and they look for sensational stories. An Israeli attack is always news, especially one on the Port. Unhappily the media people are now in full cry. Late this afternoon our security police arrested a *Le Monde* reporter. He has found out a good deal. For example that the dead men were Syrian army officers.'

'In the name of Allah! Why were we not told?'

'I gave instructions that you were to be. It was late this afternoon. Our people cut off a telephone call the reporter was making to his Paris office. At first he was only repeating the Al Hayat story, but as soon as they realized he knew more they cut him off. That was before he was able to tell Paris that the dead men—

59

but for one Israeli—were your officers.'

'What can you do to him?'

'Not much. We have to be careful with the French. But of course they are very much involved. They may not object too strenuously if we hold him. At least for some time.'

'The longer the better,' said the Syrian Minister. 'We need time. We are having a special meeting of the Cabinet tonight to consider these developments. I was anxious to talk to you first. If the truth gets out—and it looks as if it will—the political implications are extremely serious. We shall of course be guarded in any statements we release, and we shall have to consult with the French Government and yourselves.'

'Will you be disclosing the nature of the weapons?'

'I cannot say at this stage. The fact that the Israelis must now know—if they didn't already—will influence our judgement. The whole affair will have to be considered on the basis of political advantage, with special regard to international repercussions. I will keep you fully informed.'

'Thank you, my dear Samedi. I will let you know of all developments at this end. I shall instruct our police and military authorities to assume that the missing equipment may still be on Lebanese territory. We shall maintain the utmost vigilance, you may be sure.'

There followed the usual exchange of

courtesies and the conversation ended.

*   *   *

On October 8th *Le Monde* published Pierre Gamin's story: A consignment of agricultural machinery from France to Syria, said *Le Monde*, had been the objective of the Israeli commando operation in Beirut Port on the night of October 5/6. The 'agricultural machinery' had evidently been of a sufficiently confidential nature for special precautions to be taken for its safety while in the Port. So much so that five Syrian army officers, including a colonel, had been assigned secretly to protect it, although the machinery had been consigned to a well-known Beirut firm of agricultural machinery distributors for delivery to the government irrigation works at Bekàa.

All the Syrian officers had been killed in the course of the Israeli attack, continued *Le Monde,* adding sagely: *There is considerable speculation as to why Syrian army officers should have been guarding French agricultural machinery purchased by the Lebanese Department of Agriculture.* The newspaper did not explain that it was their reporter, Pierre Gamin, who had done the speculating once he had elicited a hotch-potch of facts from a member of the *Byblos*'s crew, from a policeman who had been present when the bodies of the dead men had been found in

61

Shed 27, and from an attractive secretary in the Port Captain's office.

In a leading article commenting on the Israeli raid and the strange circumstances surrounding it, *Le Monde* observed: *The conclusion seems inescapable that the 'agricultural machinery' consigned to Beirut was a French arms shipment destined for the Syrian military forces. That it was shrouded in such secrecy, and attracted the attention of an Israeli commando operation, suggests that it must have been of a very special nature. Until such time as the French Government issues a statement in clarification there is likely to be much uninformed speculation. This can only be damaging to France.*

The cat was well and truly out of the bag.

*　　　*　　　*

Intense diplomatic and media activity followed publication of the *Le Monde* report.

In Damascus the Syrian cabinet was called together for the third time in twenty-four hours, on this occasion primarily to consider the situation in the light of the *Le Monde* report. It was decided that no statement about the missing weapons should be made until the matter had been discussed fully with the French Government. The Minister of Defence was deputed to brief the Syrian Ambassador in Paris, and instruct him to call on the Minister of Foreign Affairs at the Quai d'Orsay without delay.

There was long discussion by the Syrian Cabinet on the delicacy of the situation, observing that, although directed against Syrian military personnel and equipment, the Israeli operation had taken place on Lebanese not Syrian soil. It was finally agreed that the Lebanese Government should be asked to report the incident to the United Nations Organization and to lodge a strongly-worded protest against Israeli aggression.

*   *   *

Over the weekend of October 9th/10th there were urgent cabinet meetings in Paris, Damascus, Beirut and Jerusalem. Notwithstanding intense pressure from the media none of the governments concerned was prepared to issue a statement. All enquiries were met with a firm 'no comment'.

*   *   *

On Monday, October 11th, the Syrian Minister of Defence announced that part of a shipment of arms, 'products of high technology with an exceptional potential for destruction', had been interfered with by an Israeli commando unit while in transit to Syria. No mention was made of the place or date of the incident, the

63

outcome of the 'interference', or where the arms had come from.

This guarded statement was soon overtaken by events for the next day the BBC evening news service in London carried a report that the target for the Israeli commando operation in Beirut harbour on the night of the 5th/6th October had been a consignment of tactical nuclear missiles supplied by France to the Syrian Government in terms of a secret agreement. It was understood that the Israelis had succeeded in seizing only a small part of the consignment. Accounts of the incident, continued the BBC, were as yet confused and contradictory but it had been established that a number of Syrian army officers and at least one Israeli soldier had been killed.

The Israeli Government at once denied that it was in any way involved. It repudiated in advance any charge of aggression and challenged the Lebanese and Syrian Governments to furnish evidence in support of the allegations made.

*　　*　　*

On the following day *The Times* confirmed and amplified the BBC report. The missiles supplied by the French to the Syrians were, said the newspaper, France's latest battlefield support weapon, the Pluton, a surface-to-surface tactical missile with a nuclear warhead.

64

Aerospatiale of Paris, continued the report, were largely concerned with its production, having been responsible for project management, aerodynamic studies, guidance and control systems. The propulsion units were provided by SEP of Pateaux, France. In a footnote to the report *The Times*'s aviation correspondent listed Pluton's vital statistics as:

Length: 7.5 m.
Diameter: 66 cm.
Span: 142 cm.
Launch weight, with propellant: 2,350 kg.
Launching vehicle: AMX-30
Range: 100 to 125 km.
Propulsion: dual thrust solid propellant
    rocket motor.
Warhead: AN-52 tactical nuclear weapon,
    yield 15 kilotons.

He recalled that in 1974 the French press had suggested that Pluton might be on offer to foreign countries in view of reports that the United States had supplied its tactical Lance missile to Israel, although equipped only with conventional explosive warheads.

If the technical data given by *The Times*'s aviation correspondent were not understood, at least the concluding item of his footnote was: A *nuclear warhead of 15 kilotons would be more destructive than the atom bomb on Hiroshima in 1945.*

*   *   *

At the meeting of the French Cabinet that night there was anxious and angry discussion. The decision some months earlier to supply Pluton to Syria had been hotly contested by several members of the Cabinet. They had spelled out clearly the dangers of introducing nuclear weapons to the Middle East and the international repercussions likely to follow. The Minister of Defence had on that occasion reminded the Cabinet of the United States' sale of Lance missiles to Israel and pointed out that the Israelis were well ahead with the development of their own nuclear weapon: a two-stage, surface-to-surface rocket with nuclear warhead and a range of 450 km—well in excess, he emphasized, of France's Pluton. The Israeli project, MD-660, had been in existence for at least six years. France, he said, could certainly not be accused of having initiated the introduction of nuclear arms to the Middle East. Annoyed and frustrated at finding himself under attack for what had been a Cabinet decision, he concluded, 'If we do not supply these weapons to Syria the Soviet Union will.' Having said that he produced an elegant silk handkerchief, dabbed at his forehead and sat down.

The Minister of Economy and Finance reminded the meeting that in exchange for the

66

supply of Pluton, France had secured from the Syrian Government oil concessions of the utmost importance: a contract to develop the recently discovered Syrian oilfields and to receive from that rich source an assured supply at an advantageous price during the first five years of production. 'The health of the French economy, its planned re-development, is wholly dependent upon sustaining oil supplies in the long term at prices substantially lower than those established by OPEC. Abrogate this agreement and you do irreparable damage to the fabric of France's economic structure.'

The Minister of the Interior supported him. 'This incident, the knowledge that Pluton in limited numbers is going to Syria, has been magnified out of all proportion by the international media and by governments, friendly and unfriendly, who sense the possibility of diplomatic advantage. In a few weeks it will be seen for what it is and forgotten. It is no more than a rational step by France to protect her economy, and maintain the balance of power in the Middle East.' He paused, conscious of his timing. 'It is also a calculated attempt by Israel to create a situation aimed at preventing Syria from achieving parity in tactical nuclear weapons.'

The Minister of Foreign Affairs expressed the view that, when the weapons were handed over to representatives of the Syrian Government in Marseille, French responsibility had ended. Every possible precaution had been taken to keep the agreement secret, he said. That was why the missiles and their nuclear warheads had been described as 'agricultural machinery' and despatched to Beirut, a Lebanese port, instead of to Latakia, the principal port of Syria.

The French Prime Minister, who had been persuaded against his better judgement to agree to the supply of Pluton, had shaken his head emphatically. 'Responsibility for introducing these weapons into the Middle East belongs in both moral and realistic terms to France. It did so the moment we agreed to supply. No words, no sentiments, no denials, can in any way diminish that responsibility. There is nothing to be gained by deluding ourselves. We have now to face the reality of what has happened.'

The French Cabinet discussed the realities well into the night without arriving at any particularly helpful conclusions.

CHAPTER EIGHT

The *Leros* arrived off the Piraeus well after dark on October 13th and anchored in the Bay of Athens. Next day the pilot boarded and, on a fine morning under a blue sky where feathered clouds reflected the rising sun, she entered the port and went alongside. Stevedores swarmed aboard, the hatches were opened and unloading began.

The passenger from Beirut seemed in no hurry to leave although he'd had his passport stamped by the immigration officer in the ship's dining-saloon. Instead, he stood at the after end of the boat-deck, his leather travel-bag at his feet. Leaning on the guardrail, he could see both along the quay and, obliquely, into number 3 hold.

The cabin steward who'd looked after him passed, balancing a tray on one hand. 'Not going ashore yet, m'sieu?' He smiled sympathetically. The Frenchman had tipped well.

'Waiting for a friend. He's coming to pick me up. It's nice loafing in the sun.'

'You are right, m'sieu. I wish I could.' The steward waved his free hand and disappeared down a companion ladder.

The passenger was not waiting for a friend but he was interested in the cargo being discharged from number 3 hold which he watched discreetly from the corner of his eye. It was only after a crane had hoisted the large hessian-wrapped bale from the hold and transferred it to the quay that he began to think of moving. When he'd seen the bale picked up by a fork-lift truck and carried into the transit shed, he took his bag and raincoat and went down the passenger gangway to the quay. In the shed he produced an Algerian passport at the customs barrier. The customs officer checked his appearance against the photograph, noted the name, Simon Dufour, searched perfunctorily through the travel-bag and scrawled on it with white chalk. 'Okay,' he said nodding curtly as he handed it back.

The bearded passenger went through the exit, down the steps into the sunlight. He walked across to a line of waiting taxis. To the driver at its head he said, 'Constitution Square,' and opened a back door. As he climbed in he slammed it unintentionally. 'Pardon,' he said. 'My mistake.'

The driver grunted something uncomplimentary, let out the clutch and the taxi moved off.

*   *   *

For Tel Aviv the drab, weather-stained building was old. At least thirty years old. Characterless in grey concrete, grubby, neglected and paint-blistered, it looked more. It was in a side street in the Montefiore area between the Jaffa and Shalma roads.

The ground floor windows were boarded up, the entrance doors locked and barred on the inside. Here and there graffiti competed with remnants of old posters long since eroded by sun, wind and rain. The windows of the upper floors had not been cleaned for years and behind them sunbleached blinds shut out what little light might otherwise have penetrated.

It was only the back of the building which showed signs of occupancy. There the upper floor windows were clean, though drawn venetian blinds effectively concealed what was happening behind them. Not that anyone outside could have seen. The blank back of a red-brick building, fronting on to the street on the far side of the block, obscured the view.

The backs of these two buildings were separated by a rectangular patch of sand where an old fig tree struggled for existence. The rectangle was shut in by the windowless flanks of adjoining buildings. Near the fig tree an old wheelbarrow, a decaying oil drum and the rusted remains of a bicycle lay in the yard. The only way into the concrete building was across the yard, and the only access to the yard was through a steel door in the back of the red-brick building. Anyone making the journey did so through a complicated series of internal passages and locked steel doors overseered by security guards.

Few but the initiated knew that beneath the concrete building there was an underground complex, bomb and radiation proof, with its own generators, life support and communications systems. It was the Headquarters of Israeli Intelligence.

In an office on the second floor two men sat

71

talking on opposite sides of a desk. The elder had crew-cut grey hair and a lean weather-tanned face. The younger was sleek and round. His ingenuous features and enquiring eyes suggested a mildness which did not belong. He was second-in-command to the man to whom he was listening, General Jakob Kahn, Director of Israeli Intelligence. The general had distinguished himself as a brigade commander in the Five-Day War, and as a divisional commander in the October War. On both occasions the younger man, Bar Mordecai, had been on his staff.

'We do know,' said Kahn, 'that our forces had nothing to do with the attack on Shed 27. We did not know—and I accept responsibility for this—that the Pluton consignment had already left France.'

Mordecai nodded in agreement. 'Nor did we know that they would get nuclear warheads with the first delivery—or at all. Kuper reported they'd get conventional explosive warheads, at least until they'd completed familiarization training. Even then, he said there was doubt in the French Cabinet about supplying nuke warheads unless we deployed ours.'

Jakob Kahn shifted the cheroot from one side of his mouth to the other. 'In fairness to Kuper he has a hell of a job in Paris. Security at Aerospatiale and the Ministry is exceptionally tight. In the circumstances he's doing well.'

'Of course, I agree.' In a characteristic gesture Mordecai stroked his sleek head of hair as if he were brushing it with his hand. 'But what do you make of the Syrian allegation that the attack on the shed was an Israeli operation? We know it wasn't. So what's behind it? Salamander confirms there *was* an attack. Five Syrian officers *were* killed. And the sixth body? Who was he? We know he wasn't an Israeli.'

Kahn waved his cheroot in wide circles. 'There are two possibilities. First, the whole thing may have been set up by the Syrians themselves.'

'Isn't that stretching it a bit far? Killing five of their own officers. Hijacking their own equipment.'

'Of course. But what could be more convincing? It would be worth sacrificing six of your own men if the stakes were high enough. And they are.'

'Six?'

'Yes. For the purpose of this hypothesis the dead body was another Syrian officer. This time with an Israeli identity disc, phoney Israeli documents in his pocket, and a face slashed beyond recognition. That's an easy set-up.'

'Motive, Jakob?' Mordecai was pretty sure he knew the answer but he liked flying kites. Kahn would shoot them down.

'To throw a spanner in Kissinger's works. To destroy the détente he's trying to set up between Israel and Egypt. The Syrians suspect Kissinger's is a wedge-driving operation.' Kahn stubbed out the cheroot, took another from the packet on his desk. 'Filthy habit,' he said. 'But I enjoy them.'

Mordecai shook his head disapprovingly. 'It'll kill you before the Arabs do, Jakob. You mentioned two possibilities. What was the other?'

'Yes. It's the more probable. Who in the Arab world has the greatest need to block Kissinger's efforts?'

'The Palestine liberation movement.'

'Sure. A successful détente would leave both Syria and Palestine isolated. Unable to exert pressure on Israel for their own ends. But it's not the PLO. Arafat wouldn't do it that way. Even the El Fatah attack on a Tel Aviv tourist hotel was out of character for him. That was the PLO's attempt to neutralize Kissinger. But Arafat wouldn't deliberately kill Syrian army officers or risk an operation like the attack on Shed 27. The consequences for the PLO if that failed would have been disastrous.'

'So it was an extremist splinter group?'

'Yes.' Kahn nodded vigorously. 'Habash's MPF, or Hawatemeh's PDF or,' he paused, staring at Mordecai, 'for my money, Mahmoud el Ka'ed's SAS. Ka'ed wouldn't hesitate to do

74

something like that if he thought it would kill an Egypt-Israeli détente.'

'So what do you tell the PM and CGS at tonight's meeting?'

Kahn stood up, went to the corner, filled a glass with water from a carafe, came back. 'Several things. First, exactly what I've told you. They must make their own choice. The Prime Minister has superb political intuition. Let's see how he rates the possibles and probables. Second, whatever the motive for the incident, the nuclear warhead is now in the hands of the people who hijacked it. The high probability is that it's the Palestinians. What are they going to do with it? That's the sixty-four thousand dollar question. They've got physicists. They know the technology. It's my belief they'll use that bomb—use it in Israel, because we're right next door and we're target number one. With it they can take out Tel Aviv or Haifa. That's my appreciation of the situation.'

Mordecai said, 'I've been thinking that for some time. But I didn't want to put it into words.'

Kahn stood up. 'There's another thing the Prime Minister and CGS have got to decide pretty soon.'

'What's that?'

'The Syrians have got Pluton. So now they have nuclear capability. We'd better confirm what the world suspects—tell them straight or leak it—that we've got it too. Project MD660. No need to tell them it has four times the range of Pluton. Russian and US intelligence already know that. We can take out Cairo, Damascus, Beirut and Amman if they are looking for that sort of fight.'

'It's been rumoured for some months that we've got nuclear capability. *The Times* report on October 12th mentioned it.'

'A rumour's one thing, Bar. If we confirm it they're not going to use Pluton unless they're crazy. But that's a decision for the Prime Minister.'

*   *   *

The Times report on October 12th was followed by worldwide condemnation of France's action in supplying nuclear weapons to the Middle East. The French Government's defence that Israel had already developed a nuclear capability of her own, and that the Soviet Union would have supplied Syria had France not done so, was brushed aside.

In a leading article the editor of the *New York Times* declared: *The enormity of the moral offence can only be matched by the consequences likely to flow from it.*

The unusual shape these consequences were to take, the speed with which they were to follow, were soon to astonish the leader writer.

The Soviet Government, quick to join hounds baying at the heels of the hunted, requested an urgent meeting of the Security Council . . . *to take immediate steps to preclude the proliferation of nuclear weapons in the Middle East.* By way of a sop to Arab opinion, and to ensure that France and Israel were not let too easily off the hook, it added . . . and *to censure the French and Israeli Governments for their grossly irresponsible imperialistic actions.*

*   *   *

In a statement issued the next day the Israeli Government reiterated its denial of Israeli complicity in the happenings at Beirut Port on the night of October 5th/6th.

'On the contrary,' the statement continued, 'the incident was clearly a desperate attempt by Palestinian terrorists to block progress towards a détente between Israel and Egypt.'

Israel endorsed the call for a meeting of the Security Council and censured France for initiating the supply of nuclear weapons to the Middle East.

*   *   *

World opinion appeared to attach little credence to the Israeli counter-charge which Yasir Arafat had quickly repudiated on behalf of the PLO in particular and the Palestine

77

liberation movement in general. Indeed, there was widespread agreement that the Israelis had been responsible for the attack on Beirut Port.

In Washington, the President announced that France's action in supplying nuclear weapons to Syria would compel the United States to consider making such weapons available to Israel in order to maintain the balance of power. 'Nothing is more likely to provoke aggression,' said the President, 'than the knowledge that you have a nuclear capability and your opponent has not.'

The British Government, with characteristic phlegm, urged calmness and caution, stressing that everything possible should be done to preclude a nuclear build-up in the Middle East. It supported the Soviet Union's call for a meeting of the Security Council knowing, as did the other Governments concerned, that France would veto any resolution critical of her policy.

*   *   *

On October 14th *Le Monde* announced that its correspondent in Beirut, Pierre Gamin, had been arrested by Lebanese security police on October 7th and held incommunicado ever since. The paper recalled that Gamin had, on the day of his arrest, telephoned a report of the incident of 5th/6th October and that it was he who had first revealed that France had supplied the consignment now known to be nuclear arms. *Le Monde* urged the French Government to exert pressure to secure his release. 'He has committed no crime,' wrote its editor, 'unless truth itself be a crime.'

Which excellent point was unlikely to carry much weight with the French Government, considering how angry it was with Pierre Gamin.

*　　*　　*

Three days after the *Leros* arrived in the Piraeus, the bearded man with the scarred neck walked out of the Attica Palace Hotel and set off on foot for Constitution Square. It was almost eleven o'clock and the sun was well up in a cloudless sky. When he reached the Square he sat at a table drinking coffee, watching the passers-by. He was early and it was pleasant sitting there basking in the sun. With much tension behind him, and more to come, he found it curiously soothing; the patches of shade cast by lemon, casuarina and cypress trees, the sponge sellers, curio and lottery-ticket pedlars, and the bustle of people and traffic.

But mostly he watched the steps which led down from the Square's eastern end, where the Parliament building loomed solid and rectangular. He was doing this when he heard

79

Kemal Tarshe's, 'Hullo, Zeid.'

Kemal Tarshe, a slight man with large eyes, ran Dimitri Ionides and Co., the shipping and forwarding business his wife Cleo had inherited from her father. It was a small firm. The staff consisted of Kemal and his wife and two Greek typists, one of them a woman who had spent most of her working life with the firm. Tarshe, a Palestinian, had settled in Athens soon after his marriage in 1974. His wife knew he'd been a member of El Fatah, the militant arm of the PLO, but she did not know he had been, and still was, a member of SAS—Soukour-al-Sahra', the Desert Hawks.

He pointed to a chair. 'Sit down, Kemal. It's good to see you again. You gave me quite a fright. I thought you would come down the steps.' He and Kemal were old friends. They'd been at school and university together in Beirut.

The new arrival rubbed his hands and grinned. 'I was seeing how alert you were, Zeid.'

'I'm off duty. You wouldn't have caught me like that at any other time.' He beckoned to a waitress. 'Two black coffees, please.'

When she'd gone they talked eagerly of mutual friends, catching up on each other's news in a sort of verbal shorthand. The waitress brought the coffee and Zeid paid her. When they'd finished it he said, 'Let's walk. Safest way to chat.' They left the table and started up the southern side of the Square.

Zeid said, 'Delivered yet?'

'This morning at nine-thirty.'

'Any problems?'

'No. The truck had a wheeled pallet with it. Just as well. It's a hell of a weight. Took the driver and his mate, plus four of us, to get it in.'

'Carpets are heavy, Kemal. What's the programme?'

Tarshe lowered his voice. 'I've received the letter from London requesting re-consignment to English clients since the Athens buyer has defaulted.'

'What address did they give?'

Tarshe took a slip of paper from his wallet and passed it to the bearded man. It read:

J. P. Leroux et Cie,
43 St Peter's Road,
Fulham, London SW6.

'You ask for a Miss Morley,' said Kemal.

Zeid folded the slip of paper, placed it in an inner pocket of his jacket. 'That's good,' he said. 'And now?'

'We'll sew on address and marking labels tomorrow. I'll burn the old ones when the staff have left the office.'

'Don't on any account touch the label on the right-hand side. The one which describes the contents.'

'Okay. I'll make sure of that. The truck will come for the bale on the eighteenth and take it down to the harbour. It'll be loaded on the *Student Prince* that day or the next. She sails on the nineteenth.'

They reached the bottom of the Square and began a second circuit. 'That's great,' said Zeid. 'When does she arrive?'

'She's calling at Genoa, Marseille and Gibraltar. Due to berth at Millwall Docks on October 29th.'

'Arrangements there still the same?'

'Yes. The freight forwarding agents, Morrison, Dean and Fletcher, are to clear the consignment. You'll arrange that. And collection from the bonded warehouse. Right?'

'Yes. Rudi has the van.' Zeid looked at his watch. 'Nearly one o'clock,' he said. 'Wish we could lunch together, but we can't. Better say goodbye now.'

'What passport are you travelling on?'

'Algerian—Simon Dufour.'

'When do you leave?'

'Tomorrow morning, Air France to Paris. The nine-fifteen flight.'

'I wish I was coming. May Allah be with you, Zeid.'

'I'm a Christian, Kemal. But I hope he will overlook that.'

They laughed, shook hands and parted.

CHAPTER NINE

In a small office on the first floor of 56 Spender Street, not far from Covent Garden, two men sat at a table, a tape-recorder between them.

'Play it back, Zol.'

'Okay.' Zol Levi ran the tape back, restarted it. A conversation in Arabic followed. Shalom Ascher hunched forward, pulling at his beard, a gesture which his companion knew indicated intense concentration. The tape ran on for about five minutes before Ascher held up his hand. 'Stop. Let's have that last section again. Where the voices fade. Can't get that.'

Levi ran the tape back and re-started it. They listened intently.

'It's no good.' Ascher stood up, stretched, yawned loudly. 'We'll never get it.' He went to the small table where there was another recorder, watched the reels turning, thinking what it was all about. There were already twenty reels. The recorder's mike was fed by the receiver/amplifier on the shelf beneath the table. It in turn was fed by transmissions from the bugs on the ground floor premises of the MIDDLE ORIENT CONSOLIDATED AGENCIES LTD on the opposite side of the street. The bugs—the miniaturised microphone/transmitters —were a good deal smaller than a new penny piece.

'So,' said Levi. 'What do you make of it?'

'Two things. One, the man called Zeid is mentioned again. This is the third time we've heard his name. They expect him soon. Right?'

Levi nodded agreement, watching the big shaggy man with affection. He had much respect for Shalom Ascher.

'Who is this Zeid?' continued Ascher. 'We don't know. But it sounds as though he's got something to do with the consignment.'

Levi said, 'And the consignment?'

Ascher shrugged his shoulders. 'Who knows. They don't say. The Middle Orient Consolidated Agencies Limited . . .' He rolled out the words deliberately. 'And they're expecting it from Athens.'

'That fits, doesn't it? I mean they *are* import and export agents. The name of the firm doesn't necessarily restrict them to doing business with the Middle East.'

'If they really were, you're right. But they're phoneys, Zol. We've heard them talk for two weeks—jaw, jaw, jaw—haven't we? That's the first time they chat about any goods coming in or going out. So what sort of import/export agents are they? Anyway, here they are in business at last. But with Athens—not Beirut or Damascus?' He spread his hands with an air of finality. 'Don't ask me why?'

'So we're no wiser.'

'I wouldn't say that, Zol. Notice something queer in the chat about the consignment?'

'Not really. Bits of it weren't all that distinct.'

'That's it.' Ascher stared at the younger man.

'How d'you mean, that's it?'

'Each time they talk about the consignment it's like they're talking of God or Allah, or whatever. They get serious. Full of respect. They drop their voices instinctively. There was that bit that sounded like whispering and we couldn't make it out. Right?'

Levi said, 'Yes. Now you mention it. It is like that.'

'Another thing. Here are these import and export agents doing business for the first time in the two weeks we've been listening. They're expecting a consignment. But they never say who it is for, or when it is coming, or how it's coming. Know why? Either they don't know or they're security conscious or both. And that goes for the dropped voices, etcetera.'

'What's it then, Shalom?'

Archer picked up a paper-weight, threw it into the air and caught it with an outstretched hand. 'I think the attack on the Embassy will take place not long after Zeid and the consignment arrive. And that won't be long now because Kissinger and Sadat are making progress. The Palestinians can't afford to be left out of any Israeli-Egyptian settlement that

85

Kissinger's cooking up.'

Levi pursed his lips. 'So we do what?'

'We go on watching and listening. Every second, every minute. Night and day. We have problems. We don't know what the consignment is. We don't know how it's coming or when, except they expect it soon.' Ascher sat down, a bearded, brooding figure. 'So we watch and we listen and maybe we find out.'

'Yes,' said Levi. 'That's about it.'

'In the meantime I see the Ambassador tonight.'

'What shall you tell him, Shalom?'

'What we've seen and heard. What we think. He'll pass it to Intel HQ. They'll have ideas, you can be sure.'

Levi made a face. 'More of Jakob's possibles and probables.'

'Right,' said Shalom Ascher. 'And sometimes they're good.'

*   *   *

The Air France flight from Athens arrived at Charles de Gaulle Airport at 11.57 am. It was twenty-three minutes late having been delayed in Rome with engine trouble.

At the immigration barrier the bearded man showed his Algerian passport. The immigration officer noted the name on the immigration form, 'Simon Dufour', and other answers, opened the passport with professional ease, checked the details, compared the bearded long-haired young man in the photo with the bearded long-haired original standing in front of him, closed it and passed it back. 'Bon,' he said, turning to the next passenger in the queue. The bearded man moved on through the complex of travellators which gave the new airport its science-fiction ambience, arrived at the baggage pick-up point and after some delay collected the brown travel-bag from a distributor.

He travelled into Paris in an Air France bus. At the terminal at Port Maillot he took a taxi. 'Rue des Beaux Arts,' he said to the driver. 'Hotel de Nice.' It was a small unpretentious hotel in St Germain-des-Prés on the left bank, not far from the gates of the Académie des Beaux Arts. But he would not be staying in the Hotel de Nice.

On arrival outside it he paid off the taxi, put his travelbag on the pavement, and made much of searching through his pockets. When the taxi had gone he picked up the bag, walked round into the Rue Berligny. It was a narrow street with small art galleries, picture framers, and shops given over to artists' materials for the students of the Académie.

Outside a small picture shop, the Galerie Duquesne, he paused to look at the paintings in the window. Beyond them, through the glass, he saw a young woman. She was alone.

He went in. 'Hullo, Magda.' He spoke quietly.

She looked at him, frowning, her head on one side. 'Do I know you?'

'You should. Don't you remember me? Zeid. At BUC?' They had overlapped for a year at Beirut University College.

She laughed with relief. 'Zeid! All that beard and hair. D'you blame me? There's not much left to recognize.'

'Still the same person, Magda. Where's Tewfik?'

'He's gone to the bank. At the Place Vendôme. He'll be back before long.'

'That's fine. I must see him.'

She took his hand in hers, her eyes shining. 'Oh, it's good to see you.'

He grinned to hide his embarrassment. 'But you knew I was coming?'

'Yes, of course. But I didn't recognize you.'

'Kemal sends his love.'

'Oh. That's nice. Does he still grin?'

'All the time. How are you, Magda? You look marvellous.'

'I'm fine.' She held his hand affectionately. 'It's quite a long time, isn't it? Not since you worked in France?'

'Yes. But I was also in Paris three months ago. You were away.'

'Tewfik told me. I'd gone to my mother. She was ill.'

'It's really good to see you, Magda. How is he?'

'He's fine.'

He looked towards the street, became suddenly serious. 'I'd better not stand here.'

'Sorry. This way.' She led him through the curtains at the back of the shop, up a small staircase to a room on the first floor.

'It's our room. There's a bathroom and loo next door. Knock on the floor when you're ready.'

'Good,' he said. 'I won't be long.'

When she'd gone he found the scissors and shaving gear in the travel-bag, took off his grey jacket and trousers, laid them on the bed, and went through to the bathroom in his underclothes. He got busy with the scissors and razor. When he'd finished the beard, the moustache and the long sideburns had gone. He put a towel round his waist, knocked lightly on the floor with a shoe.

The girl came up. 'That's more like the Zeid I remember,' she said. 'What a transformation. And I can see the scar.' She put her hand on his neck and touched it gently. 'Poor Zeid.'

She was very desirable, they had once been lovers, and for a moment he wanted to take her in his arms. He fought down the emotion, handed her the scissors and a comb. 'Now my hair, Magda. To here.' He turned his back and with his hand indicated the length.

'Sit on that bath stool,' she said. 'You're too tall.'

He sat down and she began combing and

89

cutting. At last she said, 'Look now.' He stood up and went to the mirror.

'That's great,' he said.

'See the mess on the floor.'

'Sorry, Magda.'

'Don't worry. I'll get rid of it.'

They went through to the bedroom. She sat on the bed while he changed into the blue suit he'd taken from the travel-bag.

'What are the flight details, Magda?'

'Eight-ten tonight. British Airways from Orly. Heathrow about half an hour later. Want the passport and ticket now?'

'Please.'

A bell rang in the shop below. 'Customer,' she said. 'I'd better go.'

She came back later with a French passport and the airline ticket. 'The passport's been in the safe since you left it there with Tewfik. He bought the ticket yesterday.'

'Good.' He handed her the Algerian passport. 'Keep this for me, Magda. Tell Tewfik I'll pick it up again. In a couple of weeks, I hope.'

She looked at him sadly. 'Is it dangerous? Your mission?'

'There is always danger, Magda. Every time one crosses the street.'

'This is different, Zeid.'

'Danger isn't. The objective is.'

She shook her head. 'How nice if you could stay in Paris for a while.'

'Just as well I can't. It might start all over again. Tewfik wouldn't like that.'

She smiled sadly, knowing he was right.

*　　　*　　　*

The immigration officer in Heathrow's Terminal 1 looked at the passport—Simon Dufour Charrier, born September 7th, 1948, Philippeville, Algeria—and his well-trained eyes checked the man's age, height and colouring, then the face on the photograph—high forehead, eyes set well apart, high cheekbones, prominent nose, mole on right cheek—against the face in front of him. Satisfied, he pushed the passport back, nodded curtly. 'Right,' he said, looking at the next passenger.

Zeid Barakat turned up the collar of his raincoat, tightened the silk scarf which so well concealed the scar, and put on dark glasses before boarding the British Airways bus which took him to the West London Terminal in the Cromwell Road. There he changed to a taxi. 'South Kensington tube station,' he told the driver.

*　　　*　　　*

After two weeks of exhaustive enquiry the Deuxième Bureau in Beirut, assisted by their colleagues from Damascus, had made no

91

progress in solving the mystery of the whereabouts of the two packing cases removed from Shed 27 during the Israeli commando raid on the night of October 5th/6th.

Nor had they succeeded in tracing the truck which had passed through the Port gates early in the morning of the 6th October, evidently carrying the missing warhead and detonator. It had been established that the truck did not belong to D.B. Mahroutti Bros. although the name of that firm had appeared on it. The Deuxième Bureau assumed that it had been re-sprayed and given new plates immediately after the incident.

Checks at Djebel Naqura, the border post between Lebanon and Israel—reserved for UN traffic—revealed that the truck had not crossed at that point. At the end of the two-week search the head of the Lebanese security police informed his minister that there were two workable hypotheses

One, the warhead and detonator had been taken into Israel by sea immediately after the attack, the use of the Mahroutti truck being a calculated diversion; or, two, the missing weapons had been taken out of the Port by the truck and were either still in the Lebanon or had been smuggled into Israel in a manner not yet known.

Digesting these facts, and with the outcry of the world's media and chancelleries still ringing in their ears, the Lebanese Cabinet decided that the Israeli attack on Shed 27 had been both politically and technologically motivated.

The Israelis' political objective had been to reveal in dramatic fashion that France was supplying nuclear weapons to the Middle East, and by so doing justify in advance any subsequent Israeli decision to equip its forces in the field with nuclear weapons.

The technological objective had been to assist Israeli physicists working on the MD-660 project by making available a recent example of French nuclear technology in a tactical weapons system.

Reluctantly, the Lebanese Cabinet had to agree with their Syrian colleagues that the Israelis appeared to have achieved both objectives.

CHAPTER TEN

43 St Peter's Road, Fulham, was an old Victorian terraced house somewhat in need of repair. It belonged to a maiden lady, Miss Katherine Morley, who took in lodgers— 'guests' she preferred to call them—provided they were what she thought of as 'the right sort of people'.

She was in the kitchen when she heard the clack of the letter-box lid and the postman's double ring. The ring was her private arrangement with him. She liked to get to the letter-box before her guests. She put down the butter dish, wiped her hands, went to the box and cleared it. Among the mail was a buff-coloured envelope addressed to *J. P. Leroux et Cie*. The name of the sender was on the flap: Benallan Steamship Company Ltd, Fenchurch Street, London EC3.

Miss Morley looked at the letter with respect. She'd no idea the nice young Frenchman—Jean Paul Leroux—who'd come to her a week ago, was a 'company'. But then he was a quiet, reserved sort of man. Not one to talk about himself or put on airs and graces. A girl with a French accent had telephoned to make the reservation some time before his arrival, saying that he was coming from Paris. Miss Morley asked him who'd recommended her. The wife of a business acquaintance in Paris, he'd said. She had stayed at number 43 some time ago. Unfortunately, he could not recall her maiden name. Miss Morley couldn't either but since several young French women had stayed with her over the years—and Mr. Leroux, though French, was a charming well-spoken man and obviously a gentlemen—she'd had no hesitation in taking him in for the week or ten days he expected to be in London.

Miss Morley placed the letters on the hall table, went back to the kitchen and got on with preparing the breakfast.

Later that morning Jean Paul Leroux took a taxi from Trafalgar Square where he'd arrived by underground.

As was his custom he paid off the taxi shortly before it reached the Aldwych, walking the remainder of the way to 39 Spender Street.

It was his third visit to the premises of the Middle Orient Consolidated Agencies Ltd since landing at Heathrow on October 20th. He rang the bell, went in through the front door, exchanged greetings with Hanna Nasour, Najib Hamadeh and Ibrahim Souref, hung up his raincoat and umbrella and accepted Hanna's offer of coffee. She poured the coffee and passed him the mug. 'Any news, Zeid?'

'Yes. The letter came this morning.' He felt more than heard the impact of his announcement.

There was a long silence, broken by the girl. 'When do you leave Fulham?'

'It'll be a few days yet. I told Miss Morley I'd be returning to Paris soon. I'll have to move in with you then, Ibrahim. Okay?'

The man with the mournful face sitting on the edge of the desk said, 'Fine. If you don't mind a stretcher.'

Zeid looked round the office with dubious eyes. The premises were poorly lit, sparsely furnished. There was a musty smell of long ago, an atmosphere of decay and neglect. Where they were in the front office there was a monk's bench, a table, some chairs, an old Royal typewriter, a stationery cabinet, two typists' desks, two four-drawer steel filing cabinets, telephone directories—but no telephone —'in and out' baskets with letters in them, a wall calendar from which gazed a breasty, sultry young lady, a number of newspapers and some periodicals. The shelves along one wall were stacked with pattern books, specimens of silks and damasks, brocades and other Oriental cloths. There were two doors at the back of the front office.

One opened into a stockroom with modest stacks of Persian and Turkish rugs, and bundles of carpet samples on shelves along the back wall. The other gave on to an open passageway which led to an outside cloakroom, and a backyard with coal shed and garbage bins. There was a gas ring on a table, near it a corner cupboard.

Zeid put down the empty mug. 'I've some telephoning to do, Najib. Can't be from a callbox. Can we go to Sandra's?'

'Of course. She'll be at work now.'

*   *   *

In the Strand they took a taxi to Rupert Street off the Bayswater Road where Najib's sister Sandra rented a two-roomed apartment.

Hamadeh, a regular visitor, had a key and knew the porter who was seldom about. They went into the apartment where Zeid got busy on the phone.

First he rang Morrison, Dean and Fletcher's officer in Fenchurch Street. The switchboard operator put him through to the clearing department and after some delay he got hold of the right clerk. 'J. P. Leroux et Cie of Paris here,' said Zeid. 'We want you to clear a consignment of carpets ex Athens in the *Student Prince*. The goods are in transit shed 14, Millwall Docks. I'll call this afternoon with the bill of lading and manifest, and arrange payment. How long will clearance take?'

'A few days. We have to prepare the custom entries, process them through the Port of London Authority's head office. You'll receive notification from the PLA in due course that the goods are ready for collection. We can arrange for a haulier to pick them up.'

'Don't worry about the haulier. We'll see to that,' said Zeid. Next he dialled a Lewisham number. A man's voice answered, 'Speedy Removals.'

Zeid chuckled. 'Is that so? Zeid here.'

'Oh, hullo, Zeid. I was expecting to hear from you.'

'Listen, Rudi. The carpets have arrived. Transit shed 14, Millwall Docks. It's going to take a few days to clear them.'

There was a pause on the line. 'Okay, Zeid.

That's fine.' The voice had become suddenly husky.

'You all right, Rudi?'

'Of course. It's just—you know—surprise. I'm okay.'

'Fine. I'll be in touch as soon as the goods are ready for collection. We'll fix then when you are to pick me up. Okay?'

'Sure. That's okay.'

*   *   *

The driver of the Bedford panel van backed it up to the loading platform behind transit shed 14 in the Millwall Dock. The black van was several years old but well kept. There was nothing unusual about it except, perhaps, the absence of the name of any firm upon it. The driver got out, went into the office and gave the foreman the J. P. Leroux et Cie's delivery order. The foreman examined it, checked through a file, found the relevant papers, handed a receipt in triplicate to the driver. 'Sign here,' he said. The driver signed with a flourish 'L. E. Jones'. The foreman looked at the signature—thought to himself, he's no Welshman, looks more like a Pakki to me— and handed over a pass which specified the goods the driver was authorized to take out of the docks.

He gave the other papers to the clerk at the desk behind him. 'Take this lot, Bert.' He turned to the driver. 'He'll show you where your load is.'

The driver followed the clerk down the shed through a maze of cargo. At the far end they found the hessian-wrapped bale addressed to J. P. Leroux et Cie. A fork-lift truck arrived. The clerk said, 'That's it, Jim.' The driver, a small wizened man, backed and filled until the fork was under the bale. He pulled a lever and the bale lifted clear. 'Where's the van, then?'

The van driver pointed to the far end of the shed. 'Down there. At the first loading platform.'

The fork-lift truck led the way, the driver and clerk following. Near the end of the shed the clerk called to two men leaning against a stack of packing cases. 'Give us a hand, lads. Got to get this lot into a van.' The men moved slowly, joining the cortège with reluctance. When they reached the Bedford the driver said, 'I've got a roller pallet inside.'

He slid the pallet out of the van. The fork-lift driver lowered the bale on to it. It took four of them, shoving and pushing, to get it across the tail-gate into the van.

The driver thanked them, put chocks against the pallet rollers, closed the van doors, climbed into the driving seat and drove off.

At the dock gates he showed the receipt and pass to the PLA policeman on duty. The policeman got him to open the van, and checked there was nothing inside but the bale specified in the pass. Satisfied, he said, 'That's all right, mate.'

The driver climbed in, started up the engine and drove away.

*　　*　　*

The van made down Manchester Road towards Blackwall at a moderate pace, the man in the cab driving with extreme care. He turned into the Blackwall Tunnel, crossed under the Thames, and took a circuitous route to the east, making for Charlton. Later he swung north and then west towards Blackheath and Lewisham. It was after six in the evening when he stopped opposite the Clock Tower in Lewisham Way. A man in a raincoat carrying a brief-case climbed into the cab beside him. The van crossed over into Lee High Road, travelled down it for some distance, turned right into Kiddey Road and later left into Pimsvale Lane. The lane was a narrow cul-de-sac leading down between rows of old, weather-worn terraced houses. At its far end, almost a hundred yards beyond the last houses, stood an old brick building once used as a workshop by glass merchants. The van driver had for some months rented a part of it; a garage with a two-roomed flat above.

He lived in the flat and kept the panel van in the garage which was a convenient arrangement for a man in the furniture removals business.

For him the place had the added advantage that there were no houses adjoining the building. It stood quite alone, its back to a small field which had somehow escaped development. The driver, known to neighbours as Rudi Frankel, was a quiet reserved young man who kept himself to himself. He was regarded as a hard-working man and those inhabitants of Pimsvale Lane who'd used or recommended him to friends spoke well of his reliability and reasonable charges. He was understood to be Jewish and to have worked in Israel for some years before returning to London where he'd been born. His parents, he'd said, lived in Birmingham.

What was not known about him was that his name was not Rudi Frankel—nor for that matter 'L. E. Jones'—nor was he Jewish, notwithstanding his Israeli passport. Which was not surprising since forged passports were more easily come by in Beirut than most other places in the world.

*   *   *

When they'd parked the van, the driver and his passenger climbed out and bolted and padlocked the garage doors on the inside. They got into the back of the van, the man in the raincoat taking his briefcase with him. He examined the bale carefully, cut away the stitches at one end of the canvas 'contents' label, turned it back and found a loose strand of carpet weave. He pulled on it until a flexible plastic tube emerged. He unscrewed its cap and exposed the end of a multicore cable.

Frankel said, 'Gives me the jitters, Zeid. Sure you know what you're up to?'

'I should know. Didn't I put this lot together in Beirut?' He looked up and laughed. 'You know, Rudi, if I passed out now and you had to carry on with the job, you'd—Jesus! I don't know. I suppose you'd be the only man in the world who'd detonated a nuclear bomb while he was sitting on it.' He laughed again with nervous hilarity. 'Know what the date is?'

'Fifth of November?'

'Yes. Funny isn't it?' Zeid shook with laughter.

'It's not funny, Zeid. It's bloody terrifying. That's what it is.'

'Sure it is. But if it goes wrong we won't know anything about it, so relax and let's get on with the job.'

Zeid pulled several inches of multi-core cable from the tube and separated the taped leads: two brown, two green, two black, one chequered. He took a cardboard box from the briefcase and placed it on the bale. Working methodically, he removed the insulation from the leads and joined them to coils of identically-coloured flex, attaching the ends of these to terminals on the plastic switchboard which he took from the cardboard box. He checked the springloaded locking device on the switch before testing the circuit with an ammeter. It was fed by dry batteries in the bale. Satisfied, he carried the switchboard forward with elaborate care, Frankel paying out flex from the coils. Zeid passed the switchboard through the small window behind the driving seat and lowered it gently into the driving-cab. The two men climbed out and locked the van's loading doors. They left the garage by an internal door which led to the staircase to the flat. Frankel double-locked that door and they went upstairs.

When they'd washed and eaten a modest meal, he slid a Skorpion 7-65mm Vzorgi into the holster of his shoulder harness and put on a denim jacket and an overcoat.

Zeid said, 'Let's go down to the van now. I'll explain how the switch works and we'll fix the phone. After that I must go. Don't leave the garage until Ahmad arrives. Okay?'

'Sure. Sure. I know.' Frankel's voice was hoarse with anxiety.

*   *   *

When Zeid had gone Frankel latched open the garage door leading to the staircase and got into the driver's cab. With nervous hands he checked the plastic switchboard and laid it gingerly on the seat. He opened a cab window, made himself as comfortable as he could and settled down to wait.

Shortly before eleven o'clock he heard gentle knocking. He climbed down from the cab and went through to the front door of the flat in stockinged feet. 'Who's that?' he called through the letter-box.

'Ahmad Daab.'

It was a familiar, expected voice. Frankel unlocked the door and a tall man wearing a duffel coat and cloth cap came in.

The new arrival took off his cap, rubbed his hands together. 'Phoo—it's cold. Can't take this climate.' He had bushy eyebrows, a mandarin moustache and an easy smile.

Frankel locked the door again. 'Glad to see you, Ahmad. Go upstairs. Make yourself coffee. You know where the things are. I've drawn the curtains. Don't put on lights in the living-room. It's okay to use them in the kitchen and bedroom.'

The newcomer stared at him. 'So it's actually begun.' His deep voice dropped to a whisper. 'It's difficult to believe. After all that planning and scheming. It's finally here. How bloody marvellous.'

'It's more than that, Ahmad. It's the pivotal event for our people. It has cost some lives but in the long run it's going to save a great many.'

'Has Zeid put on the settings?'

'Yes. I'll show you when you take over. We can only pre-detonate. There's no time-setting yet. He'll fix that later.'

104

'Want me to take over now?'

'When did you last sleep, Ahmad?'

'This afternoon. Four hours.'

'That's good.' Frankel looked at his watch. 'It's ten past ten. Relieve me at midnight. There's a portable phone-line between the driving-cab and the bedroom. We can be in touch at any time. Got your gun?'

Daab opened the duffel coat and pulled aside his jacket. Frankel saw the Vzorgi nestling in the shoulder-holster.

Daab said, 'What's the drill for a pee on watch?'

'There's a bucket under the garage workbench.'

'Okay.' Daab grinned. 'You think of everything.' He lumbered up the stairs.

Frankel went back to the garage.

CHAPTER ELEVEN

The day after the Bedford van collected the bale of carpets from the Millwall Dock, a dark clean-shaven man wearing sun glasses, raincoat and silk scarf, called at the Avis desk in Heathrow's Terminal 2. After a brief discussion he completed forms for renting a Volvo 244 Automatic, provisionally reserved by phone from Paris a few days earlier.

The business was quickly done and with a

minimum of fuss. He would, he said, require the car for a week or ten days. The Avis girl asked if he wanted full collision damage waiver at extra cost. He said he did, adding, 'I do not expect collisions, mam'selle, but here it is not like France. You drive on the wrong side of the road. This makes for us problems.'

She laughed. 'We think you drive on the wrong side in France.'

He produced his French driving licence and passport, signed the rental forms and paid the deposit.

The girl explained that the Avis courtesy car would take him across to the depot where the Volvo would be waiting. He thanked her for her help.

When he'd gone she said to the girl with her, 'Quite a dish! Wouldn't mind what side he drove with me.'

'It's the accent, love. Makes you all goosey. What's his name?'

'Simon something or other.' She looked at the form on her desk. 'Simon Charrier.'

'Sounds familiar. Pop star?'

'Could be. Never heard of him.'

*　　*　　*

It was a cold grey day, wet and windy, London at its worst, and the man and woman in the first-floor office at 56 Spender Street, kept as close as they could to the electric fire. 'It's a bloody climate.' Through the venetian blinds the man was watching the street where the light was already failing.

The young woman nodded gloomily. 'Terrible, Shalom. What wouldn't I give to be back in Tel Aviv.'

He looked at his watch. 'Three-twenty-seven. Zol takes over at five. Can't wait for it.'

She moved her chair closer to the window, concentrating on the premises on the opposite side of the street. 'I hope our Mocal friends feel the cold.'

'Must do,' growled the burly man. 'We differ politically but we come from the same climate.' He went over to the table where the two Grundigs stood. The tape-wheels of one were turning. 'Number two's almost ready for changing. Zol can play it back as soon as we've left. Maybe the last two hours will throw some light on what we heard this morning.'

She remained at the window, leaning forward in her chair, chin in hand, opera glasses on her lap. 'It's so frustrating. Cryptic references to "goods" . . . new names and things we can't place. Something's happening. We don't know what or where.'

'At least it's happening. It's taken us time to sort out "Zeid". Now we've seen him several times, photographed him. We know he's a Palestinian.'

'We don't even know his surname. What's it help to know he's Zeid?'

107

'A lot. Zeid and "the goods" are just about synonymous. They seldom mention one without the other. Be patient, Ruth.'

She yawned, stretching her arms. 'At this rate they'll have blown up the Embassy before we can do anything about it.'

'We'll hear something worth while before that. We're bound to. Law of averages.'

She shook her head in disbelief. 'Wish I could be so sure. *Where* are "the goods"? *What* are they? Who's Rudi . . . and the other guy? What's his name? Ahmad? What's all that talk about posting Christmas cards?'

'You know what I feel about that—I keep telling you. "The goods" must be explosives. If they're really out to smash up the Embassy it means a car-bomb in Palace Green. A big one. That could mean a hundred pounds of explosives, or maybe a bazooka. Who knows?'

'I suppose you're right. And the Christmas cards, Shalom. They're Moslems.'

'Not all of them. Hanna and Zeid aren't. But they could be code-words for letter bombs. Anybody's guess.' He became suddenly irritable. 'Don't ask me.' He beat his chest with both hands. She recognized the symptoms. 'Don't ask me,' he repeated. 'They're playing security. Talking shorthand.'

'Think they know they're bugged?'

He shook his head. 'Definitely not. It's their training.'

'How can you say definitely?'

'Because Hanna and Ibrahim wouldn't come back there at night and make love. Not if they thought the place was bugged.'

'I don't know.' She looked at him quizzically. 'They're in love. Why should they be ashamed to make it. It's not unnatural.'

'Would you like to make love and talk about it in a room bugged by Palestinians?'

'Might be fun.' She was flippant. 'And anyway the listeners wouldn't be able to see. Who knows if . . .' She broke off, leant towards the window. 'Look! Look!'

'What?' He went to the window, knelt beside her chair. On the coffee table next to it there was an Asahi Pentax with a telephoto lens, and a pair of binoculars.

A tangerine Volvo had stopped outside the premises opposite, notwithstanding the double yellow lines which ran the whole length of the narrow thoroughfare. Leaving the engine running, the driver jumped out, ran across to 39, rapped on the windows, got back into the car. A man and woman came out. She thrust the shopping bag she was carrying through the Volvo's open near-side front window. After that she and the man chatted to the driver and walked round the car, apparently admiring it.

Ascher aimed the Asahi Pentax, clicked the shutter, pulled the rapid wind lever, and clicked again. He did this several times, hoping there was enough light. 'Got the registration number, Ruth?'

109

'Yes,' she said. 'And the make—Volvo 244. Tangerine sedan.'

'Zeid's the driver,' said Ascher. 'Wearing his silk scarf as usual. Hanna put a shopping bag in the front seat. Not much in it. Now they're admiring the car.' He put down the camera and picked up the binoculars. 'She looks tired.'

'Must have been last night. It was a Marks and Spencer bag.'

'You've a nasty mind, Ruth. It was light. She flicked it in with her wrist.'

'Not nasty. Just realistic. Yes, I agree. Nothing heavy in it.'

The man and the woman on the pavement were waving and laughing.

'Zeid's off,' said Ruth. 'If it was a film we'd follow.'

'Yes. With a car dropped by helicopter into Spender Street. Slap on his tail. Laser beams at the ready.'

'Wouldn't that be great. The Volvo's an automatic,' she said. 'He never took his hands off the wheel.'

'Right. Get on to the Embassy. Check that registration number.'

Ruth Meyer picked up the phone, dialled the Israeli Embassy.

The man and the girl outside 39 stood talking for some moments before going back into the premises.

*   *   *

110

Normally Zeid was a fast driver but he took no chances with the Volvo. On the contrary he observed speed limits scrupulously, driving in a manner which would have earned the approbation of the Police Driving School at Hendon.

He crossed the Thames by Putney Bridge, threaded his way gingerly down the High Street and up Putney Hill to the junction with the A3. The drizzle became more opaque as he reached the Kingston by-pass and he switched on the Volvo's lights.

There was a good deal of traffic but for most of the time he stayed in the slow lane. He could not afford an accident. At the *Marquis of Granby* he turned left following the Portsmouth Road into Esher. Opposite *The Bear* he picked up the A244 and went on through Hersham towards Weybridge. Leaving Walton-on-Thames, he switched to the A3050 and drove down into Weybridge. He parked the Volvo near *The Ship*, put on leather gloves, raincoat and trilby, took the shopping bag from the front seat and locked the car.

He walked down the High Street to the letter-boxes outside the post office. From the shopping bag he took five large envelopes of the sort used by solicitors for legal documents. Having examined the addresses and checked the stamps, he posted them. On his way back to the Volvo he screwed the shopping bag into a ball and put it in a refuse basket.

It took him the best part of an hour to get back to the West End. He travelled down Piccadilly towards Leicester Square, turned into Whitcomb Street and left the Volvo in the car park at its lower end. Walking towards the Haymarket he looked at his watch. 'Eight minutes to six, Saturday, the sixth of November,' he muttered, his mind full of many things.

It was a cold night and rain fell indiscriminately on the never-ending streams of traffic and people. Zeid turned up the collar of his raincoat, pulled down the trilby and made for the Piccadilly tube station.

At the top of the Haymarket he had to wait at the traffic lights. Worried and fearful at first, he slowly relaxed, his emotions heightened by the scene: the abstract patterns of light reflected on wet streets; the subdued roar of traffic; the squelching hiss of tyres; the glistening raincoats and umbrellas; and overall the insidious odour of exhaust fumes.

All this activity, he reflected, might be brought to an end within the next few days, and the people pushing and thrusting round him hadn't a clue that he was the man who might do it. To them he was just another Londoner in a raincoat with pulled-down trilby and dark glasses.

Filled with a sudden euphoria, a feeling of supreme power, his emotions fed on themselves until all fear had gone. Now he saw himself as a man of destiny, holding in his hands not only the life of a great city, but the future of all his people.

The crossing lights went green. His mood had made him careless and he bumped into someone crossing from the opposite side. The woman he'd nearly knocked down let out a startled, 'Christ!'

Before Zeid could apologize, the man with her said, 'You stupid twit! Why don't you look where you're going.'

CHAPTER TWELVE

The morning's mail on Monday, November 8th, brought identical envelopes with identical contents to the Prime Minister at 10 Downing Street, to the United States Ambassador in the Embassy in Grosvenor Square, to the Director-General of the BBC in Langham Place, to the Editor of *The Times* in Grays Inn Road, and to the Editor of the *Daily Express* in Fleet Street.

In each instance the envelopes were opened and the contents read and examined by private secretaries. In the case of the Prime Minister and the US Ambassador the envelopes had, as a matter of routine, been security checked for strip explosives before opening. Within the

113

hour all five addressees had either read the document or had it read to them on scrambler phones. The Prime Minister was finishing a late breakfast at Chequers when his principal private secretary, Andrew Lanyard, telephoned the contents to him.

'I'll be at Number Ten in less than an hour,' said the Prime Minister. 'It may be a hoax. But inform DGSS and McGann personally—repeat personally—at once. Not a minute is to be lost. Have copies ready for them. And see that a D-notice is put on it without delay.'

'Right, Prime Minister. That will be done.'

DGSS (the Director-General of the Security Services) was the shadowy background figure who headed Britain's intelligence services. He was never referred to by name and few people were aware of his identity. Dugald McGann was the Assistant-Commissioner in charge of the Special Branch at Scotland Yard.

*   *   *

The Prime Minister was in his office in Downing Street soon after ten o'clock. Having gone through the motions of lighting a pipe, he considered the document a pale and agitated Andrew Lanyard laid before him. Immaculately IBM-typed on legal folios, it bore no indication of origin, no heading other than the single word ULTIMATUM. For these reasons the Prime Minister turned to the last page

114

before reading it. It had been signed in black ink with a felt-tipped pen, 'Mahmoud el Ka'ed.' Beneath the strong, aggressive flourish appeared the name in type, beneath that the words 'Soukour-al-Sahra'.

The Prime Minister frowned. 'Where was it posted?'

'In Weybridge. At the High Street post office. On Saturday evening.'

'Weybridge. H'm.' The Prime Minister fussed with a dead pipe, gave it up as a bad job, laid it on the ashtray. 'Interesting. Have DGSS and McGann seen it?'

'Yes, Prime Minister. They have copies. Both of the document and the photos.'

The Prime Minister's calm struck Lanyard as altogether too monumental. He doubted if it would endure through the document. It was one thing to have it read to you over the phone, quite another to see it in black and white.

'I suppose I'd better read it, Lanyard.' The Prime Minister spoke with resignation, turned to the front page and leant forward in his chair, his mind concentrated:

1. A nuclear device has been placed in an important area of London. It will be detonated in seventy-two hours commencing noon, November 8th, 1975, unless the Government of the United Kingdom jointly with that of the United States accedes unequivocally to the

115

following demands before that time.

2. All Palestine territory seized by Israel in 1948 and 1949 in excess of the 29th November, 1947, United Nations Resolution for the partition of Palestine, together with those parts of Palestine not occupied by Israel before 1967, notably on the West Bank of the Jordan and in the Gaza Strip and Jerusalem, to be returned to and assigned forthwith to the people of Palestine.

3. The territories so assigned, constituting as they do the Palestinian homeland, to be recognized as an independent sovereign state and the sum of $10bn to be made available immediately as a contribution towards the cost of setting up such state and providing the infra-structure for a sophisticated and balanced agricultural/industrial economy.

4. Although this ultimatum is addressed to the Government of the United Kingdom in view of its special responsibility as the former mandatory power for Palestine, it is acknowledged that without the assent and full co-operation of the United States the United Kingdom cannot comply with its terms. If they are not met, responsibility for the consequences will thus rest jointly with the governments of the United Kingdom and the United States.

5. The Palestine Liberation Organization to be recognized as the provisional government of the new state until such time as arrangements can be made for a freely-elected government.

6. Provided the terms of this ultimatum are

accepted in full within the stipulated seventy-two hours, and the necessary undertakings given and guaranteed formally and irrevocably by the United Kingdom and the United States, the pre-set timing mechanism for detonating the nuclear device will be rendered inoperative.

7. If the whereabouts of the device and/or the guards and technicians responsible for it become known to the United Kingdom or any other authorities or agencies or persons and if any attempt is made to interfere with the device or those responsible for it singly or severally it will at once be detonated.

8. When the necessary undertakings have been given jointly by the governments of the United Kingdom and the United States the nuclear device will remain in position in London under the control of the Soukour-al-Sahra' until such time as the undertakings have been fulfilled in all respects.

9. The demands in this ultimatum are not negotiable by the Soukour-al-Sahra' nor the PLO nor any other authority or group or agency or persons and for that reason no means of communication has been suggested or given and all undertakings in regard to the fulfilment must be made by the United Kingdom and United States by publication in The Times *and the* Daily Express *and by announcement at pre-advertised times over the BBC's home and overseas radio services.*

10. In order to establish the authenticity of this

117

document, photographs of the nuclear device and its detonating component are attached and attention is drawn to the series numbers stamped upon each by those responsible for their manufacture.

11. Copies of this ultimatum have been dispatched by the same post to the US Ambassador to the United Kingdom, to the Director General of the BBC, and to the editors of The Times *and the* Daily Express.

Signed: Mahmoud el Ka'ed,
Soukour-al-Sahra'

The Prime Minister noted that, but for the ink-written date in the first paragraph, the document was undated. He put it down, leant back in his chair. 'Now, let me see those photographs, Lanyard.'

Lanyard, tight-lipped, visibly shaken, handed them over. The Prime Minister shuffled through the photos, puffed at his pipe, then sat deep in thought for some time. 'Think it's a hoax?'

'Emphatically not, Prime Minister. DGSS was on the phone ten minutes ago. He's already checked with the CRS and the Direction de la Surveillance du Territoire in Paris—also with the French Ministry of Defence. Lassagne, the Ministry's nuclear weapons boss, has checked with Aerospatiale. The device in these photos is the Pluton warhead missing after the alleged Israeli commando raid on Beirut Port on October fifth/sixth.'

'So the Israeli denial *was* genuine.'

'It seems so, Prime Minister. DGSS believes the raid was carried out by Ka'ed's SAS. So does Anton Girard of the DST.'

'Is that belief well-founded?'

'Yes. McGann goes along with it too.'

'Couldn't the photos have been taken while the warhead and detonator were in the hands of Aerospatiale?'

Lanyard shook his head, playing his trump card with a certain boyish satisfaction, just as McGann had to him not long before. 'I think this answers your question, Prime Minister.' He handed over the last photograph. It showed the Pluton lying on a trestle in what looked like a crude workshop. At the top of the photograph, hands held an open newspaper, the tip of the warhead's nose-cone piercing it. The name of the paper and date of publication could be seen quite clearly: *Al Hayat, October 7th, 1975.*

'That's the Arabic language daily published in Beirut,' explained Lanyard.

'I know.' The Prime Minister continued to examine the photograph. 'Let us say it provides fairly conclusive evidence that these people had the warhead in Beirut the day after the raid on the Port. But what evidence is there that it is now in London? Presumably it's fairly large and heavy. How did they transport it from Beirut to an 'important area of London'? It may still be in Beirut.'

Lanyard nodded. 'DGSS and McGann thought of that as soon as they'd read the ultimatum.'

'What conclusions did they reach?'

'None in the short time they were here, Prime Minister. Except to say . . .' Lanyard hesitated.

'To say what?' prompted the Prime Minister.

'That it could be a bluff but somebody had better decide bloody quick. No use passing the buck. Those were, I think, the exact words used.'

'Sounds like McGann. Did he say who that somebody was?'

'Yes, Prime Minister. He seemed to think it was you.'

There was a meaningful silence before the Prime Minister said, 'Generous of him.' He laid down the empty pipe. 'Not an easy decision, Lanyard.'

That, thought his principal private secretary, is likely to be the understatement of the year.

'Have you checked with the other addressees?'

'Yes, I have. They all confirm having received copies. The United States Ambassador is in Scotland . . . or rather was. He's flying south. Due at Grosvenor Square at eleven-forty-five. But it's been read to him. He told his secretary he'd phone you as soon as he reaches the Embassy. They've already spoken to Washington. The Director-General of the BBC has it. So have the editors of *The Times* and the *Daily Express.* They've undertaken not to publish for the time being. But they expect to be taken into your confidence within the day.'

The Prime Minister frowned. 'Do they really?' The media were not his favourite people. He got up from the chair and stood looking at the photos. 'And the D-notice?'

'DGSS had one slapped on it as soon as I phoned him, Prime Minister.'

'Good. I want a meeting of the Cabinet at two-thirty this afternoon. By then DGSS's people and McGann will have put in five hours on this—the US Ambassador will have spoken to Washington and come back to me. By two-thirty we should have something to bite on.' He hesitated. 'Tell Cabinet Ministers that a national emergency of . . . of what? . . .' He looked at the ceiling hoping to find some helpful answer there.

'Cataclysmic proportions,' suggested Lanyard.

'Rather too much, don't you think?' The Prime Minister smiled at his private secretary. 'I daresay you used that in an OU debate.'

Lanyard grinned guiltily. 'Actually I did.'

'So did I once. I was younger then.' The Prime Minister became suddenly serious. 'This

121

is no light matter, Lanyard. These people have a cause and they're prepared to die for it. That always inhibits political solutions. Like the wretched mess in Northern Ireland. Only a damned sight worse.'

'Indescribably worse, I should have thought, Prime Minister. There are eight million innocent people in London. Why should they be put at risk? It's monstrous.'

'We won't discuss the *why* of it now, Lanyard. That's become irrelevant. The fact is they *are* at risk.'

The private secretary went towards the door. 'One moment,' said the Prime Minister. 'I want to see the Leader of the Opposition and the Leader of the House of Lords between one and two this afternoon. In making the appointments, stress that I wish to discuss privately a national matter of the utmost urgency and importance.'

'Yes, Prime Minister.' Lanyard was making notes.

'And I would like the Permanent Secretaries for Home, Foreign Affairs and Defence, the Chief of the General Staff, the Chairman of the Combined Intelligence Committee, the Commissioner of Police and the Head of Special Branch from Scotland Yard, the Chairman of the GLC and his Chief executive, and of course DGSS and George Isaacson—plus two leading nuclear physicists and nuclear weapons experts nominated by him—to be on call here during the Cabinet Meeting.'

George Isaacson was the Prime Minister's principal scientific adviser.

Lanyard went on scribbling. 'May I read that back?'

'Yes. Please.'

Lanyard read back. When he'd finished the Prime Minister said, 'Good. But I want Isaacson to bring *two* nuclear physicists and *two* nuclear arms experts. That's four in all. Is that clear?'

'Yes. I have that.'

The Prime Minister crossed to the far corner of the room. 'One more thing, Lanyard.' He smiled reassuringly. 'Keep cool. We're going to get over this somehow.' He didn't add that he hadn't the slightest idea how.

The principal private secretary nodded forlornly and left the room. When he'd gone the Prime Minister sat at his desk, head in hands, 'God help us,' he muttered. 'What an appalling situation. What impossible demands. They must know we can't meet them. The Israelis will never agree.'

Minutes later he looked at the carriage clock on his desk. There would be just time to get to the Palace, tell her, and be back at Number Ten before the US Ambassador reached his Embassy in Grosvenor Square.

Seventy-two Hours To Go

CHAPTER THIRTEEN

Shalom Ascher went slowly up the stairs of 56 Spender Street, the speed of his ascent reflecting his disenchantment with his task. On reaching the first-floor landing, he turned left and knocked on the door of the office on the right. While he waited he looked at his watch. Three minutes to two. At least he was not late. He heard footsteps in the office and knew that Zol Levi was coming to the door and would be examining him through the spy-hole. He heard the key in the lock turn. The door opened. Levi nodded. ' 'Kay. Come in.' Ascher went in. Levi shut and locked the door behind him. Ascher put the wet umbrella in the metal wastepaper basket, brushed rainwater from his shaggy head. 'Anything new, Zol?'

Levi smiled knowingly, made a circle with his thumb and forefinger. 'Listen to this. Recorded about eleven this morning. I've just played it through.' He went to the small table where the Grundigs stood. On one of them the wheels were still turning. He switched on the other, adjusting the volume until it was audible though muted.

The two men pulled chairs close to the recorder and near the window so that they could watch Mocal's premises while they listened. From the Grundig's speaker came the sound of voices speaking Arabic. The Israelis had no difficulty in identifying them. They had listened to many tapes in recent weeks.

HANNA NASOUR: How can we be sure all the cards were delivered this morning?

ZEID: They were posted Saturday about five-thirty. The letter-boxes were cleared at seven. They should all be deliverered by now.

IBRAHIM SOUREF: The addressees must have had a nasty shock.

NAJIB HAMADEH: You're telling me.

HANNA: Well. We'll soon know. Everything okay with Ahmad and Rudi?

ZEID: Yes. Ahmad phoned at eight this morning. From a call-box.

HANNA: This waiting kills me. I churn and churn inside. A high-jay's chicken feed compared with this.

ZEID: Watch it, Hanna.

HANNA: Sorry.

SOUREF: Who doesn't churn inside? But think of Rudi and Ahmad. At least we don't have to deliver the goods. Have you spoken to Brussels again, Zeid?

ZEID: Yes. Last night.

SOUREF: Anything new?

ZEID: How could there be? The action's here not there. We have to make the sale. We're committed to the contract. All Brussels

125

wants to know is market reaction once the terms are known.

HAMADEH: When will that be?

ZEID: Tonight, I imagine. It's not a thing to be delayed.

HANNA: The sooner the better. Ibby! Your hair. Put it straight.

SOUREF: Satisfied?

(Sounds of a scuffle, laughter).

HANNA: Whoops! Don't you dare. That's better. Coffee anyone?

ZEID: Not for me, Hanna. I must be going.

SOUREF: Yes. Please. With sugar. Lots of it.

HAMADEH: Please. No sugar.

(Sounds of a chair scraping, a deep sigh and footsteps.)

HANNA: It's a man's world.

(Light laughter, a door opening and shutting.)

SOUREF: Super girl.

HAMADEH: You should know.

SOUREF: Jealousy will get you nowhere.

ZEID: You must all get as much sleep as you can while you can.

HAMADEH: Easily said. It's impossible, Zeid. Too much to think about. Difficult to sleep on the edge of a volcano.

ZEID: Discipline yourself, man. It's not such a problem. It's going to be more difficult for others. How would you like to be sleeping in Palace Green tonight?

SOUREF: Thanks to Allah, I won't be. It

could be a two-way blast for them. Market reaction *and* the contract.

ZEID: It's good that its terms are not negotiable. Especially by them.

HAMADEH: I wonder what the decision would be if it were?

ZEID: No point in speculating on what might have been. Let's deal with what is. That's enough for any man.

HAMADEH: When do we see you next?

ZEID: Tonight. After the late editions have come on the streets. You listening to that radio, Ibrahim? I must go now.

SOUREF: Sure. It's turned right down but I can hear. It's just behind my ear.

ZEID: 'Bye now.

HAMADEH: Allah be with you, Zeid.

(Sounds of chairs scraping, footsteps, a door opening and shutting.)

Levi switched off the Grundig. 'That's all that's worth hearing. The rest's just chat.'

'That was interesting,' said Ascher. 'Very interesting.'

'What do you make of it? I have my own ideas.'

Ascher was watching the premises opposite. It was some time before he spoke. 'Most of it figures,' he said, 'but not all. They were playing the shorthand game. Amateurish but effective if you don't get careless. Hanna got careless. Know why? She was excited. They were all excited. Did you get that?'

'Yes, I did. And she let out high-jay.'

Ascher nodded. 'Yeah. Zeid didn't like that. So she's been on a high-jack. It's the first time since we've been listening that any of them have admitted to being what we know they are.'

'So what d'you think?' Levi frowned, watching the other man.

'Certain things stand out like a sore thumb. "The cards"must be the Christmas cards we've heard about. Letter bombs, probably. Hence the addressees' nasty shock. And the addressees? Probably prominent Zionists in the City. Okay?'

'So far I'm with you,' said Levi.

Ascher stood up, moved closer to the window. 'Rudi and Ahmad—whoever they are —are to deliver "the goods".'

'Explosives,' suggested Levi.

'Sounds like it.' Ascher scratched his ear. 'To be delivered where? The only reference to a place in that tape is Palace Green. And that's tied to to-night.'

'The Embassy's address is Palace Green.'

'You're highly perceptive, Zol.'

'I do my best.'

Ascher's shaggy head nodded in slow affirmation. 'Right. So it fits.'

Levi said, 'I'd say it does. What was all that stuff about "Brussels", "the contract" and "market reaction" once the terms are known?'

Ascher thought about that. 'Brussels? Probably a communications link. They've mentioned it before you know. The contract could be some sort of ultimatum, couldn't it?' He shrugged his shoulders. 'Market reaction? Well. They said that twice. The second time in relation to Palace Green. In both contexts it could have meant 'public opinion'. But where I come unstuck is where Zeid says, "its terms" are not for "their decision". He was referring to those at Palace Green. In other words the Israeli Embassy.'

'So?' said Levi doggedly.

'There's some sort of ultimatum associated with an attack on the Israeli Embassy. But it's not for the Israelis to decide the response. Okay?'

'It makes sense. But it's not conclusive. And who will decide?'

'Who knows. And of course it isn't conclusive. Nothing is in this game.'

Ascher looked at his watch, got up with sudden urgency.

Levi was puzzled. 'And now?'

'I'll do what I should have done ten minutes ago. Alert the Embassy. Then go up there with the tape. You stay here. Ruth should be along shortly. I'll use a call-box for this one.'

Ascher was about to go when they heard a knock on the door. Levi went to it, looked through the spy-hole. 'She's come.' He unlocked the door. Ascher thought she looked

129

very desirable, cheeks and raincoat glistening with moisture, dark eyes and white teeth combining in a vivid smile.

'Hi,' she said.

Levi shut and locked the door. She put down the shopping bag and umbrella, took off the raincoat, and hung it on a peg near the door. 'It's miserable outside,' she said, 'but I've news for you.'

'What news?' Levi watched her closely.

'I've seen him at close range.'

'Who?' It came from the two men simultaneously.

'Zeid. I almost bumped into him. In a stationery shop in the Strand. Near the Aldwych.'

'Big deal,' said Levi.

'Quite a dish at close range. He was buying a pocket-size notebook. Now I know why he wears that silk scarf round his neck.'

'Difficult to wear it anywhere else,' suggested Ascher. 'But tell us.'

'There's a scar running down the left side of his neck. One of those red wrinkled ones. Starts from behind the ear and goes down into the collar.'

'You didn't follow it below that?' Levi cocked his head on one side.

Ascher was serious. 'How could you see it, if he was wearing a scarf?'

'He wasn't at that moment. He'd gone round the corner behind a display stand and was re-tying the scarf. I could see his reflection in a mirror. The whole left side of the face. When he came round the corner he saw me and smiled. I think he'd seen me watching him in the mirror and felt embarrassed. But it was a nice smile.'

'The rotter,' said Levi. 'Trying to turn you on like that. Anyway, when contemplating his noble features in future just remember he's a bloody assassin.'

'How d'you know?' She frowned absent-mindedly. 'But don't you see the importance? He hides that scar. He knows it identifies him.'

'Keep calm, Ruth.' Ascher smiled at her as if she were a naughty child. 'We've got the message.'

She liked Ascher's face when he smiled, when moist lips and shining teeth softened the severity of the beard. 'What's more,' she said, 'I photographed him.'

She held up the lighter which was also a Minolta spycamera.

Ascher put a beefy arm round her shoulders, held her tight, kissed her cheek. 'Great, my little secret agent.'

She looked at him with disbelief. It was the first time he'd done that. She liked it, but instinctively pulled away hoping that wouldn't stop him doing it again some other time. 'And I've more news for you,' she said. 'I phoned the Embassy. On the way here. They've checked the Volvo. It was hired from Avis at

131

Heathrow by a Frenchman, Simon Charrier, a few days ago. He still has it. After some argument they gave the Embassy his London address. Forty-three, St Peter's Road, Fulham.'

'That's really good.' Shalom Ascher looked at her with approval. 'Really good. We'll check forty-three, St Peter's Road.'

'I've already done so. By phone about half-an-hour ago. The place belongs to a Miss Morley. Very refined. Takes in lodgers. "House guests" she calls them. She's never heard of Simon Charrier or the Volvo. When I began questioning her, she put the phone down.'

'Could happen we still check there.' Ascher scratched his ear. 'D'you think she was bluffing?'

'No. She sounded genuine.'

'Who is Simon Charrier anyway?' asked Levi.

'Maybe Zeid. We know he drives the Volvo.' Ascher pulled on a raincoat. 'We'll discuss it later, Ruth. Must go now. Zol will put you in the picture. Things are beginning to happen.' He unlocked the door and let himself out.

CHAPTER FOURTEEN

In the Cabinet Room at Number Ten the Prime Minister, a thick-set slightly hunched figure, sat at the head of a long table, outwardly calm and relaxed, mouthing an unlit pipe. His mind, as it happened, was anything but calm and relaxed. On his right sat the Secretary for the Home Department, on his left, the Secretary to the Cabinet. The far end of the table was headed by the Chancellor of the Exchequer, to his right the Secretary for Foreign Affairs, to his left the Secretary of State for Defence.

Along the flanks of the table sat those fourteen Members of the Cabinet who had been able to attend.

The muted hum of conversation ceased when the Prime Minister put down his pipe and cleared his throat—familiar signals that the business of the Cabinet was about to begin. He looked at the ceiling, then at his notes. 'You will, I am sure, appreciate that I would not have called you to this meeting at such short - notice with neither agenda nor supporting papers except under the most exceptional circumstances.'

The Prime Minister paused, his eyes searching the faces along the table. 'I regret to say that the circumstances are both

133

exceptional and appalling. This morning's post brought to me, as it did to the Ambassador of the United States, to the Director-General of the BBC, and the editors of *The Times* and *Daily Express*, an ultimatum. An ultimatum which threatens the continued existence of this country as a free and independent nation.

'Before I read it to you I will ask the Secretary to distribute copies. The documents are numbered and we will, I am afraid, require their return at the end of the meeting.'

When the copies of the ultimatum had been distributed the Prime Minister read it aloud, clause by clause, in measured tones. At its conclusion he said, 'That, then, is the situation which confronts us. I have some advantage in that I have had five hours in which to consider the document. During that time I have consulted with the United States Ambassador, with the heads of our security services, with Sir George Isaacson, and others including the Chief of the General Staff. For that reason, I feel I should draw your attention to certain aspects of the ultimatum before opening the matter for discussion.

'In the first place let me say that all the evidence available makes it clear that this is no hoax. We have already checked with the French Government and they confirm that the nuclear warhead depicted in the photographs is the one found to be missing after the so-called Israeli commando raid on Beirut Port on the night of October fifth/sixth.'

The Prime Minister paused, looked blandly down the rows of faces turned towards him, a sure sign, his listeners knew, that the punch line had still to come. 'Some of you may not be familiar with the background and history of this terrorist organisation. Let me explain. In 1972, a young Palestinian, Marwan Haddad, quarrelled with Yasir Arafat and broke away from the PLO. Assuming a new name and appearance, he formed the Soukour-al-Sahra'—the Desert Hawks—the most militant, ruthless and aggressive of the Liberation movement's extremist groups. The name he took for his new role was Mahmoud el Ka'ed.

'No . . .' The Prime Minister shook his head emphatically. 'This ultimatum is no hoax. There is, of course, the possibility—and our security services are well aware of this—the possibility, I say, that a certain aspect of the ultimatum may be a hoax but only, and I repeat only, in the sense that the missing warhead may not be in London. It may still be in the Middle East. But I ask you . . . can we conceivably gamble on such a possibility with the lives of hundreds of thousands of our people, indeed with the very security of our country at risk? That is the grim, the wicked irony of our situation. The warhead may well be in the Middle East. But equally, it may well be in London. Ka'ed says it *is* in London. He is a proven fanatic, a ruthless, dangerous man.

135

You may ask . . . how could this terrorist group possibly have smuggled an object of such size and weight into London? That is a valid question, but it is not one we have now to answer.

'The Government has been presented with an ultimatum. We have been given seventy-two hours, from noon today, in which to decide our response to its demands. It is for that purpose I have called you here to-day. It is not a matter which—at this stage at any rate—can be discussed in the House of Commons with all its attendant publicity. Shortly before this meeting began I had a private discussion with the Leader of the Opposition. He will of course consult his Shadow Cabinet, but he has in the meantime undertaken not to do or say anything which might add to our difficulties. I need hardly add that he fully appreciates the gravity of the situation.

'There are a number of matters which we shall have to discuss in the course of this meeting. The probable area of destruction of the warhead. The baffling problem as to where in this vast city it may be. What announcement we must make to the people of London—to the country—and when. Are we to declare a state of national emergency, to introduce martial law? Can we conceivably arrange an orderly evacuation of London in the time available? In what language should we couch such an instruction if we are to preclude,' he hesitated, 'some sort of mass hysteria? What will be the attitude of the United States Government? Clearly, their co-operation is essential if the terms of the ultimatum are to be met. And what of France, West Germany and other NATO powers?

'Last, but by no means least, what reaction can we expect from Israel . . . the country which, if the ultimatum succeeds, has to pay the greatest price.

'Ka'ed threatens—his record suggests it is no idle threat—that, should the warhead be found by us, should we take steps to deal with it, or the terrorists responsible for it, it will at once be detonated.

'The terms of the ultimatum are not, he says, negotiable, indeed there is no one with whom to negotiate. I doubt if any government, any nation, has ever been confronted with an ultimatum so devastingly ruthless, so implacably one-sided.

'It must be clear to you, as it is to me, that, if this ultimatum succeeds—and how we are to prevent it from doing so is as yet beyond my comprehension—then no great city, no nation, is safe. Historians may say that this was the final breakdown of the rule of law in our western civilisation. It is London today, it could be New York tomorrow, Paris or Berlin the next day. Indeed all the great capitals of the world, all the nations to which they belong, could be at the mercy of small groups of ruthless, mindless terrorists and criminals.

'There is no shortage of such creatures, no absence of causes or projects for which they would not be prepared to risk all.

'What then, you may ask, are we to do? And I must reply that as yet I see no solution. Whatever decisions we take . . . must be taken within the next,' the Prime Minister looked at the clock on the wall, 'within the next sixty-nine hours.

'I have already given instructions for the immediate recall of our ambassadors to the Lebanon, Syria and Israel so that we may consult with them. Sir Neville Ashton, our Ambassador in Beirut, has at my request already seen Yasir Arafat who has told him that the PLO disclaims all knowledge of and responsibility for the ultimatum which it deplores. Arafat repudiated Mahmoud el Ka'ed and his terrorist group in the strongest terms, reminding Ashton that the PLO had long-since outlawed the Soukour-al-Sahra' which it regarded as a thoroughly irresponsible and dangerous splinter group. Nothing could have been more damaging to the Palestine Liberation movement, Arafat said, than this ultimatum which he described as savage and barbaric. He did add, however, that the pusillanimity of Great Britain and the United States in regard to the dismemberment of Palestine and the tragic plight of the Palestinian peoples invited action of this sort by radical extremist groups.

'Ashton believes Yasir Arafat to be sincere. The Arab leader was, he says, clearly appalled by what has transpired.

'As soon as I had read and digested the contents of the ultimatum I requested the DGSS, the Special Branch and Scotland Yard to concentrate all their energy and resources upon discovering the whereabouts of the warhead and those associated with it. I authorized them to give absolute priority to this operation, to make use of every man available, and to take whatever steps they deem necessary. Fortunately, search without warrant is permissible where the presence of explosives is suspected—and that, in the circumstances, means the whole of London.

'I need hardly tell you that I have stressed beyond all doubt that if the warhead is traced nothing—I repeat *nothing* with all the emphasis at my command—is to be done by way of interference with it, or the persons responsible for it, without reference to me.

'During the course of this morning I went to the Palace and informed the Queen of the ultimatum. I urged cancellation of her appointments over the next few days and asked her to leave London at once. This she has done with the greatest reluctance. I am pleased to say she is now at Sandringham. A bulletin is to be issued by the Royal Household announcing that she has been obliged to cancel her appointments because of an indisposition which, while not in itself serious, requires that she should rest.

'The Duke of Edinburgh has refused point blank to leave London. I had no option but to accept this highly predictable decision which may yet prove helpful in sustaining the morale of Londoners during the ordeal which is soon to confront them.

'One more word . . . I have thought it necessary—indeed essential—to have at our disposal during this meeting those key officials whose knowledge and experience can best assist us.

'They are at present in the ante-room where they are being briefed by Sir Brynne Evans and the Head of the Special Branch. When we have concluded our private discussions I propose calling them in for the general discussion. You will have an opportunity then of putting to them any questions you may have in mind. I will now ask the Secretary to read to you their names.'

*   *   *

In the discussion which followed the formal meeting in the Cabinet Room the enormity of the problem posed by the ultimatum was discussed in all its aspects.

Sir George Isaacson, opening at the Prime Minister's request, pointed out that the basic problem confronting the Government was starkly simple. Somewhere within the 120 square miles comprising the County of London there was believed to be a nuclear warhead liable to be detonated in seventy-two hours, or earlier if those responsible for it so decided. Everything they would discuss centred around that fact.

The nuclear physicists expressed the opinion that a nuclear warhead of 15 kilotons, equivalent to 15,000 tons of TNT, detonated at ground level, would devastate an area within a radius of 8 to 10 miles. There would be grave problems of radioactive fall-out over a far greater area.

The nuclear weapons experts explained the functioning of a tactical nuclear warhead. It would, they said, be entirely practical to detonate a Pluton warhead by means of an electrical or mechanical timing device, and if necessary to by-pass that device to secure instant detonation. They explained the design, size and weight of the warhead and agreed it could have been introduced into London in a number of different ways without being detected. Adding a lugubrious footnote, they said detonation of the warhead would create an urban catastrophe without parallel since Hiroshima.

The Chairman of the Combined Intelligence Committee, Sir Brynne Evans, speaking for the intelligence services, said that there were no clues whatever as to the whereabouts of the warhead. A search on an unprecedented scale was being mounted and London would be fine-combed by more than 3,000 men. Until an official announcement had been made the operation would be hampered since searchers would not be able to say for what they were looking, nor could a general appeal be made to the public for information which might provide leads.

Sir Brian Parkes, Commissioner of the Metropolitan Police, agreed that a public announcement would do much to help and he urged one as soon as possible.

The head of the Special Branch, Assistant-Commissioner Dugald McGann, said, 'There are good reasons to suppose that the warhead came by sea. It would be extremely difficult, though not impossible, to smuggle such a large, heavy object by air. In this instance the lapse of time between the theft of the warhead in Beirut and release of the ultimatum here strongly suggest a sea passage—and a slow one at that. 'The warhead,' he went on, 'may still be in a ship or other vessel somewhere in London Docks or elsewhere on the Thames. We are, with the assistance of the Port of London Authority and the Metropolitan Police, organizing a search of all ships, barges and boats in the area concerned, and it will begin to-night. Ships which have arrived from Middle East ports are being given special priority and we are with the help of HM Customs and Immigration examining cargo manifests, bills of lading, passenger lists and immigration records on a systematic basis. We are carrying out similar checks at other major ports and airports. This is a time-consuming operation, complicated by the fact that until the public announcement is made we cannot say what we are looking for.'

There was long discussion about the possibility of a mass evacuation of London, other than personnel required to maintain essential services such as power, water, transport and sewage. The Director-General of the GLC, Andrew Watt, giving the logistics of such an operation, made it clear that it was not remotely possible.

Dugald McGann said that the Special Branch was pulling in for questioning persons known or suspected to have affiliations with the Palestine Liberation movement. In addition a number of informers were at work among the Palestinian community, particularly in London.

The DGSS said that 'his people' were in touch with Interpol, the Deuxième Bureau in Beirut and Israeli Intelligence in Tel Aviv. Neither the ultimatum nor the nuclear warhead had been mentioned to these authorities but they had been told there was a serious bomb threat. General Jakob Kahn, Director-General of Israeli Intelligence, had undertaken to give every possible assistance and had added that there was reason to believe a bomb attack on the Israeli Embassy in London might be imminent.

The Chief of the General Staff, General Sir Dyhart Tanner, said if the warhead's whereabouts became known it was possible that those guarding it could be 'neutralized' before they could take action to detonate it. He explained that the Chemical Warfare Establishment at Porton Down might be able to provide the means to do this under certain circumstances.

'Such circumstances will not necessarily apply in this instance,' he said. 'They depend upon a number of human and environmental factors, but the possibility should not be lost sight of.'

While expressing interest in the CGS's contribution, the Prime Minister stressed that if the warhead were found it would not be possible to take chances. 'We should need to be very sure that the action proposed was going to succeed before we embarked on such a course.'

There was strong support for this view.

The CGS replied that the terrorists would presumably do everything possible to avoid detonating the bomb since such an act would defeat the object of the ultimatum.

As the meeting progressed there was general agreement on the following:

(i) It would be unwise to proclaim a state of

national emergency or martial law at the present juncture.

(ii) The moral right of the Palestinian people to a sovereign independent state—not necessarily comprising the territories referred to in the ultimatum, but sufficient in size and ecology to support the 3,000,000 Palestinians in the Middle East—was acknowledged, though the methods used by Soukour-al-Sahra' to secure these ends were deplored.

(iii) Notwithstanding the virtual certainty of Israeli rejection of the ultimatum's territorial demands, there was no practical alternative to its acceptance if the warhead could not be located and rendered safe before the seventy-two hour deadline was reached. The risks involved in rendering it safe while it was still under the control of terrorists were regarded as unacceptable.

(iv) An ad hoc Committee under the Chairmanship of the Prime Minister—comprising the Home and Foreign Secretaries, the Defence Secretary, the Chief of the General Staff, the Chairman of the Combined Intelligence Committee, the DGSS, the Commissioner of the Metropolitan Police and the Head of Special Branch, the Prime Minister's Principal Scientific Adviser, the Chairman and Chief Executives of the GLC and the Port of London Authority—was appointed with power to act and co-opt other members as necessary.

145

(v) The Prime Minister to discuss the situation by hotline with the President of the United States, and the US President to be asked to make similar contact with the Chairman of the Soviet Union.

(vi) The ad hoc Committee to consult as necessary with the United Nations Organisations and NATO, and to keep these bodies informed throughout.

(vii) Prior to addressing the Nation, the Prime Minister to send for the Israeli Ambassador to acquaint him with the terms of the ultimatum, the attitude of the British Government, and the steps it was taking.

(viii) The Prime Minister to keep the Leader of the Opposition and the Leader of the House of Lords informed.

(ix) The Prime Minister to address the Nation at 8 pm that night in the manner outlined by him to the meeting.

(x) The media to be authorized to publish and broadcast the terms of the ultimatum after the Prime Minister's address, and to be asked to support the Government by urging calm and resolution, and by refraining from publishing anything which might encourage panic and disorder.

It was well past six in the evening when the Prime Minister closed the meeting. In doing so he announced that the ad hoc Committee would meet in the Cabinet Room at 8.30 pm that night.

CHAPTER FIFTEEN

Ascher came out of a call-box in the Trafalgar Square post office, flagged down a taxi, told the driver, 'Israeli Embassy', and sat back in the seat. The burly hunched figure, beard and hair hiding a hawkish face, looked more like a folk singer from the Kentucky Hills than a deep-cover agent. While the taxi growled and rumbled its way up through St James's Piccadilly and Knightsbridge towards Hyde Park, he mulled over the Mocal tape.

Most of it made sense but he was still puzzled by *contact terms and market reaction*. Some sort of ultimatum associated with a bomb attack on the Embassy? Public reaction to its terms? Was it to be a hostage operation? An exchange for terrorist prisoners? Unlikely in London. There weren't any. Not Palestinians at any rate. And there were two things terrorists knew for certain. One—the Israeli Embassy bristled with security systems. Two—the Israelis liked to shoot it out. They didn't worry too much about hostages, reckoning that dead terrorists were just about the best deterrent around for live terrorists. Other countries, big powerful ones like West Germany, Britain and Italy, negotiated, haggled, bargained, waffled about the sanctity of human life to people who didn't know what the words meant, released terrorists convicted of murder, paid huge ransoms, laid on aircraft to fly them to destinations of their choice and, if need be, sent their own diplomats along as guarantors of good faith.

The Israelis shot it out. An eye for an eye, a tooth for a tooth. It still worked as it had done through history. Even terrorists were motivated by the desire to remain alive.

The taxi passed the Albert Hall and at the end of Kensington Gardens turned right and stopped at the gates at the foot of Palace Green. Ascher showed his pass to the top-hatted commissionaire who waved the taxi on. The driver stopped outside the locked gates of No. 2, Ascher settled the fare, showed his pass to a security guard at the gates and to another at the main entrance. He rarely visited the Embassy. Only a few senior officials knew who he was. None had any knowledge of his assignments other than the Ambassador and Ezra Barlov, Head of Intelligence. The Ambassador was known to treat Ascher with respect. Other officials took their cue from the Ambassador. Shalom Ascher was evidently an important person.

Today he was expected. The security guards had been briefed and there was no delay. He was ushered into the First Secretary's office by an almond-eyed young woman whose assured manner suggested she was used to taking charge.

When she had gone the First Secretary, a balding man with cold eyes, held out a limp hand. 'Good afternoon, Ascher. What can I do for you?'

Ascher shook his head. 'Nothing. I want to see the Ambassador.'

The First Secretary smiled thinly. 'Pity you didn't mention that when you phoned. He's in Liverpool for Marcus Friedman's funeral.'

Ascher hadn't the faintest idea who Marcus Friedman was, nor did he care. 'I realized he might be away. Ezra Barlov will do.'

Another thin smile came from the First Secretary. 'Barlov's up at Holy Loch. Looking at the latest US nuke. It has the Poseidon missiles.'

Ascher spread his hands in a gesture of impatience. 'Who's left in ID then?'

'Michael Kagan.'

'Micky Kagan! When did he come here?'

'Ten days ago.'

'He'll do. Call him down. And let's have a recorder in here.'

'Certainly.' The First Secretary eyed him coolly as he flicked a switch on the desk intercom. 'Ask Captain Kagen to come down, please, Miss Simons. And bring in a tape recorder, please.' He put heavy emphasis on the 'pleases'.

Soon afterwards there was a knock at the door and the almond-eyed girl came in with the tape recorder. 'Captain Kagan,' she announced.

The man who followed her was young and slight with spaniel's eyes which blinked with deceptive meekness. 'Hullo, Shalom.' he said. 'What the hell?'

The two men grinned, shook hands warmly. They'd spent three weeks together in the October War disguised as Bedouins, moving about behind the Syrian lines on the Golan Heights.

The girl set the recorder on the desk and plugged it in. When she'd gone Ascher took the Mocal tape from his pocket and put it on the machine. 'It was recorded this morning. Don't ask me how, where or by whom because I won't tell you.'

When the tape had been played through he gave his interpretation, told them of his doubts, explained what it might be about. There was a long discussion after which the First Secretary said, 'Right. We'll assume it's laid on for tonight. I'll brief Joe Kowarsky. He'll tighten up security and let the Yard know.'

'Not about this tape, he won't,' said Ascher grimly. 'I'm not having my cover blown. This operation is top secret—and I mean top.'

'There was no intention of mentioning you or the tape.' The First Secretary was irritated. 'They'll double-check vehicles coming into or parked in and around Palace Green. Kowarsky will see to the rest. Terrorists won't get much change if they try anything here.' Joe Kowarsky was the Embassy's chief security officer.

There was a discussion about possibilities and probabilities which would have gladdened the heart of Jakob Kahn, Ascher missing no opportunity to knock out of the ground any loose ball bowled by the First Secretary. When the clock over the door chimed four he got up. 'I must go now,' he said. He looked at the First Secretary. 'Put the Ambassador in the picture when he arrives.'

'Of course,' said the First Secretary coldly.

'When's he due?'

'At seven. He's got a dinner party at eight-thirty.'

Ascher watched the First Secretary with critical eyes. He didn't like the man. A cold fish. Too precise. The antipathy must be chemical, he decided. He went to the door. 'See you,' he said in a toneless voice. He smiled at Kagan. ' 'Bye, Mick. Watch it boy.'

Kagan smiled back. 'You, too, Shalom.'

When Ascher had gone the First Secretary said, 'Know him well?'

'Very well.'

'What's he like?'

'A ruthless bastard but a good friend and a bloody good agent.'

'What makes him so good?'

'He's highly intelligent, very industrious and extremely patient. Never lets go.'

151

'I don't think I like him. Bad manners are unattractive.'

Kagan smiled. 'Watch it, Julius. He's a dangerous man.'

'In what way dangerous?'

'He's a killer. By practice and precept. I've seen him at it.'

The First Secretary looked at the young man with disapproval. 'I think we'd better get busy. There's not much time. Ask Kowarsky to come down.'

* * *

Soon after 7 pm a black Rover 3500 flying an Israeli pennant stopped in Downing Street. Two security guards stepped from the car and spoke to the policemen on duty outside Number Ten. A policeman rang the bell, the front door opened and the Israeli Ambassador walked quickly from the Rover into the building.

Andrew Lanyard met them in the hall. 'Please follow me, Ambassador.' He led the way down a passage to the library at its far end. The Prime Minister stood up, put the papers he'd been reading on a table and greeted his visitor. The two men exchanged courtesies and made themselves comfortable in leather armchairs beneath shaded lights flanked by book-lined walls.

'I'm afraid, Ambassador, that I have grave

152

news for you. I suggest you read this before we go any further.' The Prime Minister passed across a copy of the ultimatum with the photographs attached.

The Ambassador's face as he read the document and studied the photographs remained impassive. When he'd finished he took off his glasses, looked searchingly at the Prime Minister. 'What does your Government propose to do?' It was said quietly and with restraint.

The Prime Minister summarized the discussions which had taken place in the Cabinet Room that afternoon. At the finish he said, 'You will, Ambassador, I am sure, appreciate that we cannot under any circumstances accept the destruction of a substantial part of London and the killing and maiming of tens of thousands of our people.'

'In other words, Prime Minister, you are telling me that your Government will accept the terms of the ultimatum. That Israel alone is expected to pay the price for that acceptance. You surely do not believe that Israel will meet those territorial demands and so make impossible the defence of what remains of her territory.'

The Ambassador's eyes held the Prime Minister's.

'By no means all the price, Ambassador. The ultimatum demands the sum of ten billion dollars towards the cost of setting up a

153

Palestinian State. Britain and the United States will have to find the money. It will entail grievous sacrifices on the part of our people. Furthermore, acceptance will demand from us a price in terms of moral and diplomatic humiliation which cannot be measured.'

'Then don't accept. It may be a bluff. Even if it isn't, it's better to do what is morally right and leave the consequences to God.'

The Prime Minister busied himself with his pipe. It was a useful manoeuvre for gaining time. 'Who is to say what is morally right in such circumstances? You must know that you suggest a course of action which is quite impossible. Furthermore, you overlook a factor of the greatest importance.'

The Israeli Ambassador regarded the Prime Minister with sceptical, dubious eyes. 'And what is that?'

'Unless something quite unexpected, quite unpredictable, occurs in the next sixty-four hours we will have no option—no viable option—but to accept the terms of the ultimatum. But acceptance is not the end of the matter.'

'I don't follow, Prime Minister.'

The Prime Minister assumed the air of bland innocence to which he often resorted in moments of crisis in the House and at party conferences. 'We accept . . .' He smiled without humour. 'We give them the undertakings required of us. But consider

154

those undertakings. They will take time to implement. And it is time we so desperately need. We can add days, weeks, maybe months, to the seventy-two hours stipulated in the ultimatum. Each hour, each day, we gain increases our chances of finding the warhead, of wearing down the nerves of those responsible for it, of starving them out psychologically. Of reaching a position where we can take positive onward-going action.'

'Such as bringing pressure to bear on Israel.' The Ambassador shook his head. 'What you have told me about acceptance is—and I say this with the utmost respect—a typically political, a typically British response. What the French call *la perfidie d'Albion*.' He paused, his mind filled with suspicions of another sort of perfidy. An oil deal. The ultimatum was addressed to the United Kingdom and the United States. Was there connivance? Had this scenario been set up with the Arabs? What better, more convincing, more respectable case could be made for ditching the cause of Israel? He said, 'It will not work, Prime Minister. I think my country understands better than yours the people with whom we are dealing. Through force of circumstance we know best how to handle them. You cannot in a dangerous world always play the field from a position of safety. You must take risks to succeed. You must have a moral basis for your struggle if you are to survive.'

The Prime Minister did not like those implications. 'We have a good deal of experience of that sort of thing,' he said tartly.

'I appreciate the dilemma in which your Government finds itself.' The Israeli Ambassador, having made his point, decided to recover lost ground. 'You cannot threaten reprisals because there is no Palestine State to visit them on. Your problem is immensely difficult, appalling in its implications. For Britain, for Israel and for the world.'

'I must ask you, Ambassador, to exercise the utmost discretion in regard to my remarks about acceptance. I would not have taken you into my confidence had not Israel been so inextricably and tragically involved.' The Prime Minister stood up. 'And now I must ask you to excuse me. I have to speak to the Nation at eight o'clock.' He looked at the grandfather clock in the corner. 'That is in twenty minutes. I have had little opportunity for preparation.' He shook the Ambassador's hand. 'When I have finished speaking the ultimatum will be known to the world. Please assure your Government that we shall keep them fully informed as the situation develops.'

After they had taken their leave of each other, Lanyard saw the Israeli Ambassador to the front door.

*   *   *

The Ambassador's return from Liverpool had been delayed. On reaching the Embassy, and learning of the Prime Minister's urgent summons to Number Ten, he had left at once for Downing Street, brushing aside the First Secretary's attempts to tell him of Ascher's visit, saying it could await his return.

When he got back to the Embassy just before eight he went to his study. He switched on television as the announcement was made that the Prime Minister would address the Nation.

CHAPTER SIXTEEN

At 6 pm all television channels of the BBC and ITV—and all radio channels of the BBC—interrupted their services to put out a newsflash. It announced that the Prime Minister would address the Nation at 8 pm on a matter of grave importance. It was followed by five minutes of patriotic music, a circumstance which reminded older listeners of the prelude to Mr Chamberlain's announcement of the declaration of war against Hitler's Germany in 1939.

At 6.30 and 7.30 pm, television and radio stations again interrupted their services to remind listeners that the Prime Minister would speak to the Nation at 8 pm. This

157

announcement, like its predecessor, was followed by excerpts from patriotic and martial music. These included *Land of Hope and Glory* and *Colonel Bogey* which evoked in many listeners recollections of the Last Night of the Proms and the Bridge Over the River Kwai which was not quite what was intended.

At 8 pm the Prime Minister, looking unusually drawn and strained, appeared on television to address the Nation.

'I have to speak to you tonight,' he said, 'about a matter of the utmost gravity. Before doing so I want to stress the importance of calm and reason, particularly on the part of those who live in London. At an emergency meeting of the Cabinet today I was asked to assure you that the Government will take all and every step necessary to ensure that the peril which threatens will not occur. Of that you may have no doubt. It will not, I repeat, be allowed to occur. That is an absolute undertaking and one which I must ask you to keep in the forefront of your mind as I speak. This morning I received, as did the Ambassador of the United States, an ultimatum from a Palestinian terrorist group, the Soukour-al-Sahra'. The ultimatum was addressed to the British Government as the former mandatory power for Palestine. It claims that a nuclear warhead has been placed somewhere in London and that it will be detonated within seventy-two hours, as from noon today, unless the Governments of the United Kingdom and the United States accede to its terms. The hard core of these is dealt with in the following words. I read: *All Palestinian territory seized by Israel in 1948 in excess of the United Nations resolution of the 29th November, 1947, for the partition of Palestine, together with those parts of Palestine not occupied by Israel before 1967, notably on the west bank of the Jordan and in the Gaza Strip and Jerusalem, to be assigned forthwith to the people of Palestine.*

'That is the ultimatum's basic demand. It contains a number of other terms and conditions of a harsh and implacable nature. Since these will be published in all British newspapers tomorrow, and broadcast over the country's television and radio networks several times during the day, I will refrain from dealing with them now.

'My purpose tonight is to assure you that there is no need for panic, no cause to interrupt or vary the routine of your normal lives. Indeed, to do so can only add to the grave difficulties already confronting us. The important—I believe the decisive—contribution each of you can make is to behave as if the threat had never existed. Let "business as usual" be your watchword over the next few days.

'I can assure you that the Government is taking most vigorous and energetic steps to deal with the situation. I am in constant touch by hot-line with the President of the United States and the Heads of Governments in France, Germany and other friendly and concerned powers.

'At its meeting today the Cabinet appointed an ad hoc Committee consisting of the Home, Foreign and Defence Secretaries, the Chief of the General Staff, the heads of the Security Services, the Special Branch, Scotland Yard and the Metropolitan Police, together with representatives of the GLC and Port of London Authority. That Committee, over which I shall preside, has been given full power to act and will remain in constant session until such time as the threat has been removed. We will of course report to the Cabinet at frequent intervals.

'It is possible that this is a bluff, that there is no nuclear warhead in London. But we are proceeding on the assumption that it is not a bluff, and I give you once more the Government's unequivocal assurance that before the expiry of the seventy-two hour deadline the threat to London will have been removed.

'For obvious reasons I cannot at this stage explain to you how this will be done, but I ask you to accept my assurance, given with knowledge of all the facts, that it will be done.'

*　　　*　　　*

160

Richard Baker's face appeared on the television screen. 'And that concludes the Prime Minister's address to the Nation.' He said it in much the manner he would have used to announce the programme of a forthcoming Proms concert. 'At eight-thirty,' he continued, 'the ultimatum will be the subject of . . .'

'Switch off,' interrupted Ascher. 'Give me that transcript of the Mocal tape.'

Ruth Meyer went to the desk and began to sort through a heap of papers. 'How can he guarantee anything?' she said. 'He hasn't a clue where it is.'

Ascher was pacing up and down the living room of the small apartment near the Vauxhall Bridge, arms clasped across his chest, shaggy head bowed. 'Because he's a politician. Got to reassure the people. Of course he doesn't know where it is. That's not the point. What he does know is what he's going to do. That message came through loud and clear. All that spiel about "unequivocal assurances" and "absolute undertakings".'

'You mean?' She looked up from the desk.

'The British Government's going to accept the ultimatum. For God's sake! He couldn't have made it more obvious. Britain's not going to shed any tears for Israel. This nuke threat is just what they want. Now they can say they had to play ball with the Arabs. Maybe the Brits and the Yanks laid it on with the Arabs. In exchange for oil concessions. Like the French

161

supplying Pluton.'

'Oh. Shalom. It couldn't be like that.'

'Couldn't it hell. You tell that to President Thieu and what used to be the Saigon Government. Israel can no more depend on the US and UK than South Vietnam could. Their promises and alliances don't mean a goddam thing. Oil's the only thing that means anything now. Got that transcript? I'm in a hurry.'

She came over, gave it to him and he saw that her hand was trembling. He squeezed it for a moment. 'Don't worry. We'll find the nuke. Then we'll handle things our way.'

He sat cross-legged on the corner of the studio couch, reading through the transcript. At the finish he said, 'It all ties up.' There was an unusual light in his eyes, a sort of wildness, but he didn't sound excited. He never did. 'The "contract" *was* an ultimatum, Ruth. Not the one we thought. All that double-talk wasn't about an attack on the Israeli Embassy. It was to do with what we've just heard. That Mocal bunch aren't El Fatah or the PFLP or George Habash's MPF or Hawatemeh's PDF. No wonder we couldn't identify them. They're Ka'ed's group . . . Soukoural-Sahra'. God! That lot over here.' He got up, shaking his head as if to shuffle his thoughts, and began pacing again. He was a heavy man and the floor of the old apartment creaked and groaned with his weight.

She stood in front of him, hands on hips, eyes bright with danger. 'It's not there, is it? In Spender Street?'

'No. No.' He waved the transcript at her. 'Remember what Souref said.' Ascher began reading aloud: *'But think of Rudi and Ahmad. At least we don't have to deliver the goods.'* He stared at her. 'Rudi and Ahmad have the warhead.'

'Deliver the goods where?'

'Who knows. Could be *idiom* for having to be with the warhcad—seeing the job through. Could mean physical delivery to a specified place. They knew there'd be a search, so maybe they keep the nuke out of Central London until they need it.'

He looked at the transcript again. 'Listen to this.' He read: *'HAMADEH: Easily said. It's impossible, Zeid. Too much to think about. Difficult to sleep on the edge of a volcano.'* Ascher laughed dryly. 'It's a volcano all right.'

She stood on her toes leaning over his shoulder. 'Why did Zeid say: *How would you like to try sleeping in Palace Green tonight.* He means this very night?'

Ascher looked at her reproachfully. 'Think! He's talking of the Israeli Embassy. Up there right now at this minute they've just heard the British Prime Minister tell the world about the ultimatum. Do you think they're going to sleep easily tonight, knowing what that means to Israel?'

'I see.' She hunched her shoulders. 'Sorry. I thought there was some deeper meaning to it.'

'My God. That's deep enough, isn't it?'

'What are you going to do?'

Ascher put the transcript into a back pocket of his jeans, took a duffel coat from the back of the door, handed another to her. 'We're going to the Embassy as fast as we can. I'll phone from the call-box outside the laundrette.'

*　　*　　*

There were five of them, including the Ambassador, in his study at Palace Green. Ascher, Ruth Meyer, Ezra Barlov—who'd flown from Holy Loch that evening—and his assistant, Michael Kagan. They'd been talking for a long time: dissecting, analysing, arguing about the Mocal tape and the terms of the ultimatum. What lay behind them. Was there connivance by Britain and the United States? Through all these discussions messengers moved discreetly between the communications section, the cypher room and the Ambassador's study, bringing in and taking away teleprinter and radio tapes—high speed transmissions, computer-scrambled, two-way traffic between Israel and the Embassy. Some of the messages were exchanges between the London Embassy and the Prime Minister and Foreign Secretary in Jerusalem, but most were with Israeli Intelligence HQ, in Tel Aviv.

The Ambassador finished reading the latest tape from Jakob Kahn. 'Listen to this, Ascher,' he said, and they could tell from his voice that he was pleased. 'Jakob says he's just got agreement to the proposition that we keep what we know to ourselves for the time being. He repeats the words *time being*.'

Ascher said, 'Great. So we don't tell Number Ten or the Special Branch what we know about Mocal and the tape.'

'We don't tell anyone on this side. Not yet at any rate,' said the Ambassador. 'All right with you, Barlov?'

Barlov nodded. 'Suits me. I like it that way.'

'So do I,' said Ascher. 'The Brits could ball this one up. We don't bargain with terrorists.'

Barlov laughed. 'Don't be too contemptuous about terrorists. We were pretty good at that ourselves once.'

'That's different.' Ascher was poker-faced.

'It's always different when it's your cause,' said the Ambassador. 'I don't suppose historians will see any significant difference.' The Ambassador had taken an honours degree in History at Oxford and it was still very much in his blood. Somewhere a clock chimed midnight. He echoed their thoughts. 'Sixty hours to the deadline.' His voice was sepulchral.

A messenger came in with another tape. 'From General Kahn, sir.' The Ambassador took it and she glided away. He read it, frowned, then smiled. 'Listen to this: *Ascher*

165

must continue to keep Mocal premises under closest visual and audio surveillance since reference oblique or otherwise to whereabouts nuke probable now ultimatum is out. If location warhead becomes known take every precaution against pre-detonation and inform me instantly. While we acknowledge pre-detonation risk exists we believe it to be over-estimated. Warheads not easily come by. If detonation should take place on expiry time limit or otherwise objective of ultimatum would be defeated and future attempts with that warhead along similar lines aborted. This constitutes major psychological advantage our side.'

They discussed that message for some time and were still on it when another came in from Kahn. Once again the Ambassador read it aloud: *'Ruth Myer to fly Tel Aviv 0715 El Al tomorrow Tuesday with relevant tapes, photos and other material assist identification Zeid and report fully on situation your end. Hope return her London Wednesday latest.'*

Ruth Meyer regarded the Ambassador with mixed feelings. She was in on the ground floor in London. She didn't want to get off it. 'How will Shalom manage without me?' she asked.

The Ambassador turned to Ascher. 'What do you say?'

'You'll have to give me Micky Kagan. We can't do a twenty-four hour surveillance with less than three operatives.'

The Ambassador looked at Ezra Barlov.

166

'It's your pitch, Barlov. What do you think?'

'Ascher's right. We've nothing that takes precedence over this.'

'Good,' said the Ambassador. 'Kagan is yours, Ascher.'

* * *

When they left the Embassy an hour later they took Michael Kagan with them. Not, when he'd changed, quite the dapper well-groomed Kagan thc Embassy knew but nevertheless a cheerful Kagan. He disliked the desk work associated with the Embassy job, and hankered after action. Where Shalom was, action was likely to be. That made Kagan happy.

* * *

During the taxi journey back to Vauxhall Bridge Ascher was silent, going over in his mind the discussion at the Embassy. Questioned by the Ambassador about the nuclear warhead he had been emphatic that it was not in Spender Street. 'There are several reasons why I'm sure it's not there. One— if it was, some of them would remain with it throughout each twenty-four hours. They don't. They're still working a normal seven/eight-hour day. All go home at night. Two—if it was, some hint of it would come

167

through on the tapes. Nothing has. Three—the only taped reference so far suggests that Ahmad and Rudi—whoever and wherever they may be—have it. They are the only two we haven't seen. The only names we can't tie up. Four—we've been watching Mocal night and day now for a long time and nothing big and heavy like a nuke could have been taken in without our seeing it. The warhead's not there, Ambassador. Believe me.'

That, finally, had satisfied both the Ambassador and Colonel Barlov.

Forty-eight Hours To Go

CHAPTER SEVENTEEN

Soon after one o'clock on Tuesday, November 9th, El Al's 747 from London touched down at Lod Airport and disgorged its passengers and luggage. Ruth Meyer had no difficulty in recognizing the sleek hair and rounded features of Bar Mordecai at the baggage checkpoint, notwithstanding dark glasses, sun-shirt and sandals.

There was no greeting. He came up, took her bag and she followed him to the dusty, dented Chevrolet. They'd driven several hundred yards before he said, 'Glad to see you, Ruth. Good journey?'

'Oh, it's heaven to be here. Hot sun and dry earth.' She remembered his question. 'The journey? Okay. Usual anxiety and discomforts. Leaky loos, draughts, cigarette smoke, plastic food, plastic people. You're so tanned, Bar. Lucky you. All this sun.'

'I swim a lot. Did you bring the stuff?'

'Everything you've not already had.'

'Good. We see Jakob at once.'

'Suits me. I'm back to London tomorrow.'

'Things warming up there, huh?'

She looked at him sideways. 'Forty-eight hours to go, and the twitch count rising.'

'I know. Jakob keeps telling me. It's as if he's waiting for labour pains.'

'I wouldn't know. Never had them.'

They were old friends and for the rest of the journey into Tel Aviv they talked about colleagues, mutual friends and their work.

They passed the tall block of the Bank Leumi Le-Israel, turned left off the Jaffa Road and entered the industrial area. From long habit Mordecai followed a complex route before parking the Chev outside the red-brick building she knew so well.

'That wasn't really necessary, Bar,' she smiled. 'I know the route blindfolded.'

'I vary it every time. Call it a compulsive obsession.' He opened the boot, took her air-bag from it and led the way in. They negotiated two sets of guarded security barriers, went through a steel door at the back and arrived in the sandy courtyard. As they crossed it she saw the decaying oil drums and rusty remains of the bicycle still under the old fig tree.

'Lovely garden,' she said. 'Nothing changes. Really makes me feel I'm home again.'

'Great, isn't it?' Mordecai pressed the bell-push beside the steel door in the concrete building. They stood waiting under the scrutiny of unseen eyes. The door opened, they went in, passed a security barrier, went left and right down passageways, then through another barrier and on to the lift. They came out on the second floor. Mordecai spoke to the woman at the reception desk. 'Okay?'

'He's waiting for you. Go right in.'

*   *   *

Ruth Meyer reported to Jakob Kahn and Bar Mordecai on developments in London after the British Prime Minister's address to the Nation, in particular the Israeli Ambassador's discussions at Number Ten and his appreciation of the situation thereafter. She gave them transcripts of the latest Mocal tape, interpreting the verbal shorthand used by the Palestinians. After that she explained the set-up and routine in Mocal's Spender Street premises. Zeid, she said, the key figure and the man who'd posted the ultimatum, remained unidentified despite their efforts.

They considered the copies she'd brought with her of the morning's London dailies giving first reactions to the Prime Minister's broadcast. Little in them was new to Kahn. Earlier in the day he'd received transcripts of relevant radio broadcasts from the communications division of Israeli Intelligence which monitored radio services world-wide as a matter of routine. Kahn was discussing reaction in Washington and Moscow when his secretary came through on the intercom. 'Hassfeldt's waiting.'

'I'll see him now,' replied Kahn.

A thin man with sunken eyes and a limp came in, laid a pack of blown-up photos on Kahn's blotter. 'Top one was taken by Ruth Meyer in the stationery shop near the Aldwych yesterday,' he said. 'We've computer-selected these five from micro-files on the basis of her shot and description. The scar is key data. We've arrowed him in all of them.' He said it apologetically, the thin husky voice matching his general air of debility.

Kahn looked at the photos with a magnifying glass. Two were street shots, one a desert shot—group of armed Arabs in burnouses in the foreground, large passenger aircraft burning in the background—another was a campus picture, undergraduates sitting self-consciously in three tiers. The fifth, a portrait of a young man in cap and gown. Each was dated and captioned.

171

Kahn's cheroot trained round swiftly seeking a target. It settled on the thin man. 'Who is he, Hassfeldt?'

Hassfeldt read from a typed sheet. 'Zeid Barakat, alias Simon Dufour, alias Simon Dufour Charrier. Born September 7th, 1948, in Philippeville, Algeria. The "Zeid Barakat" comes from his mother. Daughter of a Palestinian merchant settled in Algiers. His father, Paul Dufour, was a *pied-noir*— Frenchman born in Algeria. Charrier was his paternal grandmother's name. Zeid Barakat is a top-echelon member of the SAS. Close to Mahmoud el Ka'ed. Educated Beirut and the Sorbonne where he took a degree in electronics. Worked for some time with Aerospatiale in the missile and rocketry divisions. Last operation was in September when he led the SAS raid on the Turco-Ottoman Bank in Istanbul. One and a half million dollars of bullion taken. Two bank clerks and one customer killed.'

'Give me that note. Where did the scar come from? Hijack?'

'No. He's been involved in a couple of those. But this was way back. An early operation with the SAS. Border raid on Quiryat Shmona. Knife wound, Israeli inflicted. He got away.'

'Pity,' said Kahn. 'Maybe we get him this time.' He sighed, looked at his cheroot, rubbed his chin. 'So he's Zeid Barakat. Worked at Aerospatiale. They produce Pluton. No wonder he's in charge in London.' He passed the magnifying glass and photos to Ruth. 'You've seen him at close range. Satisfied he's the man in these?'

She examined them carefully. 'Yes. That's him all right.' She smiled shyly. 'He's very good-looking.'

Kahn shook his head. 'Don't let that affect your judgement, Ruth. Maybe he's a nice guy, too. But they're all poison to us.'

'I know, I know. Don't worry.'

'Okay, Hassfeldt. That's all. Leave the photos with me. Thanks for the help.'

When the thin man had gone Kahn said, 'We know from the Mocal tape that Zeid Barakat phones Brussels. Why?'

'Shalom thinks it's a communications link,' said Ruth.

'So do I,' said Mordecai.

Kahn nodded. 'Makes sense. Barakat's in charge of the London end. He needs to communicate on a more-or-less immediate basis with Ka'ed. So Brussels acts as linkman.'

'Probably more than one link.' Mordecai winked at Ruth Meyer as he borrowed Kahn's favourite adverb.

'Like what?'

'Rome, Athens, Istanbul, Nicosia—you name it.'

'Method?'

'Phone, I'd say. To avoid radio monitoring. Trouble is we can't locate Ka'ed. Salamander

173

says the Deuxième Bureau reckon he's still in the Lebanon, most likely in Beirut.'

Kahn leant back in the swivel chair, swung it through 180 degrees to look at the large-scale map of Europe and the Middle East covering the wall behind him. 'Okay,' he said. 'Whatever the linkage the end of the line's Ka'ed—that's probably Beirut. Phone? Yes. Radio? No. We monitor all radio traffic into and out of Beirut. Soukour-al-Sahra' hasn't anything as sophisticated as computer scrambling and squirt transmission. Not because they can't afford it, but they're a hunted organization and they've no HQ. They've got to be mobile. If they use the air it must be steam radio. We monitor all that stuff and there hasn't been a whiff of this in it. So okay. It's phone linkage, probably.'

Mordecai smiled. 'Highly probably, Jakob.'

Kahn frowned, not amused, twisting the cheroot in his mouth 'We have to find Ka'ed— and damn quick. Bug his room, tap his phone—if he has one. Then maybe we get in on his spiel with Barakat in London.'

'That's the crunch.' Mordecai spread his hands in a gesture of helplessness. 'We don't know where Ka'ed is. Not for want of trying. And we're not the only ones. Others are after him. Lebanon's Deuxième Bureau and the French's DST. The CIA and the Brits' SIS. Like a pack of bloodhounds. But nothing we know of has come up so far. And the clock

174

doesn't stop.'

Kahn looked at his second-in-command speculatively, his eyes narrowing in a half smile. 'We know *something*, Bar. It came through at lunchtime. You were out at Lod.'

'What's that?'

'Salamander's found Georgette Taaran's apartment.'

'Who in hell's Georgette Taaran?'

Kahn exhaled a cloud of blue smoke. He was enjoying this. 'A girl. El Ka'ed's girl. Salamander learnt about her last night. We didn't know he had a girl friend. She lives up at Baabda in the hills outside Beirut. In her parents' penthouse in the Miramar apartment block. Father's a wealthy merchant. He and her mother are on a world cruise. Georgette has a phone.' He leant forward, his eyes bright. 'Salamander's going to bug it. Today.'

Ruth Meyer said, 'I may be dumb but how's that going to help in the forty-five hours we've got left?'

Kahn shook his head in mock despair. 'Ruth, don't you know about love? Odds are Ka'ed phones her or she him every day. Salamander listens. Finds out where Ka'ed is. Then, maybe, we chip in on his exchanges with Barakat in London. We learn, maybe, where the nuke is. We don't get anything if we don't try. It's the rule of the game. So we never stop trying.'

She said, 'Sorry, Jakob. But I think we have

a better chance in Spender Street listening to the Mocal chat. Any minute now Shalom reckons they'll give us a lead.'

'Maybe Shalom's right. Maybe we are. If we put an ear on Ka'ed's girl there's always a chance of a dividend.'

'Hope you're right, Jakob. What's Knesset policy if we find the nuke?'

'They haven't discussed it. Maybe they won't. Depends on the PM. I *can* tell you Cabinet policy. For the time being we don't tell the Brits or anyone else *anything*. We've got to find that nuke ourselves. So far we've made all the play. We've found Mocal and we've got them under surveillance. We're way ahead of the Brits, even if they're really trying, which maybe they're not. We're not sure of them or the US. We reckon this thing may have been set up as a screen for a deal. You know. The Brits and the US regret that under pressure of the nuclear threat they had no option but—of course with the greatest reluctance and tears in their eyes—to sell Israel down the river in exchange for Arab goodwill which interprets as Arab oil. If we find that nuke—and our chances of doing that don't look too bad right now—we bargain from a position of strength. There won't be any selling of Israel down the river then, I can assure you.'

'I can't fault that,' said Ruth. 'Our reaction last night in Palace Green was along the same lines.'

Kahn's cheroot moved in small circles of approval. 'You know, Ruth, ours is an intelligent race. It has to be to survive.'

*   *   *

Going down in the lift after they'd left Kahn she said, 'Salamander's a code name, isn't it?'

'Of course,' said Mordecai.

'Do I know him?'

'No, you don't. And if you did I wouldn't tell you.'

'Sorry. I shouldn't have asked.'

'You know the rule. The more you know, the more you blow. Doing anything tonight?'

She looked at him quizzically. 'I'd like to phone the family in Galilee.'

'Sorry. We don't want them to know you're here.'

'In that case I'm not doing anything.'

'Come and have something to eat with us. Lea would like to see you. I'll drive you back in the moonlight.'

'Thanks, Bar. I'll come. But no stopping in the moonlight.'

He laughed and she thought of Shalom Ascher and was sad.

*   *   *

The man in blue overalls sitting in the small

telephone department van enjoying the afternoon sunshine saw from his watch that it was five minutes to four. His was one of several vehicles parked beneath a clump of pines in a lay-by high up on the road which climbed the hill to Baabda. The stone-parapeted lay-by was a vantage point overlooking the whole spread of Beirut including the coastline from Jeideideh in the north to Shuneifat in the south. Beneath him, to his right, he could see the Miramar apartment block. He knew she was there because he'd phoned earlier. She'd answered and he'd said it was the telephone department. Defects in the automatic exchange. She said there was nothing wrong with her phone. He said the fault was in the exchange, not at the subscriber's end. The relays on a number of lines in the Baabda area were, he explained, giving trouble on the board. Not releasing automatically when the handsets were replaced. Something to do with humidity. This meant that her calls could be overheard by other subscribers if the relays at the switchboard end of *their* lines were also defective.

She expressed concern and hoped the fault would soon be rectified. He told her he would be working on the Baabda lines all day and would be calling at the Miramar apartment. She said she would be going into Beirut that afternoon at about four o'clock but would tell her servant to expect him if he'd not called by then.

Soon after four he saw her come out of the front door of the Miramar and go to the garage space under the building. Minutes later she backed a red Alfa into the driveway, turned and made off down the hill. He waited ten minutes then drove the van down to the apartment block and parked in the driveway. He lifted out a satchel of tools, went into the building and took the elevator to the penthouse. An Arab man-servant opened the door in response to his ring.

'Telephone department,' said the man in blue overalls. 'Is the occupier in?'

'No. Madame has gone into Beirut. She told me you would be coming to fix the phone.'

He went in, saw the instrument on a table in the hall. 'Are there any extensions?'

'Yes,' said the servant. 'There is one in the master bedroom.'

'Show it to me.' The telephone man was small and unimpressive but he spoke with the authority of minor officialdom. The servant took him to the master bedroom, showed him the phone on the bedside table. They went back into the hall together.

'Good,' said the telephone man. 'I'll start on this one.' He opened the tool satchel, took out pliers and a screwdriver, lifted the handset, unscrewed the mouth and ear pieces. Within fifteen minutes he'd checked both handsets,

179

carried out two imaginary conversations in Arabic with the faults supervisor at the central automatic exchange, re-packed the satchel and returned to the van.

The servant had watched him at first, then lost interest and disappeared. A Jordanian himself, he'd concluded from the telephone man's accent and light skin that he was Lebanese. The Jordanians didn't much care for the Lebanese. Not that he would have seen the telephone man insert the ELX-Mk II Busch micro-transmitters in the handsets before replacing the mouth pieces. They were about half the size of the nail of an elegant woman's little finger and easily concealed.

*   *   *

Back at the van the man in the blue overalls put the satchel into the boot and drove up the hill to the lay-by under the pines. Several cars were already there and he parked well clear of them. He estimated that he was no more than two hundred metres from the penthouse, though the distance by road was a good deal greater.

*   *   *

For some time he sat eating sandwiches, pretending to read a newspaper but watching the road beneath him. The Alfa would have to

180

come up that way.

The sun set a few minutes after five o'clock. Twilight would end an hour later. At five-thirty he switched on the van's radio. From it a concealed output fed a recorder in the dash-box. That, too, he switched on. The recorder had a four-hour cassette and there were others beneath the driving seat. Ten minutes later, through a gap in the pines, he saw the Alfa coming up the hill in the gathering dusk.

CHAPTER EIGHTEEN

By eight o'clock on the night of Tuesday, November 9th, it was evident to members of the ad hoc Committee that little progress had been made in the first thirty-two hours of the ultimatum. This was not for want of action. A great deal had been and was being done but the results were singularly disappointing.

The Home Secretary reported that, notwithstanding searches taking place on an unprecedented scale, nothing positive had yet emerged. Promising leads had been pursued with energy but without avail. He apologized for the negative nature of his report, expressing the hope that the next twelve hours might bring results.

The DGSS and the Head of Special Branch reported in more detail but in much the same vein.

Sir Brian Parkes, the Commissioner of the Metropolitan Police, said the appeal to the public for information had brought a flood of telephone calls, letters and callers. A large staff, reinforced by Army units, was dealing with these and useful leads were acted on immediately. So far nothing positive had emerged.

The Chairman of the Port of London Authority said that the systematic search of shipping in the London Docks and other parts of the Thames was proceeding well, the PLA's resources having been considerably augmented by RN personnel, patrol craft, launches and divers. So far the search had not produced anything, nor had the scrutiny of cargo manifests, bills of lading, passenger lists and customs and immigration records. But the task was far from complete and he, too, hoped the action being taken might bear fruit before long.

The Home Secretary said that searches of the same sort at other major ports had yielded nothing so far.

The Director of Civil Aviation, co-opted to the Committee, gave details of the search at airports, the checking of passenger/freight records and customs and immigration entries. But here, too, he said nothing worth while had eventuated.

The Defence Secretary, reported on the

steps being taken in the Ministry of Defence to deal with the situation which would arise if the warhead were detonated.

Contingency planning for this, in consultation with the GLC, the London Fire Brigade, Scotland Yard, the Port of London Authority, the Metropolitan Hospital Board, the London Transport Board, British Rail and other authorities was, he said, well advanced. Much of it was standard procedure already laid down in the MOD's anti-nuclear defence measures for the Metropolitan area.

Sir Brian Wallace, Chairman of the GLC, commenting on public reaction, observed that the morale of Londoners remained remarkably high. He attributed this to the Prime Minister's assurance that the threat to London would not be allowed to develop. This had been interpreted by the media as an admission that the Government, with the support of the United States, would accept the terms of the ultimatum unless the warhead was found and in some way neutralized within the time limit of seventy-two hours. With small exceptions the media had, he said, behaved well. There had been no panic, no interruption of the normal life of the metropolis, other than a certain measure of inconvenience arising from search operations. In these public co-operation had been admirable, notwithstanding the absence of search warrants.

He admitted and regretted that people were

183

leaving London in greater numbers than usual for the time of year. It appeared that most of those concerned were in the higher income brackets.

At this juncture the Foreign Secretary was heard to remark in an aside to the Home Secretary, 'That's always been the jittery lot.'

There was, continued the Chairman of the GLC, a considerable demand for hotel accommodation in the provinces, in Scotland and Wales, and in France and the Low Countries.

'Foreign Secretary,' said the Prime Minister, 'may we hear from you?'

The Foreign Secretary adjusted his glasses, looked at the faces round the table and shuffled his notes. 'This morning I concluded discussions with our Ambassadors from the Middle East. They return to their posts today fully briefed on the task now confronting them. I have in the last twelve hours been in touch with the ambassadors and foreign secretaries of France, West Germany and Italy, and the secretaries-general of UNO and NATO.

'There is agreement among them on the diplomatic strategy to be pursued in the time available. These countries, and soon I hope UNO and NATO, will exert diplomatic pressure upon the Arab states—including the PLO—to persuade those responsible to extend the time limit of the ultimatum and to meet

184

representatives of the United States and United Kingdom to discuss and negotiate its terms.

'The French and Germans—and of course ourselves—are hopeful that the United States will persuade Israel to announce immediate and meaningful territorial concessions. Not necessarily to the extent set out in the ultimatum but enough to make Soukour-al-Sahra' feel they have in the main achieved their objective. If this sounds like capitulation let me remind you of two facts—somewhere in London at this moment there is a nuclear warhead to be detonated at noon on Thursday, November 11th—that is in forty hours—unless we accept the terms of the ultimatum. That is one fact. The other is that the Palestinians— and by that I mean the whole Palestine Liberation movement and not the gang of thugs behind this ultimatum—have a claim which the world regards as morally justifiable. They are and long have been a stateless, homeless people, and for that the United Kingdom must accept some measure of responsibility.

'This afternoon I was also in touch with the Israeli Ambassador and Foreign Secretary. I'm sorry to say their attitude is predictably tough and unyielding. Their Foreign Secretary believes that this is a bluff. That the SAS will not risk detonation. Firstly, because to do so would make a nonsense of their objective, and secondly because the warhead is their most powerful bargaining weapon. With it they are a force to be reckoned with, even by powerful nations. Without it they are no more than a nuisance. They will not, he believes, destroy that weapon.

'It is the Israeli view that if we make no move to meet the ultimatum's demands, the Soukour-al-Sahra' will—towards the end of the seventy-two hour period—offer to negotiate. The Israelis may be right. *They* are in a position to gamble with the fate of London. *We* are not.'

The Defence Secretary said, 'May I, Prime Minister, come in again?'

'Please do.'

'It does not require much imagination to understand the situation in which the Israelis find themselves. The Foreign Secretary says they are ready to gamble with the fate of London. Are we not, Prime Minister, ready to gamble with the fate of Israel? Seen as a moral issue, I doubt if there is much difference. Seen as a diplomatic one, of course there is. Nevertheless, I would not like us to fall into the easy but entirely false position of regarding Israel as the guilty party, and not the terrorists.'

The Chief of the General Staffs intervened to say that the Committee seemed already to have accepted that the issue was a clear-cut one between acceptance and rejection. 'With respect, I suggest it is not. There is an area of manoeuvre between these two extremes. We may still find the warhead. I would remind the Committee that, if we do, there is more than a fair chance of rendering it safe if we use the resources available to us.

'I agree with the Israeli view that Soukour-al-Sahra' are unlikely to risk detonation. Our task is to find the warhead. Should we succeed, we will not be powerless even if they do intend to detonate on the expiry of the time limit. It is to be detonated by means of a pre-set timing device. In other words, the terrorists will leave the warhead before it is due to explode. We must assume they will give themselves sufficient time to get well clear of London. Say an hour or two. During that time our boffins can go in and make the warhead safe.'

The Prime Minister's face showed clearly enough his disagreement with the CGS's contribution which he proceeded to ignore. 'I must now inform you,' he said, 'of my talk by hot-line with the President of the United States. In doing so I shall refer also to his discussions with the Chairman of the Soviet Union.

'I spoke to the President at six o'clock this evening. This was our second talk, for I had been in touch with him at midday. In the intervening period he'd had an opportunity for in-depth consultations with his advisers, particularly with Dr. Kissinger and the

Chairman of the Senate's Foreign Relations Committee. The President's views have changed. He now suggests we ignore the ultimatum altogether, but take certain other action without delay. He thinks our search programme should be abandoned or, at most, carried forward with a low profile. He considers the risk of predetonation to be as real as it is unacceptable.

'That is the negative side of his policy. More positively he suggests that both Britain and the United States should issue communiqués announcing their determination to secure the early establishment of an independent Palestine. The communiqués should, he argues, ignore the ultimatum.

'If this is done the Soukour-al-Sahra' will, he believes, have the carpet pulled from under their feet. To proceed with their threat once such communiqués have been issued—in the form and with the guarantees the President has in mind—would destroy the chances of an independent Palestine at the very moment of its birth. This is something Ka'ed would certainly not want to do.

'He went on to make it clear that it would well suit United States diplomacy at this juncture—he is much influenced by the US débacles in Vietnam, Cyprus and Turkey, and is bent on doing something to restore the prestige of the United States—as I was saying, it would well suit US policy if the present situation could be used as a valid reason for acceding to the Arabs' long-standing demand for the return of the conquered territories and the establishment of an independent Palestine.

'In the President's view world opinion would accept that the demands themselves were morally well-founded, though the methods of the SAS were abhorrent. I find myself in agreement with his view that, since the October War, world opinion has swung in favour of the Arabs. It is now generally recognized that the balance of power in the Middle East lies with them, and there is a growing feeling that Israel should return the conquered territories—or a substantial part of them—since, only in that way, can the heat be taken out of the Middle East situation.

'The President felt that these considerations would effectively counter accusations by Israel that we have, to use his phrase, "sold her down the river". He had, he said, sounded out the Soviet Chairman on this strategy in the course of a hot-line conversation this afternoon. Not surprisingly Mr Brezhnev assured him that the Soviet Union regarded such a course of action as sensible and indeed inevitable. The Soviet Chairman stressed that, but for Israeli intransigence over the return of the conquered territories, peace in the Middle East would long since have been restored.

'Mr Brezhnev said it was the intention of the Soviet Government to issue a communiqué deploring the methods used by the SAS but offering financial, logistical and technological support for the immediate establishment of a Palestine State. To placate Israel, the Soviet Chairman said the communiqué would contain firm guarantees by the Soviet Union for the continuance of Israel as an independent State.

'In conclusion Mr Brezhnev told the President that the Soviet Union was motivated solely by a desire to see peace in the Middle East. Peace on a basis which would do justice to the conflicting interests of Israel, the Arab States and the Palestinians, and in this way neutralize the most dangerous area of confrontation between the super-powers. This, said Brezhnev, would strengthen USSR-USA détente.

'The President has no doubt that the Soviet Union's real motives are to strengthen its ties with the Arab States, and to be seen to play a central role in achieving a Middle East settlement where the United States has failed. As to the West, the President said he believed that if we follow the policies he advocates the OPEC countries will adopt a more conciliatory attitude towards the supply and pricing of oil to consuming countries, thus contributing to a solution of the energy crisis and to correcting the disastrous imbalance of western economies.

'The President said that with these

considerations in mind the United States and West Germany would be prepared to put up six billion dollars of the ten billion required. There would in addition be the Soviet contribution, and he felt sure the Arab States, overburdened with petro-dollars, would want to help. Finance, he emphasized, would not be an obstacle.

'He conceded that the main stumbling block to making rapid progress along these lines was the question of the return by Israel of the conquered territories, but he thought ways and means of imposing the necessary decisions upon Israel could be found, particularly in view of the attitude of the Soviet Union. I found the President philosophic on the morality of this issue. "The Israelis," he said, "cannot expect the United Kingdom to accept mass destruction of a substantial part of London and the killing and maiming of tens of thousands of its citizens to resist what at the end of the day the world will regard as a morally justifiable claim, notwithstanding the barbaric manner in which it has been preferred."

'The President ended with remarkable frankness. "It's going to be tough for the Israelis", he said, "but their military and economic viability is heavily dependent on the United States. They'll have no option if we squeeze. And we will—as hard and fast as the situation demands. Time is the essence of the situation. If we don't move quickly, London may be filed away along with Pompeii and Hiroshima."

'Needless to say I told the President that, while his views would receive the most careful consideration, I felt certain Her Majesty's Government would not wish to appear to be yielding to the demands of the ultimatum with indecent haste. I added that, while I could give no firm undertaking, it was probable we would pursue the policy he advised, but nearer the time the ultimatum was due to expire.'

'It is fortunate,' concluded the Prime Minister, 'That the media are revealing a concensus for settlement in the general direction suggested by the President, though they can have no knowledge yet of his views.

'I would like now to throw this matter open for discussion and suggest that before we adjourn this evening we agree on a form of words for a resolution to be submitted to the Cabinet at its meeting tonight.'

There were murmurs of approval. The Prime Minister sat down and with frowning concentration lit his pipe.

CHAPTER NINETEEN

Up on the lay-by underneath the pines at Baabda the man in the telephone department van was listening by earphone to transmissions from the Busch-mikes in the Miramar apartment. With the telephone handsets on their cradles the microphones transmitted conversation and other sounds in the hall and master bedroom. Once a handset was lifted to make or receive a call the bug on that phone transmitted the subsequent conversation. Though he was now listening to the receiver directly, this in no way interfered with the recorder in the dash-recess which taped everything transmitted by the Busch-mikes.

Soon after she'd parked the Alfa he heard the sound of a door opening, followed by a conversation in the hall. It was the Arab servant telling her of the visit of the man from the telephone department.

'That's good, Fouad,' she said and sounded pleased. She gave instructions about the evening meal, he heard footsteps, then the working of a door lock and the mike in the master bedroom took over. After that sounds of movement about the room, the slamming and banging of cupboard doors and drawers. Later she must have switched on the radio and tuned to a pop programme from Paris. The guitars and pop stars were still throbbing and sobbing when just before six the phone rang in the bedroom. She gave her number and a man's voice answered, 'Hullo, Georgie.'

She said, 'Oh, Mahmoud. How marvellous. I prayed it was you.'

'Can I come at ten tonight?'

'Of course, darling. Can't you make it earlier?'

'Impossible,' he said.

'You'll have dinner with me?'

'No. There won't be time. I'll have something before I come. Listen. I'm expecting a call at ten-thirty.'

'That's okay, Mahmoud.'

'Will anyone else be there?'

'No.' She laughed. 'Do you think I have another lover?'

'I mean friends—not that.' He was brusque.

'No one, darling. Just me and you. How are you?'

'No time now. We'll talk tonight. 'Bye.'

The man in the van heard the click of the handset returning to its cradle. Once again the sounds of movement in the bedroom came through on the earphone. 'Ten o'clock,' he said to himself. 'Another three and a half hours.' He started the engine, switched on the lights, backed out of the lay-by and drove down the hill towards Beirut. He'd had no difficulty in recognizing Ka'ed's voice. He'd taped it once before and played it back

194

several times.

*   *   *

At a quarter-to-ten he drove the van up the hill to Baabda for the third time that day. It was a night of no moon, the sky bright with stars. He turned into the lay-by under the pines. Three cars were already there. It was, he knew, a favourite place for lovers. He parked well clear of the other cars, turned off the lights, switched on the radio and recorder and connected the earphone. He heard her voice in the hall. She was saying goodnight to Fouad.

At ten o'clock he saw the lights of a car coming up the hill to Baabda. It swung left into the Miramar driveway, disappearing into the parking space below the building. Not long afterwards the ring of a doorbell, the sound of footsteps, a door opening and shutting, came through on the earphone. Then her voice, low, emotional. 'This is lovely, Mahmoud. The last two days have gone so slowly. Why did you not come?'

'You know why. It's not easy for me, Georgie.'

There was a long silence. He imagined them embracing.

'Where is Fouad?'

'Gone already,' she said.

Silence. Then his voice again. 'There's half

an hour before the call.'

'What do you want to do?'

'You know.'

'Mahmoud, darling.' She laughed. 'Is there time before the call?'

He said, 'At least we can wait in comfort.'

He heard their footsteps along the marble floor of the hall, then silence. Next the sound of the master bedroom door shutting.

For the next twenty minutes the mixture of sound and speech which came to him left no doubt what was happening and he felt curiously uncomfortable listening to something so intimate. He was no stranger to bugging but he was not a voyeur and this man and woman were in love.

Later he knew they must be lying in each other's arms for they were talking in low voices as lovers do of their thoughts and hopes for each other and a shared future.

For him all sentiment went with the sharp ring of the telephone. He jerked forward, hand cupped over the earphone, listening intently.

It was the call from Damascus.

There were no formal greetings, no names mentioned. They exchanged numbers. He knew that the number Ka'ed had given was not the number of the Miramar apartment. Then, after a moment of bewilderment, he realized it *was*, but in reverse. Presumably the caller had done the same thing with the Damascus number. This, then, was their security check.

Simple enough, he thought, if only done once.

DAMASCUS VOICE: I've just had a report about the consignment. Market reaction seems good on the whole. Moving towards acceptance in spite of some criticism of prices, particularly from our competitors.

KA'ED: We get the same impression here. I am very pleased.

DAMASCUS VOICE: The premises were inspected this afternoon. They had a quick look round. Quite thorough, I believe. All was well.

KA'ED: That's interesting. In fact it's excellent. Very good indeed.

(There was a longish pause).

DAMASCUS VOICE: Are you still there?

KA'ED: Yes. I must think about this. Just a moment.

(Another pause, longer this time).

KA'ED: Listen. We can bring forward the delivery now. Tell him to make it noon tomorrow. During normal working hours. Got that?

DAMASCUS VOICE: Yes. I will let him know. Noon tomorrow.

KA'ED: Yes. Twenty-four hours before the sale.

DAMASCUS VOICE: Is that all?

KA'ED: Yes. That's all.

DAMASCUS VOICE: Okay then.

The man in the van heard the receiver being replaced, then her anxious voice. 'Is everything all right, Mahmoud?'

'Yes. It goes well. You know what?'

'What's that?'

'The premises were searched this afternoon. There was no trouble.'

'Isn't that marvellous. Did you expect that?'

'No. I didn't. Not at all. But it's marvellous. We can bring forward the delivery now. It was to be four hours before the sale. This is much safer. Gives us a margin in case of snags. But imagine that. It must be a thorough search. It's a huge city.'

'I know. But it's the sort of area on which they'd concentrate.'

'Yes. In the centre, more or less.'

'So it's noon tomorrow?'

'Yes. Twenty-four hours before the sale.'

'I heard you say that. Was the line from Damascus good?'

'Of course. Why not? It's not far.'

'I know. But there was a man from the telephone department here today fixing it.'

There was a long pause, sounds of movement on the bed, a muffled cry or laughter, he didn't know which, before Ka'ed said, 'Is that so. Had it been giving trouble?'

'No. The telephone man said it was at the exchange end. Relays sticking or something. Apparently a number of people in the Baabda area are affected . . .'

'Oh, I see,' Ka'ed interrupted. 'Hope he's fixed it.'

The bed creaked, he heard the pad of bare feet, a door handle turning, a lavatory cistern gushing, door movement again. Then a scraping followed by a long silence. Seven minutes went by and he assumed they were in the bathroom. The mike in the hall took over. They were coming down the stairs talking and laughing, but they were too far from the mike for him to hear what they said.

They reached the hall and Ka'ed said, 'Play it now, Georgie. We've another hour to go.'

Shortly afterwards came the opening movement of Dvorak's Serenade for Strings. A minute or so passed then, against the background of cellos and violins, came the distant hum of voices. He realized they were from the living room, too far away for him to hear what they were saying.

But he'd got what he wanted. Methodically he wound the earphone lead round his fingers, pulled it from the socket, slipped it into his overalls. He opened the dash-recess, switched off the recorder, removed the cassette, put it in another pocket. He turned off the radio, started the engine, switched on the lights and backed out of the lay-by. A couple in a car caught in his headlights ducked suddenly. He turned the van and drove down the road. As he passed the Miramar, a car came down the driveway. It stopped to let him pass, its headlights full on, then turned into the roadway and followed. It hung on to the van so he increased speed. The car behind did so too, and he slowed down to let it overtake. As it passed a man in the front passenger seat leant out, shouted, and waved him to stop. He braked hard as if obeying the signal, then, as the car pulled in ahead of him, swung the van clear and banged down the accelerator.

There was a side road a few hundred metres ahead. He skidded into it, accelerating out of the turn. In the rear-view mirror he saw the lights of the pursuing car come round the corner.

*   *   *

In the master bedroom in the Miramar things had happened which the Busch-mikes couldn't transmit.

After the Damascus call, when Georgette told Ka'ed 'There was a man from the telephone department here today fixing it', he'd rolled sideways towards the phone, a hand over her mouth, his free hand signalling silence. He leant over, took the message pad and pencil from the bedside table, and wrote: *probably bugged.* He showed the pad to her, pointing to the phone.

Then in a normal voice he said, 'Is that so. Had it been giving trouble?'

She began to explain, but before she could finish Ka'ed interrupted with, 'Oh, I see.' As he said it he took her by the hand, pulled her off the bed, led her into the bathroom. He shut the door and they stood there naked, looking at each other—she puzzled and frightened, Ka'ed still holding a finger to his lips for silence. He pushed the cistern knob and while it was flushing whispered, 'Probably bugs in the phones.' She saw from the wild look in his eyes that he sensed danger. 'I'll go and check. You stay here.'

He went to the bedroom and, keeping the telephone cradle depressed, gently unscrewed the Bakelite cover of the mouthpiece. For a moment he stared at the tiny Busch-mike then, without disturbing it, screwed back the cover, replacing the handset on its cradle.

Back in the bathroom he whispered, 'It *is* bugged. Phone in the hall too, I expect.' He thought of the Damascus call. 'The bastard,' he muttered. 'The cunning bastard.' He took her arm. 'Listen. We've got to be quick.' He was pulling on socks, trousers and shirt. 'In a moment we'll go downstairs. Don't talk as we pass through the bedroom. He'll hear the doors and know we've gone. As we reach the bottom of the stairs you tell me you bought a marvellous LP today. I'll say, "Play it now, Georgie. We've another hour to go". You go into the lounge and put on any good LP. I'll go out at the back, down the fire escape to the garage. Hussein is waiting for me in the Mercedes. If those bugs are being listened to it'll be by someone in a car a couple of hundred metres from here. The only safe place for that is the lay-by immediately above us. I'll take the Mercedes up there right away. Hussein with me.' He slipped on his shoes. 'Come on. Quick. You don't need clothes.' They went back to the bedroom, opened the door and made their way down the stairs, talking and laughing as they went.

*   *   *

The road he'd taken wound through an area of private houses and occasional apartment blocks spread about the slopes of the hill. It led eventually to Khaldeh Airport and the sea. He drove furiously, tyres screaming, the small van leaping and bouncing over undulations. But it was no match for the car behind. Slowly but surely the headlights came closer and he knew that short of an accident it would not be long before he was overtaken.

With one hand he felt under the driving seat for the Sony. His fingers touched the shoulder-strap and he pulled the small two-way radio clear and laid it on the seat.

The lights of the pursuing car were no more than a hundred metres behind as he slowed for a bend, took it fast, the van lurching on to the offside wheels, bumping back on to all four as he corrected the skid and accelerated away.

The two cars roared down the slope of the hill, the road levelling off and turning to the west. They were clear of the houses now. He could see the lights of Khaldeh Airport ahead.

There was a sharp noise like dry wood breaking. Fragments of glass struck the back of his neck and road noises suddenly increased. In the driving-mirror he saw the starred holes in the small rear window and hunched lower in the seat. The other car was closing rapidly, now no more than thirty metres behind. Watching the driving-mirror he saw the big car pull out and overtake. There was the slap of more bullets striking the van and he braked violently. The pursuing car shot past and he heard the screech of tyres as it braked.

He stopped the van, leapt out, clutching the Sony, and ran down the road away from the car ahead. It was backing down the road now, faster than he could run. Before the backing lights came close enough to illuminate him he dropped into a roadside ditch. As he pulled out the Sony's telescopic aerial, he heard the slamming of car doors and the sound of men running. He took the cassette from his pocket and hurled it into the darkness, into a field away from the road. Holding the transmitter close to his mouth he called 'Juri—Juri—Juri,' and waited desperately for a reply.

The sound of pounding feet came closer, stopped and he could hear men breathing in the darkness. He took the Beretta from the shoulder-holster. If they used a torch he'd have a target. They must have known that, too, for they were searching in darkness, moving slowly, quietly, taking no chances. He turned down the volume control on the Sony, held the set close to his ear. But there was nothing. He pressed the speak-button again, held the mike close. 'Juri—Juri—Juri.' It was almost a whisper, hoarse with anxiety.

As the sound of the footsteps came closer there was an answering, 'Go ahead, Sally. I read you.' The pursuer was moving deliberately, one careful step after another, the sound of his approach just audible. The man in the ditch raised the Beretta, held the Sony to his lips. A dark shape loomed above him. The telephone man fired three shots at it, heard a sharp cry. A torch flashed from somewhere behind him. He turned to fire but was too late. A bullet struck him in the back, a heavy blow that threw him against the side of the ditch. 'Sheep . . . sheep-wresh,' he burbled into the Sony. Blood was streaming from his mouth. 'Durl . . . durlurv . . . ford . . . noo . . . un . . .' He choked on the blood, spat it out. 'Too . . . mor . . .' he gasped. Another bullet hit him with a club-like blow. Bright lights shone in his eyes, a bullet smashed into his face and he lost consciousness.

*　　　*　　　*

Within twenty minutes of the receipt of Salamander's message Juri had locked and left his apartment in the Rue Hamra and driven down the Avenue du Général de Gaulle and the Avenue Ramlet el Baida, hugging the Marine Drive, the sea to his right. Where Ramlet el Baida turned east to join Rue el Ahtal, he left the road and followed the track down to the beach. The night was intensely dark, the place deserted at that hour.

He turned off the lights, felt for a switch under the dash, flicked it and pushed the lead of a pentop mike into the car radio's control panel. Concealed behind it was a Siemen's VHF 500 transmitter. He spoke into the mike. 'Suffolk-five-nine-eight.' The response was immediate. 'Plymouth-three-seven-two. Go ahead Suffolk-five-nine-eight.'

Juri passed Salamander's message, adding, 'Sounds of shots, speech slurred, words garbled.'

The acknowledgement came and he took the mike lead from the panel, shut the switch under the seat, put on headlights and drove back into Beirut. The message would probably have been monitored, the point of transmission possibly plotted, but he was not worried. He never transmitted from the same place twice. What he was worrying about was Salamander.

*   *   *

At Intelligence HQ in Tel Aviv, Jakob Kahn

and Bar Mordecai had problems with Juri's message. The communications division had taken the transmission on tape. Phonetically it read, SHEEP . . . SHEEPWRESH . . . DURL . . . DURLURV . . . FORD . . . NOO . . . UN . . . TWO . . . MORE . . .

Kahn frowned with irritation. 'These bloody phonetics ball things up. Forget the way words look, Bar. They're only sounds. Read them over to yourself quickly. Keep doing it. See what you get.'

The two men sat in silence reading and muttering to themselves. 'Now read aloud, fast,' said Kahn.

Mordecai did. Several times.

Kahn glanced at him. 'Got it?'

Mordecai said, 'I've got *Shipwreck. Delivery forward noon* . . . but I'm not sure of that last bit . . . *two more* . . . Does that fit?'

Kahn was lighting a cheroot, making a ceremony of it. 'No, it doesn't. But *tomorrow* does.'

'Of course. Sticks out a mile.'

'Always does, Bar, once you've been told. Now let's think this over. I assume *forward* means *brought forward*.' Kahn adopted his brooding posture, arms on desk, shoulders hunched, head forward, nodding sagely. Mordecai, too, did some hard thinking. Later, they compared notes. Of certain things they became sure. One—the message almost certainly concerned Mahmoud el Ka'ed,

Salamander's principal assignment. Two—in Israeli Intelligence the code-word *Shipwreck* meant one thing only—the agent using it was in grave danger at the time of transmission. Three—the slurred, garbled words, the sound of shots, suggested Salamander had been captured or killed.

'Killed, I hope,' said Kahn. 'He knew too much.'

'He'll be difficult to replace,' said Mordecai. 'How long has he been in that telephone department?'

'Seven/eight years.' Kahn shrugged his shoulders. 'He had good cover. I hate losing him. But we always find others. Let's get back to the message. Delivery of what and where? To be brought forward. Why?'

Mordecai was tentative, judicious, flying kites. 'Possibly, I say possibly, the missing nuke.'

'Probably, Bar.' Kahn squinted at the tip of the cheroot he'd just lit. 'We know Salamander was bugging the Miramar apartment today. We know from this message that he was in bad trouble, but had to get it through. So what could it be? The nuke? I'd say "yes" to that. Why brought forward? I can't answer that. To be delivered at noon tomorrow. That's twenty-four hours before the ultimatum expires. Delivered where? We know that Zeid is Barakat. That he operates in Spender Street.' Kahn sat bolt upright, and Mordecai read the familiar signal of inspiration. 'Remember what Ibrahim Souref said in that Mocal tape?'

Mordecai did, but he wasn't out to spoil Kahn's play. 'You mean?' he asked.

'*Think of Rudi and Ahmad. They have to deliver the goods.*'

That's what he said.'

'Or words to that effect.' Mordecai smoothed his hair. 'So Rudi and Ahmad *could* be delivering at noon tomorrow to Spender Street.'

Kahn said, 'I'd rate that possible, Bar. But not as high as probable. London's a bloody great city. Spender Street may be nothing more than their work cover. The nuke could be going some place else. And it's outside the search area right now, that's why it's still to be delivered. Right?'

'Right. So what do we do?'

'Pass Salamander's message with our interpretation to Barlov. He'll contact Ascher. We brief Ruth before she leaves in the morning.' He thought of something. 'She'll miss the noon delivery if it *is* Spender Street.'

Twenty-four Hours To Go

CHAPTER TWENTY

Most of the London dailies on the morning of Wednesday, November l0th, expressed in one way or another public unease at the lack of information from the Government, observing that the ultimatum would expire at noon on the following day.

In its leader *The Guardian* urged the Prime Minister to take the people into his confidence however unpalatable the news might be. *Few Londoners*, wrote its editor, *can be unaware of the massive search now taking place. Many, perhaps the majority, may ask if this is not a fruitless undertaking, the consequences of which may be disastrous. Whatever the humiliation involved, would not the Government be well advised to call off the search and announce acceptance of the ultimatum's terms. That this would entail bowing to the will of the terrorists, so savagely and barbarically imposed, should not mask the greater truth that the claim of the Palestine people to a homeland of their own is as well founded morally as its settlement is long overdue.*

The media generally, while deprecating hysteria and urging calm and business as usual, vied with each other in painting lurid and sensational pictures of the holocaust which might result from the explosion of a fifteenkiloton nuclear device in the heart of London.

Interviews with nuclear physicists, nuclear weapons experts, recently-retired generals, admirals and air marshals, fought for space and viewing time with those of Hiroshima survivors, witnesses of Pacific atoll tests, scientific and medical luminaries and politicians of varying calibre and all parties anxious to make something of the occasion.

With the advantage of visual presentation, the BBC and ITV dominated the scene and Patrick Moore, James Burke, Raymond Baxter and other pop scientists were having a field day. If the ultimatum was doing nothing else it was educating the British public in the horrors of nuclear war.

It was not surprising that the media's exertions in this direction rather more than cancelled out its appeals for calm and business as usual in the other. As the hours dragged by the morale of Londoners began to bend and the exodus to assume serious proportions. Roads leading out of London were choked with traffic—hotel accommodation in the provinces was no longer obtainable—Londoners were staying with relatives and friends in all parts of the country—caravans could no longer be bought or hired—and motorists in their thousands were driving into the country to sleep under canvas or in their cars. The danger of disease through lack of hygiene was but one of the many problems thrown up by the crisis.

*   *   *

The consensus of world media, while sympathetic to Britain's dilemma, believed she had no practical alternative to acceptance of the ultimatum, and labelled the massive search a dangerous gamble.

In the international political arena there was, however, some opposition to a policy of appeasement, notably in France and Canada where political leaders had both publicly and privately urged the British Government not to yield to nuclear blackmail since to do so would endanger the whole fabric of Western Society. Noting this a French commentator observed: *To resist nuclear blackmail is more easily said than done, no matter how ethically correct. For France, who supplied the nuclear warhead and is herself not at risk, the role of candid critic, however tempting, is disreputable.*

There was growing though not yet formidable opposition to appeasement among politicians and military leaders in the United States. Tired of humiliation and retreat, fearful of the growth of nuclear blackmail, and as yet unaware of the US President's advice to the British Prime Minister to accept the terms of the ultimatum—advice given with the confidential backing of Mr Brezhnev—they believed such a policy to be disastrous.

In Japan there was opposition to acceptance for more or less the same reasons, reinforced perhaps by a degree of *schadenfreude*; a notion that it might do the West no harm to have a taste of Hiroshima medicine. In Israel, predictably, public and political opinion was implacably opposed to yielding to force. Indeed, the Israeli Prime Minister had that morning announced to a press conference that Israel not only had a nuclear capability but would not hesitate to use it if attempts were made to recover conquered territory by any means other than negotiation. 'We are not prepared,' he said, 'to remain idle while other nations use Israel as a bargaining counter for the solution of their problems, be they oil or something more sinister.'

The oblique reference to the ultimatum was not lost on the correspondents to whom he spoke.

*   *   *

An emergency meeting of the Security Council in New York considered an Israeli resolution condemning the Arab States, *whose harbouring and nurturing of the PLO and its terrorist offshoots has encouraged this barbaric act,* and censuring France, *whose action in supplying nuclear weapons to the Middle East has made it possible.* Predictably, the resolution was vetoed by France and the Soviet Union. A French amendment urging the Arab States to persuade those responsible to withdraw the ultimatum and come to the negotiating table was adopted.

A resolution submitted by the Arab States calling upon Israel to announce at once her intention to return the conquered territories, and so remedy the injustice responsible for the ultimatum, was adopted.

*   *   *

In a communiqué issued in Beirut the PLO once again disclaimed all responsibility for theft of the nuclear warhead and the ultimatum to the British Government, Yasir Arafat repudiating the Soukour-al-Sahra' as a dangerous and irresponsible group of militants whose activities could do irreparable damage to the Palestinian cause. He added, however, that abhorrence of their action should not mask the justice of their claim for the return of the Palestinian homelands.

*   *   *

In London the ad hoc Committee met at frequent intervals, the various searches continued to be as unremitting as they were unrewarding and contingency planning went steadily ahead. As the hours went by, behind-the-scenes diplomatic activity intensified in a number of countries. Opinion among members of the ad hoc Committee was now divided between those who favoured the soft-line advocated by the US President and those who didn't.

The President's policy was favoured by the Prime Minister, the Home and Foreign Secretaries, the Commissioner of the Metropolitan Police and the Chairmen of the GLC and Port of London Authority.

Opposed to these were the Defence Secretary, the Chief of the General Staff, the Chairman of the Combined Intelligence Committee, the DGSS, the Head of the Special Branch and Sir George Isaacson. Increasingly this group believed that the warhead must be found and neutralized. If this were not done, they said, the threat to London would remain whatever action the Government might take. It was apparent, said the DGSS, that the Soukour-al-Sahra' had no intention of parting with the warhead and he drew attention to condition 8 of the ultimatum which stipulated, *the nuclear device will remain in position in London under the control of the Soukour al-Sahra' until such time as the undertakings have been fulfilled in all respects.*

There was no guarantee, he said, that the SAS would not impose further demands on the British Government as time went on. There was, he continued, the high probability that the SAS would take the warhead to other countries—threatening detonation if interfered with at any stage—so that New York, Paris and West Berlin, for example, might well be the next victims of nuclear blackmail.

The Defence Secretary supported the DGSS and added, 'Let the United States and the Soviet Union, in pursuance of their covert policies, issue their communiqués. Let them offer to provide a new Palestine and guarantee the territorial and sovereign integrity of the State of Israel once she has returned the conquered territories.

'Let the British Government, if you wish, appear to support such a policy—*but in principle only and without commitment*. In the meantime continue the search for the warhead up to and after the expiry of the ultimatum. Continue the search, I say, until it is found.' The Defence Secretary wagged an admonitory finger at members of the Committee. 'I do not believe they will detonate that device—even if it is in London, which it may well not be.'

*   *   *

It was against this background of divided opinion in political circles both at home and abroad that the Cabinet, faced with the unenviable task of formulating a policy before the expiry of the ultimatum at noon the next day, itself began to divide into hawks and doves.

At noon on Wednesday, November 10th, the issue was still very much in doubt. During the afternoon it was, however, agreed that the Prime Minister should speak to the Nation and again give the assurance that the Government would take whatever steps were necessary to ensure that the warhead was not detonated, however unpalatable those steps might be.

*   *   *

At 5 pm the BBC and ITV interrupted their services to announce that the Prime Minister would address the Nation at 10 pm that night.

There was speculation as to the lateness of the hour. In the main people thought it had been chosen both to reassure Londoners before the onset of the final day, and because it was a time when most people were likely to be at home.

In fact the time had been chosen because Greenwich Mean Time was five hours in advance of US Eastern Standard Time. The US President and the Chairman of the Soviet Union had agreed confidentially to issue their communiqués at four o'clock Eastern Standard Time. The Prime Minister, having been told this, had decided to speak to the British people an hour later. The communiqués would, he knew, smooth the way for acceptance of the ultimatum.

216

CHAPTER TWENTY-ONE

The black van backed out of the garage at the end of Pimsvale Lane, turned and travelled up to the intersection with Kiddey Road where it stopped before moving off in a westerly direction. It was a wet, windy morning and Rudi Frankel drove with exceptional care, yet not so slowly as to inconvenience other traffic or draw attention to the van. Ahmad Daab sat next to him. They seldom spoke and then only in low voices as if afraid that, notwithstanding the noise of the engine and traffic, they might be overheard. Both were frightened, worried men. This was the most dangerous phase of a dangerous operation and slippery streets did nothing to comfort them. They would have been even more frightened and worried if Barakat had not come to the garage at nine o'clock that morning and disconnected the wires which led to the plastic switchboard. He'd taped their ends and pushed them back under the bale's 'contents' label, the loose end of which he'd stitched back into place. He'd disconnected the switch because the risk of accidental detonation was unacceptably high if the van were in collision or had turned over.

Now, with its dangerous cargo made relatively safe, it travelled down through the Lewisham Road and Greenwich High Road to the approaches to the Blackwall Tunnel. It dropped down into the tunnel and emerged on the north side of the river less than twenty minutes after leaving Pimsvale Lane. Once clear of the tunnel, Rudi turned left and hugged the Thames almost to Limehouse Pier where he veered right up West India Dock Road. As the van approached the busy intersection with the East India Dock Road the traffic lights went red and he pulled up in the nearside lane, ready for the turn to the left. The traffic was heavy and soon built up behind as he waited for the lights to change.

The amber came, then green. He let out the clutch, the van moved forward and shuddered to a stop as the engine stalled. He pressed the starter several times but there was no response.

'Christ,' said Daab. 'What's the trouble?'

'Sounds like ignition.' Rudi's voice was hoarse. He jabbed at the starter again. The engine spluttered into life and the van moved forward in a series of jerks before the engine died again, leaving the van straddled across the intersection. In desperation Rudi kept using the starter but without success. The traffic behind began to hoot.

'Name of Allah,' cried Daab. 'It had to happen now. Can't you do something?'

'Shut up. I'm doing my best.'

The hooting increased. Frankel climbed down from the driver's seat and opened the bonnet. The rain came in wet sheets, and rivulets trickled down his neck. He checked the distributor and plugs and at last found the trouble. He turned to Daab. 'Go and phone the call-box number where Ibrahim is waiting. Tell him what's happened. It's a burnt coil. We'll have to get garage help.'

Daab turned up the collar of his jacket. 'Okay. I'll do that. They must be worried.' He jumped down into the road. His nerves were jangling and he was glad to get away from the van in spite of the rain.

A truck driver came up. 'What's the trouble, mate?' The noise of electric horns drowned Frankel's, 'Coil's had it.'

A traffic policeman in oilskins arrived on a motorcycle. 'What's going on?' he shouted above the noise of his engine.

'Coil's burnt out,' Frankel shouted back. 'Can't move.'

The policeman parked his motorcycle at the kerb and walked back to the van. Frankel got down from the driver's seat. He explained what had happened. The policeman was sympathetic. 'Can't leave her on this intersection. Holding up too much traffic. Get back in,' he said. 'I'll ask the bloke in the truck behind to shove you round the corner into Gill Street. It'll be all right there.' He went back to the truck, spoke to the driver and returned to the Bedford. 'Release the brakes. Put her in neutral,' he said to Frankel. 'Keep slight pressure on the brake pedal when the truck starts pushing.'

Frankel said, 'Okay,' the policeman waved the truck forward, it bumped the van gently, pushed it clear of the intersection and round the corner into Gill Street. Frankel waved a hand to the driver as the truck backed clear and continued on down Gill Street.

The policeman stopped his motorcycle alongside the Bedford. Trickles of rainwater ran down his face. 'You'll be okay there,' he said. 'I'll get a breakdown truck along to you.' He spoke into his radio telephone and Frankel heard the answering voice. There was a brief exchange. The policeman said, 'They'll send help. I've told them it's a coil. May take time.' Something, the look of dismay on Frankel's face, his air of shaky apprehension, may have aroused the policeman's suspicions. ' What've you got in there, mate?'

'Bale of carpets,' said Frankel, hoping the fear he felt so profoundly wasn't apparent.

The policeman hauled the motorcycle on to its stand, took off his gauntlets and walked round to the back of the van. 'Let's have a look, then.'

Frankel unlocked the doors. He was praying the shakiness of his hands wouldn't be noticed.

The policeman peered into the van, climbed in and examined the hessian-wrapped bale. Near the 'contents' label there was a small tear. He pulled at it until the edges of the carpets were exposed. He poked at them for a moment before getting out of the van. 'What are you going to do with that lot?'

'Deliver it to the consignees.'

'Got any documents?'

Frankel felt in the breast pocket of his jacket. 'Yes,' he said, and produced copies of the bill of lading, the invoice and delivery note.

The policeman examined them. 'Where did you pick up the bale?'

'Millwall Docks. Came in by ship from Athens.'

The policeman looked at him for a moment before handing back the documents. 'Right,' he said, taking his motorcycle off its stand and swinging his leg across the saddle. 'Better watch that engine or you'll land in real trouble.'

Frankel mumbled a dutiful, 'Yes. Thanks a lot.'

The policeman kick-started the engine into life and rode slowly away up Gill Street.

Frankel was trembling as he watched the motorcycle go out of sight. He was wet through and his long black hair hung in dank locks. He didn't know what to do. Zeid had given instructions that the van was not to be left unattended, but Daab had no means of knowing it was now in Gill Street and would be hunting for it. Frankel hesitated for a few minutes, hoping that his companion might look down Gill Street. But he didn't, so

221

Frankel walked up to the top of the road and found him waiting in the rain at the intersection where the van had stalled. 'Where the hell have you been, Ahmad?' he asked.

'Phoning. Where's the van?' Daab's eyes were wide with anxiety.

Frankel jerked his head in the direction of Gill Street. 'Down there. A lorry gave me a shove. The policeman radioed for a breakdown truck. They'll bring a coil. Let's get back to the van.' Drenched by the rain, they set off down the road. Frankel said, 'Did you give the message to Ibrahim?'

Daab shook his head. 'I'm sorry, Rudi. I lost the slip of paper with the number. I thought I knew it, but it was wrong. No one answered. Then I tried a few combinations and some people answered, but it wasn't the call-box.'

Frankel stopped walking. 'You fool, Ahmad. You stupid fool. How could you do such a thing?'

'I know. I'm sorry. But I did. I've been through my pockets a dozen times.'

'Wait till Zeid hears.' Frankel stared at him.

Daab said, 'Look. There's still plenty of time. We'll be late, but what odds does that make as long as we deliver in normal working hours.'

'You tell that to Zeid,' said Frankel. 'Come on. We can't hang around in the rain.'

They got back to the van, sat hunched and miserable in the driving cab, arguing fruitlessly

222

about what they should do. It was a hopeless situation. There was no phone in the Mocal premises and Daab had lost the number of the callbox where Ibrahim Souref was waiting for just such an emergency. Zeid would not only be worried but extremely angry. Frankel considered sending Daab on by taxi, but the breakdown van might arrive at any moment and Zeid's strict instructions were that they were to stay with the van at all times.

So they waited, becoming more and more agitated as time went on. At ten minutes past two the breakdown truck arrived. The mechanic soon changed the coil and at 2.25 pm Frankel and Daab got back into the van and resumed their journey to Spender Street.

*   *   *

The taxi travelled down the Strand, turned into Bedford Street and made for Covent Garden, its squelching tyres throwing up spurts of water as it went. The driver drew up at the kerb in King Street, Ruth Meyer got out, paid the fare, turned up the collar of her raincoat, adjusted her headscarf, and made for Spender Street.

As she walked she was obsessed with the thought which had been with her throughout the flight from Tel Aviv. When the 747 touched down at Heathrow at 11.27, jets

223

roaring in reverse thrust, tired stewardesses adjusting hats and scarves, she was worrying about it; and later, as she travelled into London in the British Airways bus, it was nagging at her; as it was in the taxi from West London Air Terminal to Charing Cross Station where she handed in her travel-bag at the left-luggage counter . . . *has the delivery at noon been to Spender Street?* Had Ascher and his men—alerted by Jakob Kahn's urgent message to Palace Green—seen it? How had it been done? By whom? And what did the thing look like? If Ascher & Co hadn't seen it, then Jakob's no more than *possible* rating of Spender Street as the delivery point was right. And if it wasn't Spender Street how on earth would they find out where it was in the less than twenty-four hours left to them?

As she rounded the first bend in Spender Street and approached Number 56, she looked across the street to 39. All seemed normal there, the rain beating down against the dark green glass of the window front, distorting the goldleafed letters, MIDDLE ORIENT CONSOLIDATED AGENCIES LTD. She wondered what was going on inside. In her mind's eye she could see the sinister steel cone of a nuclear warhead, the Palestinians sitting round it trying to look unconcerned. But no, it would be concealed—under a stack of carpets maybe.

These thoughts were interrupted by her arrival at the entrance to 56. She turned into it,

224

went quickly up the stairs to the first floor and stopped outside the door with its sign *Ascher & Levi, Music Agents.* She knocked, heard footsteps and knew she was being examined through the spy-hole. The door opened and Ascher was there, a broad smile on his bearded face, and she wanted to throw her arms round him and say, 'Oh, Shalom, how marvellous to see you,' but she knew that wasn't for her so she said, 'Hi, Shalom,' and he said, 'Hi, Ruth,' and she went in and he shut the door behind her.

Micky Kagan, listening at the working Grundig with an earphone, sitting near the window watching Mocal's premises, turned his head and waved. She made no move to take off her dripping raincoat. She had to find out first. 'Was it delivered at noon, Shalom?' Her voice trembled.

'No. It wasn't.'

She was confused, disappointed and worried, though she'd half expected this. She took off her raincoat, hung it on the peg near the door, undid the wet headscarf and fussed with her hair. 'Hasn't anything happened since I left yesterday?'

'Yes. The British Prime Minister will speak to the Nation at 10pm tonight. Most of the media, public opinion, are pushing for acceptance of the ultimatum. I expect he will. He's an appeaser.'

'God. You sound so calm, Shalom. That's

225

terrible. Don't you realize what's happening?'

'I do,' he said quietly. 'That's why we're going to find the nuke. By the way,' he added, 'we had an interesting visit while you were away.' His expression was blank.

'What was that?' She was still thinking of what he'd said before that. She didn't understand what was in his mind.

'Two policemen and our landlord.'

'So. For what?'

'Looking for it. Nice guys. Apologized for disturbing us. Said they had to search. Explained warrants were unnecessary where explosives were concerned. They had a good look round. Asked was it just these two offices we rented. The landlord said yes. So did we. They wanted to know about our business. We explained. Mostly pop. Showed them the catalogues, the stock of cassettes, the LP and single sleeves, the recorders—we'd switched off, of course, and taken out the bugging tapes when we heard the knock. One guy wanted to know if we had any Burt Bacharach numbers. So we put *Don't Go Breaking My Heart* on the hi-fi and he said his girl was doing just that to him, and his chum said it was a great number but they had to go. We switched off and they asked had we seen anything suspicious around this locality and we said no we hadn't and they thanked us and pushed off.'

'Anything else?' She thought Shalom looked tired and didn't know he was thinking the same about her.

'Yes,' he said. Quite irrelevantly he was wondering about Johnnie Peters and experiencing pangs of jealousy. Maybe she'd be seeing him tonight. 'When they left here they crossed the street. Went into Mocal's. Spent quite a time there. Came out with Hanna and Zeid. Laughing and joking. Parted from them on the best of terms.'

Her eyes were wide. 'I wonder if that's why the delivery was brought forward. Because the premises had been searched.' She hesitated, her eyes searching his. 'What on earth are we going to do, Shalom. For God's sake, tell me.' She was pale and very earnest.

'About what?'

'The nuke, of course. They haven't delivered it to Spender Street. Where is it?'

'I don't know. But I'll tell you something in a minute. First brief us on your Tel Aviv jaunt. Quickly. There isn't much time.'

'Oh, for goodness' sake. I don't understand. I don't understand.' She held her hands to her ears.

'Like some coffee?'

'Give my soul for it.' She smiled wanly.

'You needn't do that. I'll make it for you. You start talking.' Ascher went to the cupboard and switched on the kettle. For the next fifteen minutes she told them all she knew.

'Good.' He ran his hands through his shaggy

hair. 'Get across to Palace Green right away. Tell all that to the Ambassador and Ezra Barlov. They've had the hardcore stuff from Jakob. But you've got the detail. After that make for Vauxhall Bridge and get some rest. You're going to need it soon. Be back here not later than six.'

She stamped her foot. 'Shalom! We don't know where it is. What are you doing? We're wasting time.'

He looked at her in silence. 'We don't know where it is, Ruth. But we know it's expected. Listen to this.' He switched on the spare Grundig and let it run for a few minutes before switching off. 'Recorded at ten to two,' he said. 'Just over an hour ago.'

'My God,' she said. 'Why didn't you tell me before. So Rudi and Ahmad are on their way.'

Ascher shrugged his burly shoulders. 'Should be, you heard. Due at noon. They've not yet arrived. That's what they're twitching about in Mocal right now. And that's why Zol's up at Palace Green with Ezra Barlov. They're telling Jakob on the scrambler.'

'What d'you think has happened?'

'I don't think, Ruth. Makes me tired. Better wait and see.'

'And if we see it delivered?'

'Let Jakob know at once and wait for instructions.' He turned to Kagan. 'Anything new, Micky?'

The young man looked up for a moment.

228

'Zeid's phoned Rudi's place—wherever it is— from a call-box, but gets no answer. They're getting really worried over there. Wondering what the hell's happened. They can't understand why Souref was not phoned at the call-box.'

'That makes two of us.' Shalom pulled at his beard and watched a puzzled, tense Ruth putting on her wet headscarf. He thought once again what an attractive woman she was. One day, perhaps, when there was more time, he'd tell her how he felt about her.

CHAPTER TWENTY-TWO

There was sudden urgency in Kagan's 'Shalom! Look!'

Ascher checked the time—2.47 pm—took the opera glasses from the coffee table, moved into the shadows beside the window and looked through the slots of the Venetian blind. A black van had stopped on the opposite side of Spender Street, outside 39.

'Just arrived.' Kagan was husky with excitement.

Two men got out. One went into 39, the other unlocked the van doors, pulled out a pallet and a porter's two-wheeled trolley. Before long the man who'd gone into 39 came back. He was followed by Zeid Barakat,

229

Hanna Nasour, Najib Hamadeh and Ibrahim Souref The Israelis had seen Souref leave 39 that morning, and come back at a quarter-past-two.

'The van crew must be Rudi and Ahmad,' said Ascher.

The six Palestinians gathered round the back of the Bedford, three climbed in and presently the end of a large hessian-wrapped bale appeared. The pallet was pushed beneath the tail-gate and those in the street reached for the bale while those inside lowered it with check ropes. Slowly, with much pushing and heaving, it was settled on the pallet. The men in the van joined the others and, with the aid of the porter's trolley and crow bars, lifted the front end of the pallet over the kerb. Then all six shoved and pulled until they'd got the bale to the entrance where the double-doors had been opened to receive it. They struggled to get it through, turning it half sideways because it was too wide. Eventually they got it in and the double-doors closed behind them. The two men Ascher had assumed were Rudi and Ahmad came out, climbed into the van and drove off.

Carried out in pouring rain, the whole operation had taken less than five minutes. Other than the Israelis, no one but a handful of pedestrians had witnessed it.

'Phew,' said Kagan. 'Made me tired to watch. It was heavy.'

'Must have been rollers in the van,' said Ascher. 'The pallet had rollers too. Four Israelis could have handled that lot.'

'Chauvinist!' Kagan laughed in his excitement. 'Reckon that's the nuke?'

'Of course,' Ascher said it with finality. 'They wouldn't have killed Salamander for a bale of carpets.' He was thinking that what they'd seen was strangely unreal. They'd waited so long, so patiently, watched and listened so thoroughly, even when it had seemed they were wasting their time. But his mind was too full of what lay ahead to dwell on what had just happened. He put on a duffel coat. 'You stay here,' he said to Kagan. 'Zol Levi will be along in the next half hour. I'm going up to the Embassy. We've got to get cracking before the Brits' Prime Minister announces the sale of Israel.'

*　　　*　　　*

At 5.50 pm local time on Wednesday, November 10th, a Sikorsky helicopter touched down on the outskirts of Tel Aviv, not far from the Ramat Aviv Hotel. Cars and a group of security men were waiting on the patch of open ground as two passengers stepped from the helicopter into a big sedan with armoured-glass windows.

Three traffic policemen on motorcycles moved off, a car with five security men followed, then the big sedan. Two more cars, each with five security men, fell in behind.

The motorcade travelled down the Haifa Road into Tel Aviv, picked up the Petah Tikosh road, turned left into Herzl Street and shed the motorcyclists. Soon afterwards, following a series of left and right hand turns, the sedan pulled up outside the entrance to a red-brick building while the escorting cars drove slowly on. A group of men on the pavement formed a semi-circle round the entrance while others, unseen, watched from windows above the street, sniper rifles at the ready. The helicopter passengers were ushered into the building and the men on the pavement melted away. It all seemed very casual, but it was highly organized.

A few minutes later the Israeli Prime Minister and his Foreign Secretary were in Jakob Kahn's office. They had left Jerusalem within half an hour of receiving an urgent message from the Israeli Ambassador in London. They had come to Kahn rather than summon him to Jerusalem because the situation required immediate secret exchanges with the Ambassador in London and the facility of direct consultation with intelligence staffs at either end. Only Tel Aviv could satisfy those requirements. The Prime Minister and his Foreign Secretary had come directly from an emergency meeting of the Israeli Cabinet where decisions concerning the London

232

message had already been taken.

The discussions in Jakob Kahn's office—both with him and London—concluded shortly before eight o'clock. They were as intense as they were decisive.

* * *

The Israeli Ambassador, accompanied by Colonel Ezra Barlov, was received by the Prime Minister at Number 10 Downing Street, at 6.45 pm Greenwich Mean Time. The Prime Minister had with him the Foreign Secretary and Andrew Lanyard, his principal private secretary.

The usual courtesies having been exchanged, the Prime Minister said, 'I understand you have news of exceptional importance for me, Ambassador.'

The Israeli Ambassador nodded. 'Yes, Prime Minister. We have found the nuclear warhead . . .' He paused. 'In London.'

The Prime Minister, skilled in concealing emotion, lit an already-lighted pipe with slow deliberation. 'You have, I take it, reported this to Scotland Yard?' He knew perfectly well the Ambassador hadn't, for Scotland Yard would instantly have informed him.

'No, Prime Minister. I have not.'

The Prime Minister's manner changed. 'May I suggest, Ambassador, that that was a serious omission. Where was it found?'

The Ambassador hunched his shoulders, sighed apologetically. 'I'm afraid I don't know. Only our deep-cover agents do. May I make it clear that I am acting under the instructions of my Prime Minister.'

'What are those instructions?'

'I was told to report the finding to you in these terms, personally and without delay. That was why I asked for an immediate audience. I was also to inform you that our intelligence service has prepared an operational plan to deal effectively with the terrorists guarding the warhead and to prevent its detonation. It is the earnest desire of my Prime Minister and his Cabinet that we should execute the plan in close co-operation with your authorities. If, on the other hand,' the Israeli Ambassador's eyes never left the Prime Minister's, 'that co-operation is not possible, we shall have no alternative but to carry out the operation on our own. This we will do with extreme reluctance because its execution will then be so much more difficult.'

The Prime Minister pulled himself up in his chair, took the pipe out of his mouth and stared at the Ambassador. 'Are you suggesting that your Government contemplates carrying out an operation of this sort on British soil? On the territory of the country to which you are accredited?'

'I am afraid, Prime Minister, our Cabinet took the view that if the nuclear warhead were

234

not found the measures your Government might take, encouraged by the United States, the Soviet Union and the Arab States, would threaten the security of Israel. To return to the warhead, our intelligence agents have found it and they have the capability to deal with it. Immediately and effectively. Israel appreciates that since it is your territory you would want to be fully involved. Indeed, if as we hope British cooperation is forthcoming, the entire operation will be regarded as a British one. Israel will claim no credit either for finding the warhead or assisting in dealing with it.' The Prime Minister stood up, put his pipe on the mantelpiece. Andrew Lanyard recognized the signal. The PM felt cornered, was thinking hard, playing for time. The Israeli Ambassador and Ezra Barlov watched in silence. Eventually the Prime Minister turned to them. 'I find your proposal quite extraordinary, Ambassador. I am not sure that its flavour of blackmail is any less distasteful than the ultimatum itself.'

The Israeli Ambassador shook his head in disagreement. 'Blackmail is a harsh word, Prime Minister—quite inappropriate to Israel's attitude. The terrorists' ultimatum threatens to destroy London. My Government's proposal is an explicit undertaking to remove that threat. In return we ask for nothing but your co-operation in saving your capital from destruction, its people from death and injury and your country from humiliation and

235

disaster. We do not think world opinion would consider that an unreasonable offer.'

The Prime Minister's mouth closed in a tight line. 'Your words are shrewdly chosen Ambassador, but they do not alter the facts. I will discuss the matter with my Cabinet. I must warn you, however, that it is highly unlikely they will agree to such a proposal. It is, I repeat, a quite extraordinary one.'

The Israeli Ambassador looked at his watch. 'The situation is quite extraordinary, is it not, Prime Minister? May I ask for a written reply by nine o'clock tonight. I understand you are to address the Nation at ten.'

The Prime Minister stood, chin in hand, deep in thought, before answering. At last he said, 'Please outline the operational plan, Ambassador. I shall have to explain it to the Cabinet.'

'I am afraid I cannot do that. It is an intelligence service document, not in my possession. If, as we profoundly hope, there is to be co-operation, it will of course be disclosed to those concerned by our agents.'

'I see. What will Israel do if we reject the proposal?'

The Ambassador nodded towards Ezra Barlov. 'I would like Colonel Barlov to answer that question.'

The Prime Minister's 'Certainly' was like an icy bullet.

Barlov said, 'Our men have the nuclear

warhead and those with it under continuous surveillance. They also have the operational plan. Their orders are to execute it at midnight unless they receive instructions to the contrary.'

'Who would give those instructions?'

Barlov spread his hands apologetically. 'All I can tell you, Prime Minister, is that deep-cover agents work directly under the authority of their headquarters in Israel. We do not control them.'

*   *   *

Shortly before nine o'clock that night, Dugald McGann, Head of the Special Branch, and Andrew Lanyard, were driven to the Israeli Embassy where Ezra Barlov, forewarned of their coming, at once showed them in to the Ambassador. Lanyard introduced McGann, and passed the Ambassador a letter. 'I was instructed by the Prime Minister to hand this to you personally,' he said.

The Ambassador took the letter. 'Please sit down, gentlemen.' They sat down and were silent while he opened and read it:

My Dear Ambassador,

I have come from meetings of the Cabinet and the ad hoc Committee at which I reported on our discussions this evening. The Cabinet decided that the British Government has no alternative in the circumstances but to accept your

237

Government's proposals, subject to the following conditions: One—the operation to be under British control and without reference at any stage, officially or otherwise, to Israeli participation. Two—the warhead to be neutralized by eight o'clock tomorrow morning, failing which my Government will take such action as it considers necessary.

I must add that an Operations Sub-Committee has been appointed to conduct the operation in co-operation with your representatives. Its members are:

General Sir Dyhart Tanner, Chief of the General Staff, (Chairman).

Sir Brian Parkes, Commissioner of the Metropolitan Police.

Assistant-Commissioner Dugald McGann, Head of the Special Branch.

Sir George Isaacson, my Principal Scientific Adviser.

Mr Alexander Watt, Director-General of the Greater London Council.

General Tanner will be in charge of the operation, with power to act and authority to draw on all branches of central and local government for such personnel, material and other assistance as may be needed.

In my address to the Nation tonight I shall make no mention of these developments, nor say anything which might compromise them.

The operations Sub-Committee is ready to meet your representatives immediately. The bearers of this letter will inform you of the venue and provide any other information you may require.

Beneath the 'Yours sincerely', the Prime Minister had signed his name with what those who knew him well would have described as his angry flourish.

CHAPTER TWENTY-THREE

Within twenty minutes of Lanyard and McGann's departure from the Israeli Embassy a meeting of the Operations Sub-Committee was taking place in a conference room at the Ministry of Defence in Whitehall.

The Chairman, Sir Dyhart Tanner, sat at the head of the table, to his right the members of the Committee, to his left the Israelis: Barlov, Ascher, and Ruth Meyer.

The Chairman opened the proceedings by formally introducing the British and Israeli representatives. He stressed the urgency of the situation and expressed the hope that differences of opinion, if any, would be speedily resolved. Looking at the wall clock, he said, 'It is now nine-forty-seven. We have to complete the operation by eight o'clock tomorrow morning. The Israeli Government has requested our co-operation, so I will ask their representatives to open the discussion.'

At Barlov's request Ascher outlined the operational plan. He did this succinctly, wasting neither words nor time, and soon gained the respect of his British listeners who earlier had looked askance at the shaggy-headed, bearded man in blue denims and plimsolls, who'd sat hunched in a chair doodling on a scribbling block, apparently not listening.

'Thank you,' said the Chairman. 'The plan is, I would say, ingenious and tactically sound. You have told us the warhead is in Central London—in a position which could cause devastation of possibly the most important area of the Metropolis.' He paused. 'Where in fact is it?'

There was a stir of interest. An expectant hush. A leaning forward to look at the man who knew. The question had been in all minds as Ascher unfolded the plan. He looked up from the scribbling block. 'As soon as we've agreed the plan in principle I'll give the location.' With that he resumed work on a complex doodle.

The Chairman said, 'I hope this doesn't suggest mistrust of the undertaking given by our Prime Minister.'

'No,' said Barlov quickly. 'It is simply our belief that the operational plan must be considered objectively. This is best done if we agree on the general outline now and thereafter discuss the detail.'

'Very well,' said the Chairman. 'I think we can accept that. Now let's get on with the discussion. We haven't much time.' He didn't add that he thought the Israelis were a cunning lot; holding back the prime secret until they were satisfied the operation was to be conducted in the way they wanted.

In the lengthy discussion which followed members of the Sub-Committee proposed a number of amendments to the plan. Most of these were accepted. As the meeting progressed it became apparent that confidence between the British and Israeli representatives was growing, the mutual suspicion which characterized the earlier stages having largely disappeared.

When the outline had been agreed, the Chairman said, 'I think we have a pretty thorough grasp of what has to be done. There are, of course, a number of imponderables. These will have to be dealt with as they arise.' He turned to Barlov. 'Can you now tell us where the warhead is?'

Barlov said, 'I'll ask Shalom Ascher to answer that.'

The Chairman said, 'Mr Ascher?'

The Israeli put down his pencil, leant back in his chair. 'Number Thirty-Nine Spender Street,' he said. 'Not far from Covent Garden. On the ground floor. We have two offices in the building across the road, Number Fifty-Six—on the first floor.'

'Thank you.' For some moments the Chairman considered the wall-map of London. 'It's certainly well sited. Let's get on with the detail. Please be as brief as possible.'

They were, and when the clock over the mantelpiece showed twenty past ten the Chairman was able to say, 'Now, gentlemen'— he saw Ruth Meyer's grimace, thought what an attractive girl she was, and added—'and lady.'

'Don't worry,' she said. 'I'm used to it.'

The Chairman smiled an apology. 'I think it might be helpful if I were to recap the allocation of responsibility before closing the meeting.'

There were murmurs of 'Agreed.'

He looked at his notes. 'Mr Watt will make the necessary arrangements with the local authorities—the water, gas, fire brigade and ambulance people.'

The Director-General of the GLC nodded. 'That is correct, Chairman.'

'Mr McGann will provide the Special Branch men.' The Chairman fixed Dugald McGann with a parade-ground stare.

'Yes,' said the Head of Special Branch. He was a man of few words.

'Sir George Isaacson will be responsible for the scientists, technicians and their equipment.'

The Principal Scientific Adviser looked up from the pad on which he was making notes. 'Yes, indeed, Chairman.'

'Sir Brian Parkes will see to our uniformed police requirements, the communications system and the mobile command vehicle.'

The Commissioner signified his assent, looked at his watch and frowned from long habit. There never seemed enough time to do the things which had to be done.

'Colonel Barlov will be with us in the command vehicle.'

Barlov said, 'Yes, sir.'

'The Israeli Intelligence agents—that is, Mr Ascher and his colleagues—will be at Fifty-Six Spender Street with the Special Branch people detailed for duty there, plus a Porton Down boffin and a Water Authority man. Final point—most important—we *must* begin the operation not later than three o'clock tomorrow morning. All personnel and equipment to be in position by two o'clock. Now . . . any questions? If so, please keep them brief. We have very little time.'

'Helicopters, Chairman.' The Principal Scientific Adviser pushed heavy horn-rimmed glasses back on to the bridge of his nose. 'Some of the men and equipment we need can't get here by two o'clock without them.'

'RAF,' said the Chairman. 'I'll arrange it with the duty staff at MOD as soon as this meeting ends.'

'If fast cars with fast drivers are needed, I'll supply them,' said the Commissioner.

'Good.' The Chairman looked round the

243

table. 'You all know where to apply. Any more questions?'

'Yes,' said Ruth Meyer. 'Where will the Aldermaston and other scientific and technical people and their equipment be—and the additional Special Branch men—during the run-up period? There won't be room for them in our office in Spender Street.'

The Chairman aimed his pencil at the Principal Scientific Adviser. 'Sir George?'

'They'll all be in the Water Authority vehicles. I thought I'd made that clear.'

'Not quite,' said the Chairman, gallantly covering for Miss Meyer. 'Any more? No. Then the meeting is closed.'

He gathered his papers, stood up, stretched and yawned. 'Now let's get on with it and—by the way—good luck to you all.' His eyes were on Ruth Meyer as he said it.

*　　　*　　　*

The Prime Minister's address to the Nation that night was brief and unilluminating. Prefacing what he had to say with a further call for calm, order and confidence in the authorities, he announced that the search for the nuclear warhead had been called off as from ten o'clock that night. Further consideration was, he said, being given to the terms of the ultimatum, and he would speak to the Nation again at ten on the following morning.

'I hope then,' he said, 'to have news which, while possibly unpalatable in certain aspects, will remove altogether the intolerable and barbaric threat to which Londoners have been submitted during these difficult days. Finally, I give you once more my assurance that the Government is both determined and obliged to preclude by all and every means within its power the detonation of the warhead. On that score you may rest assured.'

Later the Prime Minister's critics were to say that this was an ambiguous and misleading statement. It may have been, but every word of it happened to be true. To the great majority of those many millions who heard it, what he said amounted to an admission that the Government was about to capitulate—that he would at ten o'clock the next morning announce acceptance of the ultimatum—the course of action the US President and the Chairman of the Soviet Union had by implication advised in their communiqués broadcast an hour before the Prime Minister spoke.

It was, too, precisely what he wanted his listeners to think—particularly those in 39 Spender Street.

CHAPTER TWENTY-FOUR

At midnight the offices of Ascher & Levi, music agents of 56 Spender Street, were unusually crowded. In addition to the four Israeli agents, there were two Special Branch men—Chief Superintendent McFagan and Inspector Moynihan, the latter a fluent Arab speaker—a scientist from Porton Down, Herbert Joliffe, a small man with steel-rimmed glasses, watery eyes and a head as bald as polished marble, and a technician from the Thames Water Authority.

The Special Branch men had been the first to join the Israelis. They'd come in through the back having forced the lock of the door which gave on to Tanswill Lane. Those who came after them used this route. It was to serve for all concerned with the operation that night, both for entering and leaving. A Special Branch man was on duty on the ground floor inside the entrance.

A black-out curtain had been hung over the Venetian blinds in Ascher & Levi's main office so that the lights there could not be seen from the street. Levi and Kagan were watching the Mocal premises from the window of the adjoining storeroom which was in darkness.

A good deal of additional equipment had

been installed in Number 56 including three VHF two-way radio sets: one for communication with the mobile command vehicle—with which a landline telephone link had also been established—another on the same frequency for communication with what had been designated the Ground Force; a third on the frequency of the Metropolitan Water Authority.

The Special Branch men and the Israelis wore shoulder-holsters with hand-guns. In a corner there were two snipers' rifles with silencers and telescopic sights, a box of hand grenades and another of tear gas bombs. Nobody was quite sure under what circumstances these were to be used, but the General had felt the operation would be incomplete without them.

A sheet of white cardboard, headed OPERATION WHISKY BRAVO, was fixed to a wall with Sellotape. It gave the R/T call signs to be used during the operation, commencing with:

General Call Sign ...   Whisky Bravo
Command Vehicle ...   Whisky Bravo One
56 Spender Street ...   Whisky Bravo Two
Ground Force   ...   Whisky Bravo Three

Listed beneath these were the call signs of the other units involved.

One of the R/T speakers in Ascher & Levi's office bleeped: 'Whisky Bravo Five calling Whisky Bravo One.'

There was an answering, 'Go ahead, Whisky Bravo Five.'

'Contact entered Sea-Bee one-seven-three-nine. I repeat one-seven-three-nine. Over.'

'Roger, Whisky Bravo Five.'

A new voice came on the air: 'Tango Victor calling Whisky Bravo One.'

'Go ahead, Tango Victor.'

'We have read Whisky Bravo Five. Will do. Over.'

'Roger, Tango Victor.'

The Chief Superintendent said, 'That was the tail reporting to command vehicle. He's just seen Barakat go into call-box one-seven-three-nine. That's a Police/GPO identity tag. Tango Victor is the GPO tracing section. They'll put a tap on that call right away, punch-tape it and squirt it back to the command vehicle.'

Ascher pulled at his beard. 'I like that.'

'Useful routine,' said the Chief Superintendent. 'Good for counter-espionage.'

'We must remember that, Ruth.' Ascher lifted a quizzical eyebrow and they smiled privately.

The Chief Superintendent grinned. 'Yes. You'll have to watch it, won't you?'

'Not to bother,' said Ascher. 'Our cover's blown. We won't be operating in the UK again.'

McFagan looked at them speculatively. 'I suppose so.'

Ascher said, 'Nothing like a change of scene.'

'Good for the health,' said Ruth Meyer.

A few minutes later Whisky Bravo Five was reporting again . . . Contact leaving Sea-Bee . . . walking west on New Coventry Street . . . gone left into Whitcomb Street . . . contact entering Centrepark garage in Whitcomb Street . . .

The VHF speaker continued faithfully to relay the story of Whisky Bravo Five's vigil: Raining hard . . . Volvo emerging from garage . . . left into Panton Street . . . left into the Haymarket . . . left into Orange Street . . . crossing Whitcomb Street now, travelling east . . .

The command vehicle interrupted, ordered Whisky Bravo Five to abort task and return to base. The time was 1.54 am and it was raining.

*　　　*　　　*

Moynihan, the Special Branch Inspector who spoke Arabic, wiggled his earphones, tapped Ascher on the shoulder, held up a warning finger.

Ascher, concentrating on the conversation in 39, raised a thumb in acknowledgement.

249

IBRAHIM SOUREF: Well, he had to call Brussels at one-forty. It's fifteen minutes past two. He's got to pick up and park the Volvo. It takes time. I'm hungry. That's my trouble.

HANNA NASOUR: Here, try this apple. You greedy man.

SOUREF: Thanks. Be careful, Eve. You tempt me. (Laughter)

NAJIB HAMADEH: It's nearly twelve hours now we've had that thing. It gives me the creeps.

SOUREF: You mean Abdul. I keep imagining I hear him tick.

HAMADEH: Not possible, Ibrahim. Anyway he's not switched on yet. Must be your heart.

HANNA: Ibrahim hasn't got one. I wish Zeid was back. What can he be doing? Oh don't, Ibrahim. That hurts.

SOUREF: Sorry. Don't worry. He'll be here in due course.

HANNA: He'd better be. We could need that Volvo.

HAMADEH: You're nervy, Hanna. That's not until eleven. Another nine hours, nearly. Anyway, we can always take a taxi.

HANNA: How far can we get in one hour? (Nervous laughter)

HAMADEH: You've asked that before. Far enough. But we aren't going to need it. You heard the British Prime Minister. Search called off. No explosion. Unpalatable but reassuring news in the morning. They're going to accept, Hanna. It stands out like a camel in the desert.

HANNA: Oh God, I hope you're right. I hate the idea of the alternative.

SOUREF: Yes. Of course I'm right. It's obvious. You can be sure it's been arranged with the President and Brezhnev. Why do you think their communiqués were issued an hour before he spoke. I think . . .

HAMADEH: Ka'ed knew this. He said the US and Britain would jump at a really good excuse for an independent Palestine and ditching Israel.

HANNA: Ka'ed is a fantastic man. He's always right. But what a cynical world. Where else can . . .

HAMADEH: We can thank Allah for this cynicism if it gives us back our lands.

SOUREF: Thank Abdul, you mean. Listen to that rain.

HANNA: Pouf. It's a terrible climate. No wonder they look so serious. Come on, Zeid. (Whistling) You should have got back by now.

HAMADEH: Give him a chance. The Brussels call could be responsible. Perhaps the British Government has communicated with Ka'ed. Maybe Ka'ed wants Zeid to contact the authorities here right away. Could be anything. Who knows?

SOUREF: That's most unlikely. He'll be back in time. Your hands are cold, Hanna. What's wrong. There's nothing to fear.

HANNA: Of course there's something to fear. (Sounds of coughing) Of course I'm scared. I may be the one. I'm scared to death. Anybody who isn't at this moment isn't human.

SOUREF: There isn't going to be any need for 'the one'.

HAMADEH: Portrait of an inhuman man. (Laughter) Come and dance with me, Hanna. I'm not afraid. Let us celebrate the new Palestine. (Sounds of a scuffle and a man and woman giggling)

SOUREF: (Shouting) Keep away from that flex, you fool.

HAMADEH: Okay. No need to get excited. I was watching it.

SOUREF: You weren't. You were messing about with Hanna.

HAMADEH: Look who's jealous.

HANNA: Don't be like that, Ibrahim. We were just fooling.

SOUREF: This is no time to fool. If you fall on that it'll be the last thing you do.

HAMADEH: You forget the locking device.

SOUREF: Never mind the locking device. Zeid warned us. If the flex is wrenched out there can be a short circuit. Then you'll have something to celebrate.

HANNA: Sorry, sorry, dear Ibrahim. We are all too excited. I'm just a bundle of nerves tonight. Twenty-three minutes past two. I wonder what has happened to Zeid?

HAMADEH: Remember what I said about the Brussels calls.

SOUREF: I'm tired.(Sounds of yawning) What about some sleep

HANNA: Sleep. I'm too worked up. (More sounds of yawning)

HAMADEH: We must get sleep. Tomorrow is already here, but we've still got seven hours of darkness. It's going to be a long day.

While Ascher listened, Moynihan gave the Chief Superintendent a brief summary of the conversation. There was a lot of discussion about what 'the one' meant, and in the end agreement.

*　　　*　　　*

The mobile command vehicle was parked in a deserted loading bay off Henrietta Street, a relic of Covent Garden's former glory as a market. The small armoured windows set high on the rain-drenched sides of the big six-wheeler were blacked out, the driving cab door locked.

From the outside there was no sign of life in the vehicle. Inside things were different. It was brightly lit and much alive. One end was dominated by the communications system, the other by the operations table. From a console the controller could select frequency channels, switch transmitters and receivers, activate loud-speakers, handle landlines to the telephone

253

exchange, and oversee transcribers. Between the two ends there were built-in desks with cupboards beneath, bookshelves over; yacht-like settees found space along the sides, and vertical map screens with sections of London stood on either side of the operations table. On it there was a large-scale plan and blown-up aerial photo of Spender Street and its immediate surroundings.

The five members of the Operations Sub-Committee and Barlov sat round the table, the General at its head. They were supported by Commander Barrington, Head of the Yard's bomb squad, two Special Branch inspectors, a Metropolitan Police inspector, a scientist with burn scars on a face which had neither eyebrows nor lashes, and an official from the Thames Water Authority, Bob Yale, an ebullient Yorkshireman with a complexion like raw beef. The low voices of those in the command vehicle, the intermittent chatter of loud speakers and the hum of petrol-driven generators, wove a distinctive, never-ceasing pattern of sound.

The console operator tore a transcriber tape against the cutter bar and passed it to the General. 'From GPO Tracing Section, Sir, by landline. Transcript of the Brussels conversation.'

The General read it against the steady buzz of R/T chatter. Gale was talking by radio to Whisky Bravo Seven—one of the three

Thames Water Authority vehicles standing by in the area. The man with the facial burns was murmuring technical jargon into a hand-mike. At another Dugald McGann was talking by telephone to 56 Spender Street. The Special Branch inspector was still handling Whisky Bravo Five.

One way and another a lot was happening.

The General passed the transcriber tape to George Isaacson. 'It's in French. Barakat's Brussels chat. Brussels wanted to know local, US and Soviet buyers' reactions to the terms of sale. Barakat said favourable. He expects a firm offer in the morning. He asked Brussels if there were any changes in the original terms of sale. The Brussels man said, "No, no changes." Barakat said, 'Still the lots?' and Brussels replied, "Yes. I'm afraid that's essential. There is definitely no change, but from what you say they're not going to be necessary." He wished him good luck, said goodbye and that was that.'

Isaacson said, 'Is your French good?'

'I hope so. I was military attaché in Paris for two years. In Brussels with NATO for another two.'

'Sorry,' said Isaacson. 'Mine isn't highly reliable. I wanted to make sure. It's evident they expect acceptance. That exchange on top of the chat just recorded in Fifty-Six. What do you make of the reference to "lots"?'

'Most interesting bit of the conversation, I

thought. Might be a code word. *Lots* could be used in the context of a sale.'

'It's possibly more basic than that.' Isaacson blinked at the General through thick lenses. 'Brussels said, "I'm afraid that's essential". *Afraid*? Isn't that an expression of regret?' The Principal Scientific Adviser leant forward on the operations table. 'They're a fatalistic people. It could mean drawing lots, something unpleasant. Sacrificial.'

'You may well be right. Fits in with Hanna and Souref's references to "the one".'

'*One* remains behind.' Isaacson made a steeple with his fingers. 'I seem to recall your belief, General, that there would be a period immediately before the expiry of the time limit when all the Palestinians would have gone. You thought our bomb disposal people could then go in and make it safe.'

'I was wrong,' said the General. 'Nice of you to remind me.' He turned to Barlov. 'Ask Ascher what he makes of "the one".'

Barlov called Ascher on the landline and put the question.

Ascher's reply was immediate. 'Yes. That was Jakob Kahn's assumption when he outlined the operational plan. Someone, he said, would probably remain behind to deal with an electric failure or outside interference.'

'Extraordinary idea,' said the General.

'Not really,' said Barlov. 'The sacrificial concept is strong in terrorist philosophy.'

Dugald McGann put down the phone he'd been using. 'They're all set to start in Fifty-Six. Just waiting for the word from you, General.'

'Good. I think we should go to fifteen minutes notice. Is that agreed?' It was, and the console operator transmitted "alert fifteen" on the Whisky Bravo general call-sign. The acknowledgements came through, and he said, 'There's a hitch on Whisky Bravo Seven.'

The scientist with the burn scars reached for a mike. He spoke in the gentle voice which was becoming familiar to those in the command vehicle. When he'd finished he said, 'They're changing a defective valve on a cyclinder. Another ten to fifteen minutes.'

The General looked at the clock. 'Brings us to two-forty. That's acceptable. We want the water to come on stream at two forty-five.'

'No problem,' said Gale.

'Has Whisky Bravo Five finished with Barakat yet?' asked the General.

The Special Branch inspector said, 'He's just reported Barakat crossing Whitcomb Street, Sir . . . travelling east . . . it's still raining.'

'Good heavens,' said the General. 'Tell him to abort at once and return to base.'

'Will do, sir.'

The General spoke to the Commissioner. 'No point in following him now. The object of the exercise was to monitor the chat with Brussels. I imagine tailing's a dodgy operation at this time of the morning. Don't want to alarm Barakat. We know he's returning to Spender Street. The sooner he gets there the better.'

Dugald McGann said, 'Special Branch tails aren't easily spotted, General.'

'Here we go then,' said the Commissioner. 'Violin music, please.'

'They're a sight better than your CID tails,' muttered McGann.

'What's that, Dugald?'

'Nothing, Brian. I was thinking aloud.'

'Bad habit for a Special Branch man.'

'Come, come,' said the General. 'Do I detect inter-service rivalry?'

*   *   *

There was knocking on the front entrance to 56 Spender Street. Parry, the Special Branch man on duty in the darkened hallway, waited, puzzled. The front door was not to be used during the operation. Who would be wanting to come in that way at twenty to three in the morning? He wondered if it was the landlord, but then recalled that he had a key.

The knocking grew louder, more urgent. Parry went to the door, unlocked and opened it. A tall man in a rainsoaked overcoat, water streaming down his face, stared at him. Parry, conscious that someone in the Mocal premises opposite might be watching, said, 'Come in.'

258

The tall man hesitated, the Special Branch man reached out, pulled him in and shut and locked the door. He shone a torch in the man's face. 'Who are you and what do you want?'

'Never mind that bull. I want to see her. And take that bloody light out of my eyes.'

'See who?' Parry smelt liquor.

'You know who. Ruth Meyer. Where is she?'

'Never heard of her. You've been drinking, haven't you?' Parry took his arm.

'Don't touch me, you stupid bastard.' The tall man pushed the hand away. 'You've got her upstairs. I've been checking up. She comes to you at any old time, doesn't she?' He glared, swaying and belching. 'Randy bloody Casanova, aren't you?'

Parry's tone changed. He took a firm hold of the other man's arm. 'That's enough,' he said. There was a sharp scuffle, heavy breathing, cursing and then the handcuffs were on. The Special Branch man said, 'You're under arrest. Attempted break-in.'

'You lying bastard. You let me in. What's going on?' His eyes were frightened and angry at the same time.

'You'd better co-operate unless you want to land yourself in worse trouble. Now. Let's have your name and address.'

'Get stuffed.'

'Right. We'll soon fix that.' Parry felt inside his raincoat, brought out a mike, spoke into it.

'Parry here. Ask the Chief to come down for a moment. It's urgent.'

There was the sound of a door opening on the first floor. A torch beam shone from above and a man came down the stairs. It was Chief Superintendent McFagan. 'What's the trouble, Parry?'

'This man, Chief. Trying to force the front door. I've put him under arrest. Attempted break-in.'

'We heard some knocking. Thought it was the back door,' said McFagan.

'He's lying,' said the tall man. 'I knocked on the door. He let me in. I want to see Ruth Meyer.' He belched. 'It's my bloody right, isn't it? She's my girl. I know she's here.'

The Chief Superintendent shone a torch in the man's face. 'You've been drinking. There's no Ruth Meyer here.' He turned to Parry. 'Hand him over to the uniformed constable in Tanswill Lane. He's to be held at Bow Street overnight for SB questioning in the morning. They're not to take a statement. We'll see to that. Make it snappy. I'll keep an eye on things here until you get back.'

The tall man, querulous and chastened, went quietly, muttering about his Member of Parliament, the Ombudsman and the Association of Advertising Consultants.

*   *   *

'He wanted to see you, Ruth.' The Chief Superintendent looked at her quizzically. 'Tall chap. Dark moustache. Not bad looking. Advertising man, I think.'

Ruth Meyer's eyes went wide with surprise. 'My God! Johnnie Peters. How on earth did he know about this place?'

'Says he's been checking up on you. Know him?'

Ascher said, 'She knows him intimately.'

'Drop dead, Shalom.' She glared at him, turned back to the Chief Superintendent. 'Yes. I do know him. Where is he now?'

'On his way to Bow Street. Handcuffed. He'll spend the night in a cell. Cooling off.'

'Oh, poor Johnnie.' She was torn between tears and laughter. 'Is that really necessary?'

'Essential,' said Ascher, looking rather pleased with himself. 'All this scenario needed was your drunken boyfriend doing his Romeo to your Juliet. Business and pleasure don't mix, Ruth.'

'Get lost. It wasn't my fault.'

'Love's Labour Lost, more likely,' said the Chief Superintendent. 'He might have wrecked the whole show.'

CHAPTER TWENTY-FIVE

Barakat replaced the handset in the call-box in Leicester Square, turned up the collar of his raincoat and set off for the parking garage in Whitcomb Street. It was raining but he scarcely noticed it. The Brussels call had left him disturbed. Somehow he'd hoped there *would* be a change. Admittedly the outlook was good, but they were dealing with politicians and there could be delays. Yet the message was 'no change'. Ka'ed was making no allowances for delays or any sort of negotiation. If the ultimatum was not accepted by noon, that was it. After the Prime Minister had spoken at ten o'clock they'd know. Then, if there was to be no acceptance, they'd draw lots. Barakat was not afraid of that. In a way it would be better, much better, to die. He was deeply troubled about the morality of what they might have to do. Even in the planning stage he'd had reservations about that, but Ka'ed had talked him round. Now that the climax was approaching the implications bore on him in a frightening way. It was one thing to take part in an operation where a few people might be killed. That was part of the price for an independent Palestine. But to kill and maim hundreds of thousands? That would be something with which he could not live afterwards. It would be better to die with them than to live. In the few minutes since he'd left the call-box he'd made his decision. He would elect to stay if that were going to be necessary. There would be no lots.

He collected the Volvo in Whitcomb Street, drove it down to the exit barrier, paid the parking fee, bade the attendant 'goodnight', got an answering 'it's morning, man', and accelerated out through a curtain of rain. At Panton Street he turned left into the Haymarket, travelled down it to Orange Street where he went left again and travelled east along it. His destination was the National Car Park in Drury Lane, one within easy walking distance of Spender Street.

Blown by a south-westerly wind the curtain of rain became denser and he leant forward to put the screen-wipers to FAST. This must have unsighted him for he had no warning of the car coming in on his left from St Martin's Street. Fortunately neither car was travelling fast and the collision left them stopped on the intersection, front ends locked. Before he could get out, two men tumbled from the other car and wrenched open his door.

'What the bloody hell d'you think you're up to?' demanded the driver. He was a big man with long, black hair.

'Stupid twit,' said his bearded companion. 'You drove straight into us. You weren't bloody looking.'

Barakat sensed danger. The men were angry and excited. They had two women in the car with them. This was presumably the return from a night on the town. They'd certainly been drinking. The last thing he could afford was trouble. The intersection was in a backwater, its thoroughfares more or less deserted at that hour. He was determined to do nothing provocative.

'Get out,' said the big man.

'You've scared the tits off our birds,' complained the bearded man. 'Sods like you shouldn't be allowed to drive, except a pram or a hearse.'

Barakat said, 'I'm sorry. It was the rain. I didn't see you coming.'

'Blooming wog,' muttered the bearded man.

'You didn't bloody look,' said the big man. 'What's your name and address?'

Barakat opened his diary, tore a page from it, wrote *Simon Charrier* and the address in Rupert Street where Najib Hamadeh's sister lived. He handed it to the driver who went back to his car, while the bearded man leant into the Volvo and inspected the dashboard. He took the keys from the ignition lock, looked at the tag. 'Hey, Joe,' he called out. 'It's not this bloke's car. It's an Avis hire job.'

The big man was checking on the damage to his Austin Allegro. Barakat joined him and saw that it was slight. It hadn't been a serious collision thanks, he had to admit, to the prompt reaction by the other driver.

Barakat said, 'I accept all responsibility. I've got full insurance cover with Avis. It won't cost you anything.'

'You're bloody right it won't, mate.' The big man got into his car, started the engine and moved it clear of the Volvo. He drove it forward for about a hundred yards, then backed up to the kerb. 'She seems okay,' he said. 'But it'll cost at least sixty quid to put this lot right.' Barakat realized the figure was not far off the mark. The big man said, 'Got sixty quid on you?'

'I've got about forty.'

'That'll do as a deposit. Don't try and get away with the rest though, unless you're looking for trouble.'

Barakat took a wallet from his pocket and produced four ten-pound notes. The man took them, went back to the Austin and said something which made the girls laugh shrilly. Both men came back and he thought they were going to attack him. But he was wrong. While he looked on helplessly, they let the air out of the Volvo's tyres.

'You've been a bloody nuisance to us,' said the big man. 'Smashed up our car, scared our women, got us soaking wet. I reckon you could do with a bit of trouble yourself.' He and his companion got into the Austin and drove off, shouting to him as they passed. The girls waved and shrieked something he couldn't understand. Anxious for peace, he'd not asked the driver for his name and address. The man's failure to offer it, and the demeanour of his companions, caused Barakat to wonder if the car was a stolen one.

With a sigh of resignation, he examined the Volvo. The damage was slight. A crumpled nearside wing, a buckled fender and a smashed headlamp. He knew he wouldn't be able to drive with flat tyres, but he got into the driver's seat. He had to know if the engine was working.

It was only then he realized that the men in the Austin had driven off with the Volvo's keys. He couldn't start the car or open the boot to get at the tyre pump. The Volvo couldn't even be pushed clear of the intersection because the ignition key locked the steering. There were, he knew, spare keys in the glove-box but he'd locked that and the key was on the ring they'd taken. It was a hopeless situation.

Frightened and anxious he looked at his watch. It was a quarter-past-two. It would take about fifteen minutes to walk to Spender Street, but the Volvo was their get-away car. If the ultimatum wasn't accepted by noon that day, they were going to need it badly. There were alternatives. They could take a train from Charing Cross, or a taxi, or hire another car—but the first two were risky and the third time-consuming. And there was very little time. There was also the problem of the Volvo. He

266

couldn't leave it where it was. The last thing he wanted was trouble with the police or the Avis people. He must, he realized, somehow or other get it going again.

He remembered that an Avis car carried AA membership. The collision had taken place not far from the AA office near Leicester Square. He set off up St Martin Street. When he reached the AA office he found it locked. A notice on the door gave the emergency service number. He went to a call-box and dialled it. It was engaged for some time and it was fully ten minutes before he finally got through. He told the duty clerk of his troubles. Yes, he would send an AA patrol van. Barakat should return to his car, lift the bonnet and wait. It might take a little time.

At two-thirty an AA patrol arrived. It didn't take the patrol long to pump up the tyres. Then came the problem of the locked ignition and steering. 'That's not so easy,' said the patrolman. 'The difficult we do at once. The impossible takes a little longer.' Barakat laughed feebly. The patrolman was as good as his word. Before long he'd forced the lock on the glove-box, taken out the spare keys and started the engine. He waited while Barakat test-drove the car for a short distance, only leaving when it was evident that the collision had not affected its road-worthiness.

It was 2.53 am when Barakat parked the Volvo in Drury Lane and made for Spender

Street. The rain had stopped but he was wet and miserable. He walked fast, sometimes breaking into a trot.

*   *   *

Spender Street was a little-used thoroughfare. Narrow, it ran from north to south, twisting as it went, its northern end higher than its southern. Numbers 39 and 56 faced each other in the lower part of the street, some distance below the point where it curved to the north-west.

At about a quarter-to-three that morning a small service van belonging to the Thames Water Authority stopped near a man-hole at the higher end of the street and two men got out. Some fifty yards further up it a policeman stood in the shadows watching. Having erected traffic barriers and diversion signs, they lifted the cover from the man-hole. One of them eased himself down into it while the other passed him tools. A few minutes later the man inside climbed out. The steel cover was replaced, the men got into the van, started the engine, drove a few yards and stopped. The driver then worked the engine up to maximum revs, and the noise all but deadened the dull thump of an explosion. They got out and walked back. Several feet from the manhole there was a gaping hole in the road from which water poured in a powerful stream.

'Never thought I'd do a thing like that,' said the Water Authority man. 'What a wicked waste.' He shook his head sadly. 'I suppose you people know what you're up to?'

The Special Branch man said, 'You needn't worry about that. We'll wait here now. Keep an eye on things. If anybody asks what we're up to, we've checked the report of the burst water main and asked for assistance.' He got into the van, picked up a mike, pressed the speak-button. 'Whisky Bravo Nine calling Whisky Bravo One.'

'Go ahead, Whisky Bravo Nine.'

. 'Have located burst water main. Please send assistance.'

'Roger, Whisky Bravo Nine. Will do.'

*   *   *

The inside of 39 Spender Street, dimly lit by the red light of a camping torch, was a good deal untidier than usual. Empty tins and wrappers shared waste-paper baskets with apple and orange peel and scraps of foodstuff wrapped in newspaper spills. The smell of food, coffee and human bodies hung in the air like an invisible pall. There were four people in the front office and they lounged on chairs with outstretched legs or sat on desks. A portable radio churned out pop music between hourly news broadcasts.

Hanna Nasour went to the corner cupboard

in the stockroom and poured herself a cup of water. She came back, sat down next to Souref. 'What on earth has happened to Zeid?'she pleaded.

'In the name of Allah. Don't go on about that,' said Ibrahim. 'He's late. There can be a dozen reasons. Even if he doesn't arrive we can manage.'

'I don't like it. It's . . . it's odd.'

Ahmad Daab rolled his eyes. 'Rubbish, Hanna. You're suffering from nerves. Have you ever known an operation go smoothly? No hitches? Of course you haven't. Anyway, what's eating you? We can manage. If Zeid's not back, we can switch on and Najib can make the ten-thirty Brussels call. Apart from that all we need do is listen to the radio. There may be announcements before the Prime Minister speaks at ten.'

'I'm tired,' Souref yawned. 'Wish I could sleep.'

Najib Hamadeh yawned in sympathy. 'You and Hanna are supposed to be resting now. While Ahmad and I . . .'

Daab's warning hand interrupted them. 'Sheesh, sheesh. Turn that radio down.'

Hanna switched it off. They heard a car stop in the street, the slamming of doors, the sound of men's voices.

'What's that?' Hanna's was a frightened whisper.

'Put out the torch,' Hamadeh stood up. 'I'll

take a look.'

The light went out and he went to the front of the office. They had long ago scratched a spy-hole in the dark paint on the inside of the window. A bit of black masking tape covered it. He pulled the tape aside, put his eye to the spyhole. 'Police car,' he whispered. 'They're looking into the gutter. It's running with water. Like a small river. Must be a burst water main up the street.' He paused. 'They're walking back to the car. One of them is speaking into a mike. Reporting the trouble, I suppose.' There was a long pause before he said, 'Now they're going . . .'

The Palestinians heard the police car drive away. Souref switched on the torch.

'Phew . . .' Hamadeh pressed the palms of his hands against his stomach. 'That worried me. I thought they might be coming in here.'

'Thank God.' Hanna's eyes were half closed. 'Oh, thank God.'

'You Christians,' said Daab. 'What about Allah? Turn up that radio.'

*　　　*　　　*

The Thames Water Authority man hung up the mike and took out his earphone. 'Whisky Bravo Nine reports task completed, sir. They're standing by.'

'Good,' said the General. He looked at the time-table. 'I see your maintenance vans are

271

due to move at five past three.'

'Yes, sir. I've given them the stand-by.' It was warm in the mobile command vehicle and the Water Authority man mopped his face with a bandana. His discomfort was not altogether due to the temperature. What happens, he was thinking, to the wife and kids if this lot goes up? A number of people in and around Spender Street were asking themselves the same question and most of them were arriving at the same answer. If it did at least they wouldn't know anything about it. Which was about the best human beings could be expected to do in the circumstances.

Barlov, talking into a microphone, listening with an earphone, tapped the console operator on the shoulder. 'Put Whisky Bravo Two on a speaker, Jim.'

The operator flicked a switch and Ascher's throaty voice came on the air. 'The gutters outside are running with water. Presume Water Authority has been notified. Brown John has not, repeat not, arrived. Suggest you collect. Over.'

'Tell him we will,' said the General.

Barlov pressed the speak-button. 'Roger, Whisky Bravo Two. Will do.' Brown John was the code-name for Zeid Barakat.

Barlov looked at the operations clock. 'It's five minutes to three, General. What do we do about him?'

The General twiddled a ball-point and

272

considered the plan of Spender Street. 'It won't do to have him walking into Mocal after three o'clock. If he turns up now we'll have to pick him up as soon as he enters Spender Street.'

The Commissioner said, 'I'll see to that right away.'

The scientist with burn scars said, 'The defect in the valve has been made good, General.'

'Splendid. Your people know they must get involved with the digging party, don't they? Must appear to belong to them.'

'Yes. They're briefed on that. And dressed for it.'

'What about the transfer of equipment? Any snags?'

'None that we haven't foreseen, I hope. The dig is on the Mocal side. A little bit up the street. Say twenty feet.' The scientist's pencil hovered over the blown-up photo of Spender Street. 'The van with the equipment will park further up on the same side. When the dig is under way, they'll take equipment in through this lane.' The point of the pencil touched it. 'From there, through the back into Thirty-Seven.'

The General said, 'Good. They'll be out of sight of anyone in Mocal?'

'Yes,' said the scientist.

'Three o'clock.' The General looked at the operations clock. 'Five minutes to go.'

273

CHAPTER TWENTY-SIX

It was two minutes past three in the morning when Barakat rounded the corner into Spender Street and saw the traffic diversion signs at the foot of the street, beyond them water tumbling down the gutter and disappearing into a drain.

Late and worried he paid little attention to the two men working on the flicker-lamps, until one of them stepped on to the pavement. Barakat saw the revolver and with disbelief heard the words, 'Put your hands up.'

He did. The second man frisked him, found the handgun in the shoulder-holster and whipped it out.

'He's clean now,' he said, holding a mike in front of Barakat as if interviewing him.

'What's your name?' asked the first man, poking the revolver into Barakat's stomach and pulling the silk scarf from his neck.

'Simon Charrier.'

'Address?'

'Seventy-three Rupert Street. Off the Bayswater Road.'

'Why are you armed?'

'For protection.'

'Against what?'

'I'm a stranger. This is a big city.'

'What is your nationality?'

'French.'

'Where do you live?' The man pressed the revolver more firmly into Barakat's stomach.

'In Paris.'

'Is it normal for Frenchmen visiting London to carry handguns in shoulder-holsters?'

'I don't know.'

'Where did you get that neck scar?'

'Car accident.'

The frisker took away the mike and spoke into it. 'Is it him?'

'Yes,' came Ascher's disembodied reply. 'That's his voice.'

The man who held the revolver said, 'Zeid Barakat, you'd better come along with me.'

*   *   *

At seven minutes past three, two Thames Water Authority maintenance vans towing air compressors came up Spender Street from its southern end, rounded the first bend of its 'S', and parked outside the adjoining premises of numbers 35 and 37.

Workmen climbed out, erected traffic barriers, signs and lights, unloaded airlines, jack-hammers, axes, forks, shovels and crowbars. The foreman drew chalk lines on the road surface to indicate the limits of the trench to be dug. It was to run parallel to the water-filled gutter, and to extend from number 35, down the road to number 41.

While they got ready for their task they

275

talked, laughed and shouted to each other. An observer would have concluded from the unhurried but deliberate way they set about things that this was something they'd done many times before.

The compressor trolleys were uncoupled and manhandled into position. Their diesel engines were started up, airlines connected, and workmen began to break up the hard surface of the street with pneumatic jack-hammers. As they moved forward they were followed by men with forks and shovels who cleared the loose rubble. The excavation of the trench had begun.

The boom of the compressors was soon lost in the deafening clatter of the jack-hammers. It was fortunate that Spender Street was not a residential one, for heads might otherwise have hurled abuse from upper windows.

*   *   *

While some worked on the trench, others, dressed as workmen, stood watching, waiting for tasks yet to come or moving between the burgeoning excavation and the maintenance vehicles. Among these were two nuclear weapons scientists from Aldermaston, two bomb disposal experts from Aldershot, three Special Branch men and a technician from the Metropolitan Gas Board.

A service lane ran in from Spender Street

between numbers 35 and 37, its entrance opposite the thirty feet or so of space left between the parked vans. From time to time a workman walking between them with equipment would slip into the lane and become lost in the darkness at its far end. There he would enter 37 through a side door. It had been forced by the Special Branch soon after the vans arrived.

In this way the Gas Board technician and the Special Branch men had by 3.25 am assembled with their equipment in number 37 which shared a wall with 39. They were joined soon afterwards by Ascher, Levi, Chief Superintendent McFagan and Herbert Joliffe, the scientist from Porton Down. They arrived singly, entering Spender Street at its northern end which they'd reached by means of a detour from Tanswill Lane. With their arrival the Ground Force was complete. Its equipment included gas cylinders, coils of plastic piping, electric drills, anti-gas respirators, a radio receiver tuned to the frequency of the bugs in 39, and a mike and earphone connected by long leads to the R/T set in the nearer of the two maintenance vans. This made it possible for those in 37 to talk direct to all Whisky Bravo stations.

For the main part the members of the Ground Force worked in silence as they made ready their equipment but when they did speak they had to raise their voices to make themselves heard above the din outside.

* * *

Hamadeh said, 'Zeid won't risk coming now. Not with all this business going on.'

Souref nodded. 'You're right. Too risky. Someone coming into business premises at three o'clock in the morning.'

'Three-fifteen,' said Hanna. 'They would have to choose *this* morning.'

'You can't choose when water mains burst, Hanna.'

'You know what I mean, Najib.'

In the street the deafening noise of the jack-hammers rose and fell from one crescendo to another, the occasional intervals of their silence filled with the thump and roar of the compressors.

Three of the Palestinians had moved into the stockroom to get away from the worst of the noise, but they kept the door half open so that they could see into the outer office where Daab sat at a desk near the big bale of carpets, the plastic switchboard at his elbow.

Souref was sitting on a pile of rugs peeling an apple. 'We have to . . .' He paused.

'We have to what?' interrupted Hamadeh.

'We have to admit they're prompt. I mean they lost no time in getting here.'

'How do we know?' Hamadeh worried at his side-burns. His nerves were frayed and his tone was challenging. 'That mains could have burst long ago. We wouldn't have known about it if the police car hadn't come. The water could have been running all night.'

'Have it your own way.' Souref adjusted the shoulder-holster strap which was chafing his armpit, and yawned. He turned to the girl on the rug beside him. 'Are you all right, Hanna?'

'No. I'm not.' She made a face. 'This room is terribly stuffy and I'm allergic to rugs next to my face. And that terrible noise . . . it's impossible.' The frustration in her voice gave way to pleading. 'Tell me, Ibrahim. What d'you think can have happened to Zeid. I'm frightened. I can't bear to think of the hours ahead.'

He stroked her cheek, looked into her troubled eyes. 'Don't worry. All will be well. They are going to accept. We shan't have to use it.'

'And if they don't?'

He could see in the dim red light how frightened she was but hadn't the heart to deceive her. 'If they don't—well—you know— we *shall* use it. El Ka'ed has no reservations about that. We are at war, Hanna. This is not a diplomatic exchange. It is a calculated act of war. They know that, too. And they know Ka'ed's record. He doesn't bluff. They will accept. If you don't believe me, think of the US President's and Brezhnev's communiqués. There is every reason to accept. But for the

279

loss of face I am certain the British—like the USA—welcome the ultimatum as a means of getting Israel off their backs, settling the Palestine issue and ensuring good oil terms for themselves. How many times must I tell you these things?'

'I'm sorry, Ibrahim. But Zeid? Where is he?'

'How should I know. He may have been delayed by the Brussels call. He could have asked Brussels to put a question to Ka'ed for immediate reply. Brussels has to relay the question to Istanbul—then Istanbul to Damascus—Damascus to Beirut. The answer has to come the same way. It can be a long business. And even when it is settled—which it may already have been—Zeid comes back here, sees the activity on the street and has to keep away. There's always a reasonable explanation to these things.'

She put out her hand, touched his face. 'Thank you, Ibrahim. You are very patient with me. I'm supposed to be tougher than I look. But I sometimes wonder. This is so different from anything we've done before. It's like a bad dream. A very bad dream, when you come to think of it.'

Ahmad Daab called out from the front office, 'You two keep talking. You're supposed to be resting. No wonder Hanna's nervy.' He sat back again, his ear to the radio receiver, his thoughts confused by the pop music which poured from it, the noises from the street, the difficulty of hearing what his companions were saying, his thoughts about the carpet bale behind him, and the sight of the black switch at his elbow.

*   *   *

'About there.' Ascher made a cross with a pencil low down on the wall which number 37 shared with 39.

'What's the height of the shelving?' asked Joliffe.

'About two metres. It's filled with pattern books.'

'Can you recall seeing any metallic objects along that side of the wall? Plumbing, heaters, anything like that?'

'No. Nothing like that which I can remember. But I couldn't see behind the shelving.'

'You're certain it's in there?' said the Gas Board man.

'Absolutely. We know from the bug-chat when they brought the bale of carpets in. They couldn't get it through the door into the stockroom. Too big.' Ascher ran his hands through his hair. 'And we've heard enough in the last few hours to confirm that it's in the front office. Right in there with them.'

'Good. That's the site for number one inlet, then.' The Gas Board man put a white chalk mark over Ascher's pencilled cross.

Joliffe poked tentatively at his steel spectacles. 'Ideally, the second inlet should be approximately six feet . . .'

'Two metres,' interrupted the Gas Board man staring at the scientist's bald head.

Joliffe blinked nervously through thick lenses. 'If you wish. As I was saying . . . about six feet to the left of the first inlet—that is, towards the centre of the compartment.'

The Gas Board man's chalk hovered. 'That's right, then?'

'A little lower,' suggested Joliffe, adding, 'That's it.'

'Any snags at that point on the other side, Ascher?'

'Not that I know of. Still can't guarantee the wall behind the shelving to be free of obstacles.'

'Of course,' said Joliffe. 'One understands that.'

'Best carry out the test before we go any further.' McFagan pulled out a pipe and tobacco pouch, looked at them speculatively, changed his mind and put them away.

The Gas Board man unplugged the lead on the drill and moved to the wall separating the front office from the one at the back. 'I'll drill at this point,' he said, indicating it.

Zol Levi went into the back office, shutting the door behind him. The Gas Board man drilled the hole through the wall.

Levi came back. 'Couldn't hear a thing,' he said. 'The jack-hammers win by a ton.'

'Good.' Joliffe cleared his throat. 'I feel we should now make a start, gentlemen.' It was as if he were inviting them to sit down to the first course.

'Okay with me,' said McFagan. 'How about you, Ascher?'

'Fine. Let's go.'

The Gas Board man unplugged the lead and they moved back to the wall which 37 shared with the Mocal premises.

He plugged in again, placed the bit on the chalk mark and began drilling while Joliffe and his assistant moved the cylinders and coils of plastic piping into position. Levi was thinking what a weird scene it was: dim red light reflected on men doing strange things while others watched, and outside the ceaseless staccato of jack-hammers. He wondered if those around him suffered as he did from a heart which thumped against its rib-cage, and breath which came unevenly.

The Gas Board man felt the bit break through and released the trigger. He looked to the desk where Ascher was sitting, a hand cupped over the earphone as he listened for indications of disquiet on the far side of the wall. Evidently there were none, for the Israeli cocked a thumb in an 'all's well' signal.

Before withdrawing the drill, the Gas Board man slid a steel clip along the bit until it touched the wall. He nodded to Joliffe and the Porton Down boffin took the open end of a plastic pipe which led from a gas cylinder and worked it gently into the freshly-drilled hole. When he judged it to be half-way he stopped, clamped the pipe in position, and sealed the space around it with a malleable compound.

The Gas Board man shifted the drill to the mark for the second inlet and triggered the drill. Shortly before he expected the bit to break through it came up against a hard object. He stopped, withdrew the bit, examined its tip. 'It's no good,' he said to Joliffe. 'There's something metallic on the far side.' He exchanged the old bit for a new one.

'Try a foot to the left—and six inches higher,' suggested Joliffe.

The Gas Board man selected the new position and began drilling. There was no problem this time, the bit soon broke through, and Joliffe fitted the second pipe into the hole. He clamped and sealed it, then checked the pressure gauge readings on the cylinders. 'We're ready now.' He took a stop-watch from his pocket. 'On respirators, please. Then, as soon as you give the word, I'll open the valves.'

They were busy putting on respirators when there was a sharp hiss from Ascher and his hand went up in urgent warning.

'Stop everything.' He spat the words at them.

Eight Hours To Go

CHAPTER TWENTY-SEVEN

Ascher had heard Hanna Nasour complaining about the impossibility of resting, let alone sleeping, while the noise in the street persisted. 'I haven't slept for twenty-four hours,' she said, adding with a touch of hysteria, 'This noise is driving me round the bend.'

Souref had backed her up, suggested that those off watch should rest in the cloakroom in the back-yard. They could take rugs and make themselves reasonably comfortable. At least there would be freedom from the worst of the noise.

After some discussion Hamadeh and Daab had agreed, undertaking to call them at five o'clock when they were due to come on watch. It was when Daab said, 'That's right, Hanna. Take those Kashan rugs, they're soft,' that Ascher had hissed his warning and held up his hand. When he was satisfied that the off-watch Palestinians had left the front office, he gave Levi the task of listening to the Mocal bugs. To McFagan he said, 'There's a complication. I must get on to the command vehicle at once.' He picked up the mike, gave the call sign, got an answering, 'Go ahead Bravo Whisky

Three,' and asked for Barlov. Moments later he heard the Colonel's voice.

Ascher said, 'We have a complication here. Have stopped work temporarily. I'll report again shortly. Over.'

Barlov replied, 'Roger, Bravo Whisky Three.'

The members of the Ground Force removed their respirators and Ascher outlined the problem. 'This is serious,' he said. 'We have an entirely new situation. Hanna and Souref have gone to rest in the cloakroom at the back of the yard. They get there through a passageway open to the sky. It's about twenty-five feet long. Bounded on one side by the walls of the stockroom and cloakroom. On the other by an eight-foot brick wall.'

'What's on the other side of that?' asked McFagan.

'A more or less identical passageway. It belongs to number Forty-One. Occupied by a firm of coffee brokers.' Ascher fidgeted with his beard. 'A little more than halfway down the Mocal passageway there's an open yard, about fifteen by ten feet, off to the right. The cloakroom door opens on to its south side. The cloakroom is about ten by six. A WC at the far end occupies roughly one-third of that area. The remaining two-thirds has the hand basin, wash-up sink, roller towel, etcetera. Adjoining the WC there's an old coal shed. No longer used. Now a junk store.'

'Interesting,' said Joliffe, 'but disastrous. HXC324 is a splendid toxic agent, odourless, colourless, lethal, but like most gases it won't run down open passageways.' There was a tense discussion then on the possibility of introducing gas into the cloakroom, but it was soon dismissed. The Palestinians on watch would be relieved in about an hour. There was no safe place from which to drill into the cloakroom. Street noises made by the trench diggers would not reach so far back with the intensity needed and, finally, Joliffe was doubtful if his two cylinders could produce enough gas for a second operation.

At this stage the Special Branch man operating the R/T was heard to say, 'Go ahead, Whisky Bravo One. Over.'

The others watched him closely, heard his 'Roger, Whisky Bravo One. Will do.' He spoke to McFagan. 'Message from the command vehicle, sir. Two men are on their way over. They'll be here in a few minutes.'

The 'two men' who arrived soon afterwards, turned out to be the General and Colonel Barlov. Ruth Meyer, listening in Number 56 to the Mocal bugs, had heard the decision that those off watch should rest in the cloakroom and reported immediately to the command vehicle. As it was not practical to discuss this with Ascher over the air the General and Barlov had come to 37.

'Well.' The General rubbed his hands with

the air of a man about to do business. 'Let's have your appreciation of the situation, Ascher. You know the lie of the land next door, you know the Palestinians and their habits, and you've heard all they've said.'

Ascher described the lay-out of 39 and dwelt on the limitations imposed by the new situation—two Palestinians with the warhead in the front office, two resting outside—and no possibility of getting at the latter with Joliffe's HXC324.

'What are the possible courses of action?' Instinctively the General addressed his question to Ascher who appeared to have assumed command.

'Only one worth considering. The watches change at five. That's in about forty-five minutes. If we introduce gas into the front office now, the Palestinians outside may come back at any moment and find Daab and Hamadeh unconscious. Joliffe says his gas requires from three to five minutes to induce unconsciousness, ten to fifteen to kill. Taking the first factor, there'd be time for Hanna and Souref to detonate the warhead before they lost consciousness.'

'What is your proposal?'

'We delay the introduction of gas. I know the lay-out at the back. I've been over it before. We use one of the Water Authority vans. Get into it and ask the driver to back down Spender Street past 39 and park outside

41. We force the door of 41, go in through the premises to the passageway at the back. It runs parallel to 39's and shares an eight-foot wall with it. When we're in position at the far end we give the go-ahead by R/T and Joliffe opens the gas valves. Five minutes later we go over the wall and drop down outside the cloakroom.'

The General said, 'And then?'

'We knock on the door. They'll think they're being called to go on watch. They'll come out.'

'And when they do?'

'We kill them.'

The General frowned in parade-ground fashion. 'Sounds rather drastic. Is that really necessary?'

'How else can we make sure they won't warn those inside?'

'Killing can be a rowdy business, Ascher.'

'Not the way we do it. And not with those noises in the street.'

'I don't much like the idea.'

'Do you like the idea of hundreds of thousands of Londoners being killed and maimed?'

The General looked into the intense eyes set deep in the bearded face, bathed in the red light of the camping torch. In that moment he was glad he wasn't resting in 39's cloakroom. 'You're satisfied you can deal with the two outside without disturbing those inside?'

'As satisfied as we can be. There are no

certainties in this situation. And there are no alternatives.'

'Other than to give in, Ascher. The politicians like the idea.'

'Of course they do. And we know why. But, if they did, what guarantee would they have that other, probably more extravagant, demands would not follow? Blackmailers aren't interested in the one-off business.'

Ascher was preaching to the converted. This was a point the General had hammered home at meetings of the ad hoc Committee.

'That, Ascher, is a very good question. One to which I believe there is no satisfactory answer. Now tell me. Who will go over the wall?'

'Zol Levi and myself.'

The general sat chin in hand, deep in thought, before he turned to Barlov. 'What do you think of this, Barlov?'

'I agree with Ascher's view.'

'I thought you might. Yours, McFagan?'

The Chief Superintendent didn't answer immediately. By instinct and training he preferred to think things over before expressing a view. 'I agree.' He said it cautiously. 'Subject to Moynihan and Barrett acting in close support. Things can go wrong. We have an overriding responsibility. With my men there, the chances of failure are reduced.'

The General nodded. 'I support that.'

Ascher frowned. 'I'm not too happy about

290

that. In my experience the smaller the number engaged in cloak-and-dagger stuff the better.'

There was some discussion then, but McFagan was insistent and in the end Ascher gave way on condition the Special Branch men kept well behind and only interfered if such action became absolutely essential.

'Respirators?' enquired the General.

'They cramp a man's style,' said Ascher. 'We shouldn't need them. Moynihan can keep some on his side of the wall. We'll shout if we want them and he can throw them over.'

The General asked his final question. 'Weapons?'

'Coshes, combat knives, automatics.'

'Handguns are noisy.'

Ascher smiled. 'Not ours.'

CHAPTER TWENTY-EIGHT

The wind from the south-west had freshened, bringing more rain, heightening the darkness so that the men standing inside the doorway at the back of Number 41 could see nothing.

Ascher said, 'Give the CV the go-ahead.'

Barrett, the Special Branch man, pressed the speakbutton. 'Whisky Bravo Five calling Whisky Bravo One.'

There was an answering, 'Go ahead, Whisky Bravo Five.'

291

'Water main requires new valves,' said Barrett.

From the command vehicle came, 'Roger, Whisky Bravo Five. Will do.'

Ascher looked at the illuminated dial of his watch: 4.25 am. The gas would be going in within seconds. By four-thirty they should be able to go over the wall. In the darkness he touched Moynihan's arm. 'Fine. We'll get into position. As soon as Barrett receives the okay, come down and join us. Okay?'

The Special Branch Inspector said, 'Will do.'

Ascher said, 'Come on, Zol.'

He and Levi disappeared into the darkness, moving silently in stockinged feet, hugging the wall to their right, feeling their way along it as they went. Ascher had done a reconnaissance five minutes earlier. Now he was counting his strides. Seven covered the length of the passageway. He stopped at five, crouching against the wall, so tense that the steadily-falling rain and his wet stockinged feet went unnoticed. He looked at the watch again: 4.26 am. Four minutes to go. From long experience he knew the time would pass slowly now, the minutes dragging. He concentrated his mind on the lay-out of the premises on the far side of the wall, on what had to be done once over it, thinking in terms of time and distance. While his mind was busy with this check list, he took the Maxim silencer from a pocket of his denim jeans and with a quick twist of the interrupted thread locked it on to the Mauser automatic. His fingers touched the handle of the sheath-knife on his belt, eased the cosh-thong round his wrist, patted the torch in his hip-pocket. He wouldn't be able to use that until they'd dealt with the two Palestinians in the cloakroom. He had a mental picture of them. They were people he felt he knew quite well. He'd often seen them in the last few weeks, more often heard their voices. He harboured no feelings of animosity, no emotions of hate or anger. This was war. They represented forces bent upon dismembering Israel. They had to be eliminated. Hanna was very much a woman. Attractive, a pleasant voice, amusing at times, irritating at others. The sort of girl he could have gone for in other circumstances. Ibrahim Souref was a decent enough young man, conscientious—worried always about the girl—too adolescent perhaps, probably not hard enough, for the role in which he'd been cast. Daab and Hamadeh were the tough guys, Zeid Barakat the brainy one. Ascher looked at his watch: 4.28 am— hopefully only two minutes to go.

In some respects the pictures in Levi's mind resembled those in Ascher's. For him, however, a persistent one was the big bale of carpets. He saw again the Palestinians struggling to get it through the double-doors that afternoon, lifting one side to reduce its width. Thanks to the Mocal bugs the Israelis knew where the bale had ended up. In the outer office, against the shelving on the right-hand wall, closer to the stock-room than the street. In Zol Levi's mind there was a well-defined picture of the warhead lying inside the bale, Daab sitting at the desk near it with the firing-switch, the electric timing device clicking away the hours and minutes to noon. Crouched against the wall in pouring rain, Levi knew that he was now within thirty to forty feet of the warhead. There was one certainty. If it went off he'd know nothing about it.

In the midst of his fear, he grinned. He would be at the centre of the 'hot-spot'. What would his mother say to that? She was always complaining that he didn't look after himself properly. 'Why Zol? It is absurd not to take an undervest when you are going to that awful European climate.' His thoughts switched to the Palestinians in the cloakroom. Though separated from him by two brick walls they were, he knew, no more than ten feet away. He wondered what they were doing. Sleeping? Making love?

As he fitted the silencer to his Mauser he was thinking it would be better if things worked out so that he killed Souref, and Ascher killed the girl. He looked at his watch. The minute hand was almost on the thirty mark. He stiffened, tightened his grip on the automatic and with his free hand checked the knife and cosh. It would be any second now.

* * *

'Whisky Bravo One calling Whisky Bravo Five.'

'Go ahead, Whisky Bravo One.'

'New valves for water-main now on their way.'

'Roger, Whisky Bravo One.' Barrett clipped the mike back into an inside pocket. 'That's the okay, Inspector.'

Moynihan said, 'Right. You stay here. Keep your eyes and ears open. I'll join them.'

He stepped outside, feeling his way along the left-hand wall, counting the paces. The Israelis were quite close, only fifteen feet down the passageway. Ascher had said, 'It's twenty-five feet long. The garbage bins are at the end. Keep clear of them. We can't risk noise.'

Moynihan had gone only a few paces when his left knee hit something. There was an appalling crash of empty tins falling on to the concrete surface of the passageway. Horrified, he stopped. He remembered the rows of 20lb coffee tins on the shelves in the outer office of Number 41. He must have bumped into a stack of empties. But how was it the Israelis had avoided them?

Ascher had said hug the right-hand wall. He'd done that—or had he? Oh Christ!

295

What had Ascher meant by 'righthand' wall. Moynihan had taken it to be the wall on the right looking towards Spender Street. Not the wall on the right as you went down the passageway.

*   *   *

Ascher heard the loud clatter and froze against the wall. The next moment Moynihan reached him. His hand touched the Israeli's shoulder. 'Sorry. Sorry.' He was hoarse with repentance. 'Barrett's received the okay.'

There was no time for recrimination. Only one thing counted now and that was speed. In spite of the noise made by the trench diggers, muted though it was by distance and the intervening walls, the Palestinians in the cloakroom could have been disturbed. If they had been they would investigate. The Israelis had to get over the wall before that happened.

Ascher said, 'Now! Quick!' and Levi leant against the wall. Ascher stood on his back, reached up, grasped the top of the wall and drew himself on to it. He sat there for a moment looking down into the rain-drenched darkness, shifting the automatic to his right hand, then lowering himself from the wall with his left.

Levi, using Moynihan's back, went up on to the wall seconds afterwards.

296

She knew from his heavy breathing that Ibrahim, lying beside her on the Kashan rugs, had fallen asleep. How could he sleep under such circumstances, she asked herself in a burst of resentment. The place smelt lavatorial, and though the rugs kept out the cold they did little to soften the hard floor. And that was not all. Noon was less than eight hours away—eight decisive hours. The Prime Minister's broadcast at ten o'clock should resolve the dreadful uncertainty, but in the meantime tension was building up to levels she found intolerable. Far more so than in any other operation on which she'd been engaged.

This was the great gamble. Ka'ed's Final Solution. For them it was win or lose it all. If it came off they would have achieved at a stroke the seemingly impossible . . . the return of the lost lands . . . a sovereign independent Palestine . . . a new life and hope for three million people. If it failed? Her mind turned away from the prospect.

Yet, with all that at stake, Ibrahim could lie there fast asleep, even snoring. She looked at the illuminated dial of her watch and saw it was four-thirty. They would be called in half an hour. It was awful of him. She so badly needed his companionship, his assurances. After all they were in love . . . Why did he?

She was startled by a sudden noise. A

metallic clatter close by which sounded above the distant hammering in the street. Maybe it was Hamadeh or Daab coming to the cloakroom and dropping something, a kettle perhaps? Or a cat dislodging the lid of a garbage tin? She sat up, listening intently, her hand on the butt of her revolver. She was very conscious at that moment that the cloakroom had a lock but no key.

'Ibrahim, Ibrahim.' She whispered into his ear as she shook him.

Souref grunted, turned towards her in the darkness. 'What's wrong?'

'There's a noise outside. Quite close. I think someone's there.'

That brought him to his feet, awake and alert. 'I'll check. You cover me.'

She heard the complaining squeak of rusty hinges and cold wet air blew in her face as he went out. She stood for a moment in the doorway before stepping into the yard, gun in one hand, torch in the other. Once there she remained quite still, waiting.

*   *   *

After he'd dropped down into the passageway of Number 39, Ascher stood in the dark with his back pressed to the wall, his faculties concentrated on the cloakroom door less than ten feet from him. He was about to move towards it when he heard, above the blanketing sound of the jack-hammers in the street, the slow squeak of door hinges. The noise came from ahead and to his left, and was followed by the faint scrape of shoes on concrete. Someone was moving from the cloakroom into the passageway. He edged forward, one silent step after the other. There was a dull thud behind him and he realized that Zol Levi must have slipped on landing.

A torch flashed from the darkness to Ascher's left, followed by the mildly explosive *phut phut* of Levi's silencer. Spurts of flame leapt in answer from the passageway ahead as Ascher knelt and fired. There was the high whine of bullets passing close by, the thud of their impact on brick walls. There was no time for stalking now, it was a matter of seconds. Snatching the torch from a pocket, he flashed it ahead. The beam settled on a man crawling towards the back door of 39. He turned his head and Ascher saw that it was Souref. The Palestinian rolled suddenly to one side and Ascher saw his gun hand coming up. They fired simultaneously. The Israeli felt a blow in his stomach as solid as a kick. He stumbled forward and Souref fired again. The impact of the second bullet knocked the gun from Ascher's right hand and drained all feeling from the fingers. He dropped the torch, drew his combat knife with his left and threw himself at the Palestinian. He felt the man's hot breath and stabbed blindly at his face.

There was sudden searing pain beneath his left ear and warm blood flushed down his neck. He let go involuntarily and Souref resumed his crawl. The Israeli tried to stand up but couldn't, so he followed on all fours, pursuing the noisy rattle of the Palestinian's breath. Souref must have somehow opened the door, for Ascher could see him now silhouetted against dim red light.

The Israeli's mouth and throat were choking with blood. He spat it away, gasping for breath, knowing with awful certainty that he was dying, that Souref was not far from the firing switch.

With a supreme effort he rose to his feet, staggered a few paces and lurched on to the Palestinian, grasping him in a bear-like hug.

CHAPTER TWENTY-NINE

Hanna Nasour heard a dull thud to her right, aimed the torch through the drizzle of rain and switched it on and off. In that brief instant of illumination she saw the two men, the nearest heavy and bearded; to his right, kneeling, a slimmer man whose automatic was pointing at her. She threw herself sideways, saw the spurts of flame, heard the *phut phut* of the silencer. She fired three times, rose to her feet and made a dash for the coal shed. As she ran she heard shots lower down the passageway. They must be Souref's she decided; the others were using silencers.

She reached the end of the yard, felt for the doorway to the shed—the door had long-since gone—slipped through and squeezed herself into the nearest corner. She would have the edge there on anyone coming in after her.

There were no warning steps, just the sound of his laboured breathing and the scuffle of hands on the cedarwood planking. He began to vomit and she realized she'd wounded him. But was it him, or was it Souref? She felt sudden panic, controlled it, moved into the doorway, aimed the torch and switched on. It *was* the slim man. He was leaning forward, supporting himself with two hands against the planking of the shed, his face pressed to it, his body sagging, the automatic at his feet. She held the torchbeam steady, aimed her pistol at his back. Slowly his head came round and he looked at her with glassy eyes. A trickle of blood from his mouth formed globules under his chin before dripping away.

She pushed the pistol back into the shoulder-holster, drew a knife and stabbed him in the neck. He grunted and fell.

She picked up his automatic and threw it into the coal-shed.

*　　*　　*

301

When Moynihan and Barrett heard the shots in 39's passageway they assumed it was the Palestinians because the Israelis' guns had silencers. Using a chair for a step and wearing respirators, the two Special Branch men went over the wall at a point opposite 39's back door.

Moynihan sprinted through the open doorway, gun in one hand, torch in the other. Barrett followed close at his heels. Once inside it was apparent that neither guns nor torches were necessary. The red light of the camping torch, dim though it was, showed all there was to be seen: Ahmad Daab slumped over a table, head resting on his arms, his cheek on the black firing-switch. Near him, Najib Hamadeh lay curled, foetal-like, on the floor.

In the corner behind the stock-room door Moynihan saw the bale of carpets. Ascher and Souref were sitting side by side, their backs against it. Blood dripped from wounds in their faces and necks, and saturated their clothing. Moynihan shook his head. 'Give me the R/T, Jim.'

Barrett opened his jacket, took the leather strap from his neck, and handed the walkie-talkie to the inspector.

Moynihan spoke into the mike. 'Whisky Bravo Five calling Whisky Bravo One.' His voice was wheezy from recent exertion.

The command vehicle responded at once. 'Go ahead, Whisky Bravo Five.'

'Give me the Super,' said Moynihan.

'Will do. Stand by.'

Soon afterwards the speaker crackled and Dugald McGann's deep voice came on the air. 'Go ahead, Whisky Bravo Five.'

'We're inside at Thirty-Nine, sir. Firing switch is . . .'

A shot rang out and Moynihan's voice trailed away as he slumped on to the desk behind him.

Hanna Nasour stood in the doorway, wild-eyed, gun in hand. As she ran towards the firing switch, two more shots sounded in quick succession. She screamed, put out a hand, touched the wall and slid slowly to the floor as if she were performing some gymnastic feat in slow time.

Barratt stood at the stock-room door, a thin wisp of smoke spiralling from the barrel of his .38 Enfield. He moved swiftly to where the girl lay, turned her on her back with his foot, knelt down and felt her heart. Next he went to where Moynihan lay across a desk still clasping the R/T set, his eyes staring at the ceiling. Barrett felt the inspector's heart, examined the eyes, and took the R/T set from his hands. He pressed the speak-button and asked for the Chief Superintendent. Dugald McGann answered at once. 'We heard shots,' he said. 'What's going on there.'

'Okay now, Chief.' Barrett was breathing heavily. 'No more resistance. Firing-switch still locked. Timing device presumably on stream. Suggest you send boffins over double quick. And an ambulance.'

'What are the casualties?'

'Two gassed. Four dead. One missing.'

'Christ! Who are they?'

'Moynihan and Ascher killed.' Barrett was having difficulty with his voice. 'Levi missing. Probably wounded or killed.'

McGann's voice softened. 'And their lot, laddie?'

'Hanna Nasour and Souref killed, Hamadeh and Daab gassed.'

There was a pause at the command vehicle end. Then the Chief Superintedent's reply, 'Get your respirator on again, Barrett. You don't sound too good. We're coming over right away. The Spender Street lot are listening. They'll reach you first.'

Barrett said, 'Roger, Bravo One.' He released the speak-button and sat down at the desk. 'My God,' he said, holding his head in his hands. 'What a bloody awful business.'

*   *   *

She sat in a corner, the two men watching her uneasily.

Kagan went across and touched her shoulder. 'No point in your coming with us, Ruth. Only upset you more.'

She pushed his hand away, stood up, took

304

the raincoat from the hook beside the door. She pulled it on with slow, laborious movements. 'Of course I'm coming.' Her voice was strained but she was dry-eyed. They went down the stairs in darkness and she allowed herself a few unnoticed tears. Oh God, she thought, why him?

It was cold and dark outside where the trench diggers were still busy in the rain, the clamour of their jack-hammers shattering the silence of early morning and masking the sound of water which continued to run down the gutters in a steady stream until it disappeared into the drain at the foot of Spender Street.